RED DIRT Paradise

a red dirt novel

BROOKE COWAN

This is a work of fiction. Names, characters, businesses, places, events, locales, and incidents are either the products of the author's imagination or used in a fictitious manner. Any resemblance to actual persons, living or dead, or actual events is purely coincidental.

Copyright © 2021 by Brooke Christensen Cowan

Red Dirt Paradise

brookechristensen13@yahoo.com

ISBN: 978-1-7366810-1-5

All rights reserved.

This book or any portion thereof may not be reproduced or used in any manner whatsoever without the express written permission of the publisher except for the use of brief quotations in a book review.

Cover Design by German Creative
Cover Image by Aleshyn_Andrei/shutterstock.com
Formatting by Enchanted Ink Publishing

Printed in the United States of America

First Printing, 2021

For **Pop**, who taught me many **valuable things**. Among those things, how to farm and how to use my **imagination** are the ones I appreciate the most.

"Every life has a measure of sorrow, and sometimes this is what awakens us."

—Steven Tyler

Chapter 1

May 1984

Alice Cooper's out-of-school anthem rocked the speakers, welcoming summer break with every howling lyric and strike of a guitar. I sang along, appreciating the Texas breeze as it rushed freely into Lexie's blue metallic T-top.

Lexie stole a glance in her rearview mirror, swiping her rollerball gloss across her lips until the sun gleamed off them. She smacked a few times before starting to chant the same thing she'd been chanting non-stop since spring break. "We're proud to say we rule this place, sorry freshman, that's the case. We're coming for you, raise your glass, class of eighty-five kicks ass!"

I took the wheel, avoiding a run-in with a polished purple Pontiac. "But first, it's summertime." A zing of excitement bolted through me as I spoke the word. *Summertime*.

"Yeah, I'd be happy, too, if I had to spend three months

with my grandparents." She rolled her eyes, slowing to a stop at an intersection down the road from our high school. The humid, sticky air was almost suffocating when the car wasn't moving, and I was glad when she punched the gas to give us a breeze again.

"Seriously, Austin." She tilted her head back with a dramatic groan. "What is it that makes you want to leave me for some little town a million miles away? Am I that boring?"

"It's just a summer, Lex. I'll be back before you know it."

"That doesn't tell me anything. I need reasons. Why do you like it there so much?"

I had reasons. I had a hundred reasons. I could've told her about the sunrises that peek over a rusted round-top barn, or the sweet smell of fresh-cut alfalfa. I could've described to her the caramel and fiery orange sunsets that make you stop what you're doing and stare at the sky with a grateful heart, or how the wheat looks when it dances in rhythm on a hot, windy day in June. I could've retold Grandpa's grand stories about the old days or bragged on one of Grandma's blue-ribbon apple pies.

Instead, I shrugged. That seemed easier than offering up an explanation she wouldn't understand anyway.

She flipped the top on her new pack of cigarettes, jamming the box into my chest. "Since we're *seniors* now, how about a cig to celebrate?"

"You know I won't smoke one of those."

This was an ongoing battle between the two of us. She smoked like my grandpa's old flatbed Chevy, and I hated the smell.

She lit her first smoke of the drive, took a smooth drag, then turned down the volume on the radio. "I caught Brad looking at you in science today."

I sighed, annoyed she thought she should even tell me. "He knows I'm not interested."

"You're impossible."

"I'm just not into him."

"He's the most popular guy in school."

"That doesn't matter to me."

"He's so cool, though."

"Not really."

"He's got a nice ass."

"Lexie." I laid my head back against the headrest, exhausted. Lately, conversations with her always seemed to turn to Brad, or Davey, or Scott, or some other jock she tried to pass off on me. It was starting to get old.

"So, you're really turning him down?" she asked. "I don't see why. He talks about you *all* the time and begs me to hook you guys up. Just go out with him."

I pictured Brad, the baseball star with slicked-back hair and eyes as blue as wild bluebonnets, pleading with Lexie to hook us up. "Yeah . . . he's not at all my type."

"Then what *is* your type? I've tried to hook you up with every babe in school, only for you to turn down every one of them."

Actually, that wasn't too far from the truth. Lexie and I had been best friends since the sixth grade, and I was pretty certain she'd tried to set me up with every boy we'd ever passed in the hallway since junior high.

I fiddled with the radio, flipping through every number displayed on her dash, all while ignoring her question. Because if I did try to answer her question, she'd only suggest ten more guys who were *her* type, not mine. That's usually how it went, anyway.

When Aerosmith blew through the speakers, I smiled and leaned the seat back nearly flat on the floorboard. I put my hands behind my head and pictured Steven Tyler, dressed in zebra-striped spandex and wrapped in silk scarves, singing every note of "Sweet Emotion" on a big stage somewhere. I bobbed my head along to the beat, his gravelly voice giving me chills even in the sultry Texas heat. This song was the ultimate summertime tune. It was the ultimate *anytime* tune.

She snickered, turning the radio back down. "You're still mad about me setting you up with Curtis, aren't you?"

I stirred from my daydream at the sound of that name. "You could say that."

Curtis Wray, the famed state champion wrestler from the next school district, wasn't exactly the guy I wanted to kick off summer break thinking about. Just the mention of him made my lip curl. Him with his wavy brown locks, Prince Charming appeal, and mock sweater turtlenecks. He could've been Patrick Swayze's double in *The Outsiders* and no one would've noticed—the only thing setting them apart being Curtis's stud diamond earrings he always wore that were bigger than silver dollars.

Unlike how Lexie described him to be, I'd discovered on our one and only date that he was nothing but a self-absorbed, unmannerly jerk. He was more interested in his latest hair gel than making decent conversation, and I'd hardly forgiven her for putting me through a dinner where all he talked about was how good he was at everything and how he could get any girl he wanted. His copping a feel as I left his car was almost more than I could handle.

I swore to Lexie after that I'd never date another jock, especially one suggested by her.

"Brad is a good guy," she insisted. "Just go out with him one time."

"You said Curtis was a good guy, too. Look how that turned out."

"But Brad's different. I'd only *heard* Curtis was a good guy. But I *know* Brad. He won't be a disappointment."

I sighed, knowing Brad was no different than Curtis. And even if he was, I was too burnt out on the good looking, good-at-everything, only-want-one-thing kind of jock to give it a shot. "No," I said stiffly. "He's just not for me."

Lexie threw her arms in the air with a grunt but didn't protest. Surprisingly.

"How about you and Gunner?" I asked, changing the subject.

She blew her smoke through a cockeyed grin. "He asked me out today. Can you believe he finally did it?"

"I can believe it. You've only been giving him the look for weeks."

She laughed guiltily, peeling out of a four-way stop like we had somewhere to be.

Lexie had a way with the boys. Her sleek black hair, pouty lips, curvy figure, and undying confidence always worked in her favor, making the opposite sex kneel at her feet like she was queen of the Lone Star State. She loved the attention, using her looks that kill—as Vince Neil would say—to her advantage.

She pulled into my neighborhood two wheels off the ground, skidding to a stop just inches from the mailbox. I breathed a sigh of relief every time she didn't nick one of our vehicles or level the fire hydrant in front of our house.

"I take it you're not coming to visit me?" I smiled, knowing the answer according to her scowl.

"Not a chance." She leaned over the center console, giving me a quick side-hug. "Oh, and if you meet a boy up there, make sure he's not one of those hillbillies." She moaned like it'd be pure torture if that happened. "I just could *not* deal with that."

"I'll keep my distance, but scope one out just for you and give him your number," I joked.

"I would *die*."

I sputtered a laugh, imagining Lexie on the arm of a redneck. *Yeah, right.*

I stepped out of her car, throwing my bag over my shoulder. "Tell Gunner I said hi. I know you two will be spending plenty of time together this summer." I winked at her, knowing he'd be the center of all our phone conversations to come.

"You got it." She slapped on her Ray-Bans and revved the engine like she was channeling Bo Duke from *The Dukes of Hazzard*. "Send me some postcards from Nowhereville. I'll send you some from Gunner's bedroom." She gave a goofy smile, then punched the gas, barely missing the mailbox once again.

Lexie was one of a kind.

I turned from the street, stepping from the curb to the narrow brick walkway that led to our dark-stained, oversized front door. The flowerbeds along the sides that were bare this morning were now full of pink daisies, bluebonnets, and petunias. Their touch of spring color brightened my walk to the front of the house, where there were now two magnolia trees planted in front of the pillars. The flowerbeds in front of the porch had also come to life since I'd left for school, showcasing bushes filled with white flowers that mimicked large, fluffy pom-poms. A newly-budded redbud and a new river-rock flowerbed laid around a marble angel figurine, and a palm tree that was taller than me was planted near the garage. I noticed my Uncle Jay's BMW parked in the driveway and wondered what his thoughts were on all the new landscaping.

I walked the few steps up to our door, pausing to admire the window boxes overflowing with violet poppies, and let myself in. I spotted Jay in his study doing paperwork, which was something he did anytime he was home early. I'd discovered long ago the oil business kept him busy, whether he was downtown at the office or not.

After crossing the shiny hardwood floor, so spotless I could nearly see my reflection, I stopped outside the glass French doors that led into his favorite room of the house.

"Are you ready for your trip in the morning?" Jay asked, peering over a steaming coffee mug and thick-rimmed bifocals. Whenever his briefcase was open and business was spread on the table, he was usually stressed and incapable of carrying on the simplest of conversations. But now it seemed he'd put his work aside, if just for a few moments, to give me his warm smile.

He knew how excited I was about this trip, and I was relieved he wasn't fighting Aunt Steph about letting me go. He wasn't exactly thrilled when I'd told him that Steph—after six months of me begging—had finally okayed the trip.

"I'm going upstairs to pack, and then I will be," I answered, making my way to his long mahogany desk.

He laid his papers down, diligently fastening them with a paperclip, then took his glasses off. He swept his thinning red hair to the side and folded his hands in front of him as if in afternoon prayer. "I know at first I wasn't all for you leaving us, but . . . I've come around. I realize now that you deserve a little break before your senior year. Pretty proud of you, kid. You have a good time this summer." He smiled, the shallow creases around his soft gray eyes revealing he'd meant every word.

"Thanks, Jay. I will." I gave him a fist bump, which was a

sentimental hug in our world. "The landscaping looks good, by the way."

He smiled, rocking back in his saddle-brown leather chair. "Well, it better look good with as much as your aunt spent on it. By God, it better look like a Kennedy lives here!"

I chuckled, looking out the window above Jay's head. It looked like a construction zone in the backyard, where Steph was doing some major renovations, unlike the few plants that were added to the front. She was having an in-ground swimming pool put in and a hot tub installed under a gazebo, along with an outdoor kitchen. "For hosting all of your dinner parties, Jay," she'd said when he asked why she needed all these new amenities. Jay didn't believe it was necessary, but of course didn't argue. He never argued with her. Just laughed under his breath and wrote out a beefy check that satisfied her until she came up with something else to splurge on.

Steph called from the kitchen, her voice high-pitched and tinged with a kind of excitement. "Austin? Come in here."

I left the study, and before I could make it past the dining room, she met me with open arms.

"My favorite senior," she said, squeezing me so hard I had to fight for my next breath. "I can't believe this day is here, can you?" She pulled away, brushing my hair behind my ear. "This year is going to be fantastic, isn't it? There's winter formal shopping, prom dress shopping, graduation shopping, senior trip shopping, new car shopping . . ." She stared off, her liquid brown eyes dazzling with the mention of all things shopping.

I forced a smile, dreading the thought of anything to do with it. Only until now had I been able to push back the realization of what senior year *really* entailed: going shopping to please Steph, wearing expensive clothes to please Steph, and applying to colleges to please Steph and Jay both. Though I loved my aunt and uncle more than words could say, a summer away couldn't come fast enough.

"Now, you know, you can still back out of your trip and stay home with me, right? Mom and Daddy won't be mad. They know this is a busy time for you. Or maybe you just want to shorten your trip? A few weeks? A month? What do you think, huh?"

She pushed her wispy brown bangs from her thick-lined eyes, then grabbed me by the shoulders like she was prepared to shake some cooperation out of me. She stared into me as if doing so could brainwash me to stay, nodding her head in a hopeful manner. I almost fell for it, but then I thought of all the shopping and store-hopping we'd be doing. *Not this time, Steph.*

"We'll have all school year together before I go to college," I said. "It's just three months, and I'll be back in August." I smiled and backed out of the dining room before she could suggest a lengthy vacation somewhere that wasn't the one place I wanted to go: Oklahoma.

I walked the grand staircase to my room and threw my school things in my closet, glad to be done with them for a few months. I was beyond tired of tests, homework, studying, and trying to decide my future after high school. What university did I want to go to? What would my major be? What were my goals? Questions I had no answers to, yet ones that were asked on a daily it seemed. Jay was right—I deserved a break.

I walked to my stereo and put in my Hank Williams Jr. cassette, letting Bocephus take me back to a small-town frame of mind. I smiled, thinking how Lex would be tormenting me about my choice of cassette if she were here.

Her obsession with Madonna was getting a little disturbing, so we never could quite settle on music.

As "Outlaw Women" played on the stereo, I packed my suitcase. A few pairs of jeans I didn't mind ruining, a couple pairs of cutoffs, some T-shirts with tour dates on the back, and tank tops of every color. I threw in my black cowboy boots and white Reeboks, then sifted through what I'd already packed.

Singing in my best southern twang—which was nowhere near Reba McEntire's—I played dress-up in a few of my new outfits. I pulled on a tank top and changed into a pair of faded jean shorts, hoping they fit as well as they had in the dressing room.

Naturally, they didn't.

Did anything *ever* fit like it did in the dressing room? Was I the only one with this problem?

I glanced at my reflection but didn't dwell on the baggy shorts. I was so used to pants being too big in the rear or too short in the legs that I couldn't care less anymore. What I did dwell on was the zit on my chin. *Ugh*. I hated those more than anything. Even more than eight-tracks.

I pulled my hair up in a topknot and went to my closet to see if there was anything I was forgetting. I thought about packing some nicer clothes—maybe the cute striped shirt I'd worn to the sports banquet or the silk green top I'd chosen for that infamous Curtis date—but decided against it. I wouldn't need them on the farm anyway.

When I'd finally finished stuffing my suitcase, all neatly organized and packed in as tight as I could get it, I remembered one of the most important things I'd left out. I walked to my closet and dug through the mountain of shoes that were never worn until I found my work boots buried at the bottom. As I pulled them out, the familiar smell of diesel and summertime filled the air. I smiled and tossed them toward my bag, ready to get some good use out of them in the next couple months.

Chapter 2

I walked out the glass doors of the airport, spotting Grandma stepping out of the family vehicle—a '69 Ford pickup. Cherry red with a dent in the fender from a mad momma cow, it was my favorite truck on the farm, and the one I'd claim for the summer.

"Goodness me, you look so grown up," Grandma said, smoothing my hair. She pinched my cheeks like any typical grandmother would, then wrapped her arms around me in a warm, southern-style embrace.

I buried my face in her broad shoulder, reveling in the scent of her soft floral perfume. Honeysuckle with maybe a hint of . . . lavender? I wasn't real sure. But it was the same body mist she'd used since I could remember, and it had a sort of nostalgia to it that dreams were made of. It smelled like mornings sitting next to her in the patio as she shucked corn or evenings kneeling beside her as she pulled weeds from the flowerbeds. The days of following her around in the garden and dragging a wagon behind me to hold all the fresh vegetables came to mind when I caught a whiff of it. I was glad she never left the house without a dab or two on each wrist, just so I could take in the smell all the way to Greenfield.

"Look how long your hair is getting!" She grabbed the pale yellow tips nearing my waist and tugged on them. "It looks a little blonder, too. And that *lovely* new smile you have. What a beautiful young lady you've become."

Grandma's compliments always made me feel good, even though I knew she was biased. I looked a lot more plain than she ever let on.

"You look pretty today, Grandma," I told her while I loaded my suitcase in the back.

She looked younger somehow, as if she'd shed ten years of age since my last Christmas visit.

"Well, thank you. I did my hair a little different at my last appointment."

I could tell it was freshly dyed, a little darker than normal, with a perm of soft curls that were kept pinned back in her usual updo. The darker hair color matched well against her tanned olive skin, which was a trait her Cherokee ancestors passed on to her.

"Doll, are you sure you want to spend all summer with your old grandpa and me?"

Grandma had called me *doll* ever since I could remember, and I loved it almost as much as her peach cobbler.

"I'm sure. It's nice to get out of the city for a while. You know I like it better here, anyway."

"I know you do." She pulled out of the airport with a

smile on her sun-kissed face. "And we're sure glad to have you."

We started the long drive home, picking up fast food and Cherry Cokes on the way. I stared out the window for most of the ride, mesmerized by the blue sky and lack of traffic on every road we drove down. Merle Haggard played softly on the radio, a sense of peace filling the truck as we listened to his untainted voice.

"Steph tells me the renovations have started," Grandma said as we neared the countryside. "How are things looking?"

I took a big drink of my Coke, getting a mouthful of shaved ice along with it. The ice was always the best part. "The front looks good," I said with a crunch. "The back is a disaster, but it'll look better when it's finished in a couple months."

Grandma smiled, shaking her head. "Oh, Stephanie. Jay sure is a patient one, isn't he?"

I nodded. Jay was the most patient man I'd ever known, especially when it came to Steph's impulsive purchases.

"It sounds like her photography has taken a back seat with all this renovating," she said.

I shrugged. "She has a shoot in Arizona next month and a couple in Colorado after that. I think she's trying to stick close to the studio until the house is finished, though."

"Arizona will be hotter than a pistol next month. Who's going to be in her shoots? Anyone famous?"

Steph had photographed plenty of celebrities since she became a bigger name in the industry about ten years earlier. But Grandma's definition of "famous" was always a little dated and didn't quite fit Steph's up-and-coming model portfolio. While Steph might have been photographing Elle Macpherson, Grandma would've been a lot more impressed if it was Doris Day.

"She didn't say who they were," I said, crunching more ice. "They must not have been too big of names."

"Hmm." Grandma slowed to a stop at a dirt road intersection, looking both ways several times. I smiled to myself at how cautious and unhurried she was. She wouldn't know what to think if she ever took an intersection somewhere in the heart of downtown Houston. Half the time I didn't know what to think about it, and I'd lived there since I was six.

"Oh! I almost forgot." She took a careful left-hand turn, then checked her rearview mirror. "Your grandpa has hired an extra hand. He doesn't want you working too hard."

"He didn't have to do that, Grandma. He should know I want to work."

"I know, I know. But it's not every day you get to come down and spend a summer away from the city. We want you to enjoy it. Make some memories while you're here."

I watched as endless acres divided by ancient bodark posts and rusted barbed wire passed through the window. Truthfully, making memories this summer anywhere outside a fenced-in pasture hadn't even crossed my mind. It was nice of them to think of that for me.

"Yeah, I guess you're right."

Her Cheshire grin spoke volumes as she looked seconds away from bursting out a forbidden secret. "His name is Billy. He's quite the little worker and right around your age. You're going to like him."

"He's my age?" Suddenly, the coming months took on a different perspective. I wasn't sure how I felt about that.

Grandma's voice was chipper, and her cheeks were rosy as a child's. "He's been working for us since this spring, and he asks about you a lot. I catch him looking at your pictures in the den."

Red Dirt Paradise

    I blushed, for not only was Lexie trying to hook me up, but Grandma was now playing matchmaker, too. *Unreal.*

    We drove deep into the country until there was nothing but miles of wheat fields and lonesome dirt roads. My heart warmed as I gazed at the emptiness of the open blue sky featuring puffs of white clouds scattered like sheep. The stillness of the cottonwoods, the dust that stirred from the tires—every little detail of the world around us reminded me of why I preferred Greenfield over Houston. There was no comparison when it came to this middle-of-nowhere beauty.

    I noticed the crops were already turning golden brown, hinting harvest time was near. I smiled in anticipation of taking my rightful place on the combine seat.

    "Harvest is coming soon, isn't it?" I asked.

    "It'll be here before you know it," she said with a smile.

    My grandparents lived off a red dirt road on the family ranch Grandpa pegged "Red Dirt Paradise." He named it in the early '50s, and it was made official when he painted the words on a wooden two-by-four that was now situated next to the mailbox.

    I smiled as we passed it, noticing my improvements had held up. Last summer, I'd traced the letters with rusted barbwire and nailed them to the plank, resulting in a project I was quite proud of. When I'd presented it to Grandpa, he smiled as if I'd singlehandedly paid off the farm.

    The driveway snaked between two rows of massive oak trees that'd been rooted there for years. A little brick home was nestled at the end, where rosebushes and vines covered the entire front like a leafy, thorny wall. Grandma was proud of her rosebushes, treating them as if they were part of the family. When she wasn't slaving over a stove, she was weeding, mulching, and hoeing in a jungle of red, peach, and pinkish blooms.

The front porch always looked inviting, equipped with a few rocking chairs and an antique swing older than the dirt in the nearby field. There was something about sitting in that tired swing that always made a person feel better. Its faded paint, split wood, and rusted chains could always soothe a troubled soul, no matter the damage. Maybe it was because so many people had enjoyed a peaceful sunset or hummed a hymn while swinging back and forth to the beat. Either way, it was a type of therapy for anyone willing to share a few moments with it.

Grandpa spent more time on the porch than anyone else. In the summertime, he never missed a sunrise. It was tradition for him to start every day with a cup of hot tea—no sugar—and the weekly newspaper. I joined him most mornings when I visited, as we seemed to have our best talks while the sun came up. In the evenings, if he got off work in time, you'd catch him on the creaky swing, staring out into the horizon. He'd be sipping on that cup of hot tea—so hot I'm not sure how he had any taste buds left—ready to share stories that would make you laugh harder than you ever had before, and some that would bring tears from wishing you could've seen those times yourself. Some of his tales may have seemed impossible, some a little farfetched—like the time he told me he once went to school with a girl named Ima Pig. But there was one thing for sure about Grandpa's stories: you'd never forget them.

As we pulled up to the house, the weeping willow in the front yard swayed in the wind as if to welcome us. The gentle rustle of the branches seemed to whisper in greeting. I smiled, cherishing this piece of heaven that God had handpicked just for me.

If only I could live in this moment forever.

Grandma parked the Ford in its usual spot to the east of the house underneath the carport. "Grandpa's on the tractor behind the house. You're sure welcome to take his spot."

"Okay," I said cheerfully. After all, I never turned down an opportunity to drive the tractor.

I walked behind the house, where the smell of freshly plowed dirt filled the hot air with an earthy scent. Grandpa had already driven up to the fence, so he must have seen us pull into the driveway. He jumped down from the ladder and started my way, water jug and lunch pail in hand. Although he was in his early sixties, he could still work just as hard as any man thirty years younger. He was the toughest man I'd ever known, and I'd always respect that.

"Hey, gal. You wanna take my spot? I've got some business to do at the co-op." His quiet voice and gentle eyes made me feel right at home.

"You bet." I gave him a hug, though Grandpa wasn't much of a hugger. He was the type who shared his love through a cheesy joke rather than a squeeze.

I held him close for a few seconds, breathing in his familiar scent that was thick on his decades-old Western shirt. To most people, he probably didn't smell too good—a mixture of grease and diesel and sometimes cow manure. But to me, it was something more than that. It was hard work, hard-earned money, and most of all, home. My grandpa would always be my home.

"How's that shootin' arm comin' along? You're aimin' for the backboard on those block shots, aren't you?" He squeezed my bicep as if to make sure there was enough muscle to aim properly.

"Always. We should go to the gym some this summer, just you and me."

Grandpa loved all things sports, especially basketball. He

was such a stud back in his day and still talked about his state championship win from '41 every chance he got.

His eyes lit up, his rosacea-red cheeks beaming like a July sun. "We'll do just that." He grinned like I'd just made the rest of his summer, tipping his head back with a silent chuckle. "Be good," he said before shuffling off to the barn.

I crawled up the steps of the old John Deere and sat on the torn, grease-stained seat. It felt good to be able to do that again, even if I was still wearing my nice jeans. I'd never hear the end of it from Steph if she caught grease stains on the overpriced designer jeans I told her not to buy me.

I looked to my right, where the hydraulic levers were positioned. Touching the controls, I quietly refreshed my memory of how all of them worked. I looked at the plow as I moved the front hydraulics up and down, then did the same with the back. I checked the gauges, making sure the water and oil temperatures were sound, then lifted the plow out of the ground. I held the clutch and put the tractor into gear, looking over my right shoulder. Slowly, I lifted my foot and slid the plow in the ground. Dusty red topsoil rolled over and turned to dark brown slabs as the moldboards worked their charm, and I couldn't help but smile to myself. There was nothing prettier than a plowed field.

I finished up the field by five o'clock and headed back toward the house. Getting off equipment by five was early for this time of year, and it would seldom happen as the summer progressed.

"JoAnne called earlier," Grandma said as soon as I stepped into the doorway. "She wants you to call her as soon as you can."

JoAnne—Jo for short—was a friend I'd met years ago. We'd gone to Bible school together when we were kids, and ever since then, we'd stayed close. Whenever I visited my grandparents, we went to the gym to shoot hoops or to the drive-in to see a movie. We'd call each other with life updates every few months, write letters back and forth, and plan summer get-togethers. I loved hanging out with Jo. Her crooked smile and unique giggle were my favorite things about her.

I walked to the phone and dialed her number with ease. I'd had it memorized for years.

"Hello?" said a voice as sweet as pineapple pie.

"Hey, Jo," I answered.

"You're in trouble! Why didn't you tell me you were coming for the entire summer?"

I laughed at how distraught she sounded. "I was going to surprise you."

"Well, I'm surprised! I'm on my way out to the gym. Coach wants us practicing a couple times a week until summer camp. You wanna meet me there?"

"Sure."

"Okay, I'm bringing a couple friends from the team to shoot around, too. See you there."

I changed into my red gym shorts and tied the laces on my Reeboks. Grandma gave me a sweet smile before I headed out the door with the keys to the Ford.

I approached the city limits sign, taking in old sights that always warmed my spirit. There were many things about this little town that comforted me and brought the innocence of childhood back to life, and I loved revisiting those cherished memories every time I drove on the blacktop streets. The Greenfield Library was where Grandma had taken me to all those reading programs in the summers. It's where my love for a good book was spawned. The grain elevator was where I'd eat sugar-glazed donuts dipped in cold chocolate milk with Grandpa on Saturdays, and we spent a lot of time down at the drive-in watching movies and stuffing ourselves on popcorn and frothy root beer floats. There was an old gym-turned-skating rink in the middle of town where I roller-skated when I was younger. I smiled remembering how I'd chase the O's the disco ball made on the wooden floor and collect rabbit's foot keychains from the twenty-five-cent vending machines. I'd skated a million or more circles to the Bee Gees and Donna Summer before it suddenly turned to KISS and Tom Petty with a change of ownership in the late '70s.

As I pulled into town, I noticed the old, abandoned building I'd driven by many times before. The parking lot out front was usually empty, and there was nothing fun or glamorous about it. But as I neared it, I saw that the parking lot was full of flashy cars, and people my age were sitting on tailgates and skateboarding around the rubble. It put a new spin on the building and gave it life again, making it seem like it still served a purpose. I rolled down the window, and I could hear Billy Squier's "My Kinda Lover" blaring from a black Datsun. It made me want to stop in.

A few minutes later, I pulled into the small-town gym. The building might've been an antique—the paint chipped, the bricks cracked, and the A/C imaginary—but the floor was always waxed and welcoming.

There was a white Camaro parked in the driveway and a truck I knew to be Jo's right next to it. I put the Ford in first gear before shutting it off, then walked toward the doors.

Jo and two other girls greeted me as I walked in. I hadn't seen Jo since last summer because she was gone when I'd visited for the holidays, and she looked like a totally different person. She seemed taller than she was a year before and was now just under my chin. Her hair was dyed an autumn auburn red, and just like me, she'd graduated from a mouthful of metal.

Jo smiled her lopsided grin and introduced me to the friend that was closest to her. Chocolate brown hair fell to the girl's lower back, pinned halfway up in an easy, pretty way. She was thin, with blemish-free, porcelain skin that seemed to radiate under the gym lights. She looked like a model—like the ones that cover every issue of every magazine on the racks at grocery store checkout lines.

"I'm Annie," she said, showing off her bleach-white teeth with a full smile.

I wanted to know how she got them so white but decided it might be weird if I asked.

"Jo's told us a lot about you, so why haven't we met before?"

"I'm not sure," I answered. "I guess when I'm here, I'm usually with family or working."

The other girl, who was standing next to Annie, held out her hand.

"I'm Sam," she said in a singsong voice. She had short platinum hair styled like Debbie Harry's, and she scrunched her nose like a kid when she smiled. Her eyes were bright, and her freckles were almost as muddled as my own.

"Nice to meet you guys," I said, giving them a smile.

"Where do you work?" Annie asked, twirling a silk lock of hair around her finger.

How does she get it to shine like that?

"I help my grandpa on the farm."

"Oh." She said it like she was already bored of the conversation. It was the same response I might've gotten from Lexie. "Well, let's go shoot around. I've got places to be and people to see tonight." She flipped her hair before turning and dribbling toward one of the baskets.

I shot Jo a look, but she didn't seem to notice Annie's attitude. She must've been used to it.

We started a game of two on two, and as we played, we talked about Greenfield and Houston. There weren't a whole lot of similarities between the two, but the differences kept the conversation bouncing from topic to topic.

"I've never been to Houston," Annie said. "But I can imagine it's a lot better than this hellish place." She made an attempt to dribble between her legs but lost control of the ball.

"Actually, I prefer it here," I said.

Annie picked up the loose ball and held it on her hip. "You mean to tell me you like it out here better than the city? *Why?*"

Sam rose from a defensive stance, raising an eyebrow like she didn't believe me.

Jo's mouth tugged in a smile. "Austin's just a country girl stuck in the city."

"But *everything's* better in Texas," Annie argued. "Don't you watch *Dallas?*"

"Yeah," I said, "but that's just TV."

Annie gasped. "Well, then we can switch places anytime you want. Because I'm just a city girl stuck in this tiny little hellhole that smells like cow shit every time the wind blows out of the east."

"Feedlot," Sam said with a shrug.

No sooner did Annie lose the ball again, the chat turned to boys. I listened and tried to learn the local gossip, and that was when things got interesting. Apparently, in small towns like this one, everyone dated the same person—usually more than once. They dated their own exes, they dated their best friend's exes, and Sam was currently dating her cousin's ex. They talked about each other's exes, who were also their own exes, and then they talked about who would probably end up being their future exes. To be honest, I couldn't keep up. It was like a soap opera. Something I *was* clear about was that Jo was seeing a boy named Tim and had been for a few weeks. He was Sam's ex, but surprisingly not Annie's. Although that'd probably change, considering the past.

We played and chatted for about an hour, up until Annie decided it was time to go. I figured she was getting tired of all three of us beating her in every game of H-O-R-S-E, so I didn't blame her. Plus, she said she needed a smoke break.

As we walked back to our vehicles, she pulled out a pack of Camels.

"You smoke?" she asked, waving a cigarette my way.

"No, thanks."

"Neither does Jo." She rolled her eyes and lit it for herself.

"Not all of us are as cool as you, Annie," Jo said, smiling over at me.

"Do you have a boyfriend?" Annie asked bluntly.

"No . . . I don't." I felt my face redden, and I wasn't sure why. It wasn't like it was something to be ashamed of, yet the more intimidating Annie's look became, the hotter my face felt.

She nodded, then took a slow drag. "Well." She blew her smoke while holding her cigarette high in the air, reminding me of Cruella de Vil. Even the attitude was similar. *Striking.*

"That'll change if you hang around us long enough," she said.

Jo turned toward me. "Wait, what about Pete?"

Pete was a guy I'd dated last fall. He was the only boy I'd ever considered a boyfriend, and the only boy I'd ever really kissed. He was the first one off the bench on the basketball team, a key member of the debate team, a lover of all things Larry Bird, Star Wars, and Mexican food, and only ate "the blue M&M's." Pete was awkward until you got to know him, had some of the biggest hands I'd ever seen, and used those hands on me a lot more than I was comfortable with. I broke up with him when I'd had enough of it. And that was the end of Peter the Petter.

"Oh, we aren't together anymore. We didn't have that much in common, really."

"You'll find a replacement while you're here," Annie said.

"Well . . . I'm not really looking." I tried not to sound rude, but I wasn't sure it'd worked.

Sam laughed like I'd said something hilarious. "Oh, the guys are gonna *love* you."

Annie handed Sam a cigarette, then stuffed the box back in her fringe purse. "We're going to the barn after we change. Come with us."

"The barn?" I asked.

Sam's eyes widened. "You've never been?"

"I don't think so. Whose barn is it?"

Annie laughed, which made me feel dumb for asking. "Just meet us at Jo's."

I agreed I would, then drove back to my grandparents' house. When I got there, I washed my face and put on some clean jeans. I brushed on some mascara and told my grandparents where I was going, knowing they wouldn't mind me going out. They were always happy when I hung out with Jo, so it was never a problem with them. I hopped back in the Ford and started down the road to her house, only a few miles south and over a ramshackle bridge.

I arrived a few minutes later and walked up to the door. Jo answered, and to my surprise, she looked as if she were going to a ball instead of a barn. Her hair was crimped and teased, and she wore heavy makeup and clothes that were nowhere near casual.

"How about we dress you up?" she asked, obviously noticing my style was a little more relaxed than hers.

"Dress me up?"

"Come on. I've never seen you dressed up before."

"I'm not really one to—"

"I *promise* you'll love it if you let me give you a makeover. Pleeease?" She locked arms with me and pulled me inside.

I opened my mouth to turn her down, but she was already telling me what she was going to do with my hair—combing it this way, teasing it that way. I laughed under my breath at everything she thought she was going to do to it, knowing my hair wasn't going to do any of it. I had seventeen years of proof it wouldn't do a thing but lay flat against my back, straight as wheat straw and lifeless and limp.

She led me through the living room, still linking her arm with mine, and we made our way down the hallway and into her bedroom. Annie and Sam were sitting in front of different mirrors, each getting ready by smoothing on lipstick shades darker than Grandma's roses. They were wearing clothes similar to Jo's, looking far too dressed up for the occasion. What kind of barn *was* this?

"Put this on, Austin," Annie said, handing me a white crop top and acid wash jean skirt. She never looked away from the mirror and shook the clothing when I didn't grab it right away.

"You think I should wear *this*?" I held up the shirt—or lack thereof—with half a mind to refuse.

"I know you should wear this." She smiled devilishly, as if she knew she was tormenting me. The Cruella de Vil theme song played in my head.

"I don't know . . ."

"Just do it," Annie urged.

I looked at Jo, who gave me a smile that was hard to turn down.

"You'll look good, I promise," Jo assured me.

I groaned low enough no one could hear me, then snatched the clothes and walked into the bathroom. I changed into the borderline sleazy outfit, and without even looking in the mirror, walked back to Jo's room.

"You look great!" Jo squealed.

"I feel naked."

She laughed, straightening my skirt. "I promise you've never looked better. Now, for makeup."

Foundation went on first, then came powder. It seemed to me she'd put on extra blush, and there was a big possibility my eyeshadow was caked so thick I wouldn't be able to blink. I couldn't be too sure, but I had a bad feeling I was going to resemble a Stephen King character before this was over with.

"You know I want to be a cosmetologist, right?" Jo said, lining my lips.

"I thought you wanted to be a coach?"

Jo used to talk about how she could coach basketball better than her own basketball coach. She always said she'd come back after college to prove it.

"Nope," she said. "Change of plans. I could give makeovers all day. It's my favorite thing to do. I practice on my sisters all the time."

Ah. So *that's* why I was dressed like a Valley girl and sitting in a makeshift makeup chair. Now things made a little more sense.

"Well, you'll be a good one," I said. I had no idea if she'd be a good one or not, but the way she was so focused on my face, and then on my hair, made me think if she wasn't talented in this area, she could probably practice enough to be decent.

"Okay, now put on those heels over there and go look in the mirror," she said, smoothing my brow with her fingertip.

She sprayed one last shot of Aqua Net for good measure, and then nodded her approval.

"Heels?" I said. "You think I should wear *heels?*"

"I know you should wear them!" Annie yelled from the bathroom.

Jo smiled and crossed the room for the shoes.

I'd only worn heels once in my life. It was for one of Jay's million dinner parties, and I somehow ended up breaking one of them while walking downstairs. I'd tumbled down the last few steps, ripped my new skirt, and dislocated my little finger. Steph never made me wear them again.

I took a deep breath, braced myself for another broken bone, and slipped on the white heels with little triangle prisms on the toes that Jo had dropped at my feet. Thankfully, they weren't as high as the ones I'd taken a tumble in, and they were slightly more comfortable. The thin ankle strap seemed to hold them in place a little better, too. And those were the only reasons keeping me from completely refusing them.

I walked to her full-length mirror about as clumsy as a newborn calf, with little hope and full of fear. I sucked in a breath, sure I would regret agreeing to this once I saw my reflection, but shockingly, that wasn't the case. When I took a peek, the doubts in my head took a left turn, and I was pleasantly surprised. It was safe to say I was out of my comfort zone, but I was shocked at how Jo had been able to put me together. My hair was parted on the side and thrown over my shoulder, looking better than it ever had before. And the best part of it?

Volume.

She'd even done a pretty impressive job on my makeup and applied bright-red lip stain to my lips to top off my new look. I'd never worn red lipstick before and it was definitely different, but it was something I could get used to. And though my stomach was pasty, my legs looked long and decent in the heels.

"Told you," Jo said smartly.

After everyone was finished over-applying mascara and layering on cheap lip gloss, we walked out the door toward Jo's truck. Dusk had come and went, and the stars above us dazzled the night sky. It was hard to see any stars over a city like Houston, so I was always left astonished by the diamonds that flickered above Oklahoma.

We all crowded into Jo's truck, and the choice of cassette was left to Sam. She couldn't decide between Olivia Newton-John and the soundtrack from *Flashdance*, so she broke the tie with Michael Jackson. We cranked up "Thriller" like it was Halloween night and did all the dance moves together. Jo was the best at them, even while driving. Not one of us could hold a candle to her zombie claw moves.

Chapter 3

To my surprise, we didn't pull into some farmer's old tin barn on the outskirts of town. Instead, we pulled into the parking lot of the abandoned building I'd driven by earlier. Only now, there were double the people standing outside, and cars were packed so tight we had to search for a spot to squeeze in.

When we finally found one on the far side of the old building, a boy in a plaid shirt walked up to us almost immediately. He was tall and thin, with a dark brown, broker-style comb-over gelled to the nines. His eyes were deep-set and dark as black coffee, and his lashes were so long and thick they could've been feathers. He greeted Jo with a side-hug and handed her a beer.

"This is Austin, my friend I was telling you about," Jo

said. "She's here for the summer. Austin, this is Tim, my boyfriend."

I shook his hand as he tried to give me a beer, which I politely turned down. He didn't seem offended, and I was relieved he didn't push me to take it. One taste of Lexie's beer freshman year was enough to turn me away from the stuff for a lifetime.

"Yeah, Billy told me you were comin' to town," he said, grabbing Jo's hand.

"Billy?" I said.

"Yeah, he works for your grandpa."

Oh. *That* Billy.

"Billy works for Austin's grandpa?" Jo asked.

Tim raised a brow. "Yeah, you didn't know that?"

Jo shot me a grin, and I could see the gears cranking in her mind. "No, I didn't. But this is too good."

Jo leaned in close so Tim couldn't hear and whispered, "You'll like Billy. He's *gorgeous.*"

"Oh yeah?" I said, not giving it much thought. I was more interested in the fact that a guy had just ridden up to the party on a bay horse. I definitely wasn't in Houston anymore.

Tim led us over to a Dodge Challenger, the citrusy orange paint shining like it'd been waxed and polished by Mr. Miyagi. He patted the hood, cooing to it like a baby before going to turn the radio up.

"Tim loves his car more than he loves me," Jo said. "I honestly think he'd die for it. And I wish I was exaggerating."

I laughed, watching him rub a bug splatter out of the side mirror with a handkerchief. When he was done, he smiled to himself, then lit the one-hitter he pulled out from his jean pocket.

When he walked back over to us, I could smell the marijuana as smoke rolled from his mouth. I wasn't too fond of it, but I was also so used to it that the stench didn't bother me anymore. Lexie was a proud member of the cannabis club and had been since the seventh grade.

"So, why is this called the barn?" I asked Jo.

"It used to be called Bobby's Barn. It was an old bar back in, like, the thirties. After prohibition. If you walk inside, there's still old barrels and bottles and stuff. It's cool."

"That *is* cool. Has it always been the hangout place in town?"

"Not always. It used to be the cemetery south of town where all the guys would race their cars. But that stopped after someone jumped the fence and plowed over a tombstone. So, now we hang out here, and they race on the road north of town."

"Does anyone hang out at the skating rink anymore?"

Tim let out a snorty laugh.

"Trust me," she said. "I'd love for that to still be the hangout spot, but once you're outta junior high, it stops being 'cool' to hang out there. You come here for beer and to hook up, or just to hang out."

"You girls and your skating rink," Tim said, pinching Jo's cheek like she was a little kid.

"I miss those days," she said. "I'd still be there if Tim would come with me."

"Not a chance," Tim said.

I looked around at the crowd, taking in the small-town groove and noticing how our clothing didn't really match everyone else's jeans and T-shirts. I would've fit right in had I come straight from my grandparents'.

"So, why did we all dress up?" I asked Jo. "Is that something you guys always do on Friday nights?"

"Annie dresses like this all the time because she thinks

she's Brooke Shields. Sam does whatever Annie does. I like looking hot for Tim . . . even though he doesn't notice."

"I notice," Tim said, pulling on Jo's off-the-shoulder top. "Lookin' good."

Jo rolled her eyes. "He doesn't notice," she mouthed.

I looked around the party, checking out all the guys who were checking out all their cars. I noticed a lot of them wearing the same Greenfield FFA shirt, and most of them sported shaggy hair tucked under a ball cap. Several looked like they'd just gotten off work on the farm, covered in dirt from hat to toe. It was a nice change from the boys I was around every day—boys who were clean and dressed in designer threads.

"Do all these guys farm or something?" I asked Jo as she sipped on her bottle of beer.

"Some of them do, yeah. Like Jimmy over there. Duncan's a mechanic at the body shop, and Penrod works there, too. The Walker boys farm. Cliff . . . he's just dirty." She shrugged. "Why do you ask?"

"Just wondering."

"You're used to city boys, huh?" She smiled, reading my mind.

Oh, if she could only see the polo shirts and knit sweaters at our hangouts back home.

"So, what do you think of Tim?" she asked.

He'd wandered off and was now talking to a group of guys leaning over the hood of a Trans Am.

"He seems nice. He's got the longest eyelashes I've ever seen."

She ducked her head with a laugh. "That's the first thing everyone says about him. The first time my dad met him, he asked him if they were real. As if he'd be wearing fake eyelashes! It was *so* embarrassing."

Annie came to stand next to us as I continued to gawk at the crowd. She chugged her beer and yelled across the parking lot to a group of guys tossing around a football. "Turn it up, Tim!" she yelled. "Not everyone can hear it!"

"I don't think he heard you," Jo said, watching as Tim completely ignored her. Possibly on purpose. "I'll go turn it up."

She left, cranking the tune up even more. It was so loud that cheers erupted from the people who weren't anywhere close to Tim's car.

One boy in particular caught my attention as he gave Jo a thumbs-up.

He was sitting on the tailgate of a battered black Chevy pickup. His jeans were ripped to shreds, and his Aerosmith T-shirt was stained. His dark blond hair hung to about his shoulders and swayed back and forth as he bobbed his head along to the beat. It was greasy and tangled, but it smoothed as he ran his fingers through it. There was a bottle of beer between his legs, and a cigarette separated his thin lips, which he puffed on between fits of laughter and storytelling.

"Annie," I said over the music. "Who's that guy over there?"

"Josh?" She pointed to a redhead standing beside the boy I had my eye on. "You should go talk to him!" She dropped her cigarette butt on the ground and smashed it under the glittery toe of her shoe. "I knew you couldn't resist finding a guy for the summer. Who could?"

Wait.

She thought I couldn't *resist*? As if I couldn't *help myself*? As if I was on the lookout for this hot summer romance and out of the blue sat this guy who looked like he belonged on tour with Van Halen?

No. That wasn't the case.

Aerosmith guy brought a leg up on the tailgate and rested his arm on his knee. He took a drag off his cigarette and sang along to Led Zeppelin while bobbing his head like Robert Plant at Woodstock.

Oh, but maybe that is the case.

"No, not him," I corrected her. "The guy sitting on the tailgate."

She looked toward Aerosmith guy. "Uh, what?" There was a hint of amusement behind her piercing eyes when she realized who I was talking about. "The guy on the tailgate?"

I nodded.

"Why? Do you think he's cute?"

"Well, I . . . I guess," I stammered, feeling that same intimidation from earlier at the gym. "Kinda."

"Well, you don't wanna talk to him." She pulled out another cigarette, without an explanation as to why I shouldn't.

"Oh. Why . . . not?" I asked cautiously. *Is she into him?*

"He's an asshole."

Guess not.

I flicked my eyes back to the Chevy and watched Aerosmith guy throw his head back in laughter and clap his hands like he was shooting the breeze with Cousin Eddie from *National Lampoon's Vacation*. The way he smiled made me smile, and I wondered how hard it would be to catch his eye. I wanted to talk to him. I wanted to meet the guy who looked a little bit country and a whole lot rock 'n roll.

I stood where I was and acted interested in what Annie was saying but continued stealing glances at him in hopes he'd notice me. I didn't spot any girls around him and hoped one wouldn't make her way up to him.

After a few more minutes and an earful from Annie about how Josh was the one for me, I finally caught his attention. He did a double take, and that same contagious smile spread across his whiskered face. I smiled back, hoping it'd encourage him to make a move. My heart raced as his eyes skimmed me over, and blood rushed to my face when he sang the words to "Whole Lotta Love" without taking his eyes off me.

"Let's get a beer," Annie said, grabbing my hand. She pulled me out of my trance and out of sight of Aerosmith guy.

"I'm fine," I said, irritated.

She rolled her eyes, jamming a cold can into my chest. "One beer isn't going to kill you. Come on and drink it."

I took the beer with no intention of opening it. Of course, that didn't matter because she popped the top for me.

"Hey," said a voice from behind me.

I swallowed hard, my heartbeat racing. It was Aerosmith guy, I was sure of it. Because who else would it be?

Just be cool. Tell him you like his shirt. Or hair. Or smile.

When I turned around, still rehearsing in my head the perfect thing to say, I was only disappointed by who stood in front of us.

"Josh!" Annie shrieked. "This is Austin. Show her around, get to know her, all that good stuff." She walked away, but turned around and said, "Drink the damn beer."

I raised the can, then set it down on a nearby tailgate when she was out of sight.

"Annie can be . . . well, I think you got it." Josh smiled, fidgeting with the tail of his FFA shirt.

I nodded, glad I wasn't the only one who noticed how bossy she was.

"So, your name's Austin?" He ran a hand up his opposite arm, his eyes darting nervously from mine. "That's a cool name for a girl. I have a cousin named Austin, but he's a guy. Not that you have a guy's name or anything. I mean—" He brought his palm to his forehead, turning bright red.

So far, he reminded me a lot of Pete. From his awkwardness to his fair skin and copper-colored hair. His nose was even a little turned up at the end like Pete's was. *What are the odds?*

"What I mean to say is, I like your name." He said it slowly, as if to keep from messing up his words. After he'd gotten them out, he took a deep breath.

"And what I mean to say is, are you hittin' on my girl?"

I turned to see Aerosmith guy strolling up behind me, his smile sly and his eyes focused on Josh. He put his arm around me like we'd been together for years, and my heart skipped a beat from being so close to him.

Is this really happening?

"Austin's your girl?" Josh asked, looking from Aerosmith guy to me.

I froze, unable to answer anything he could've possibly asked.

"I don't know . . . are you?" Aerosmith guy looked at me for an answer, his lips inches from mine. The warmth from his body, the way his nose crinkled when he smiled, how he seemed so relaxed and confident and at ease—all of it made a breath catch in my throat.

"I . . . uh . . ." I glanced at Josh, who looked confused, and back to Aerosmith guy, whose smile never left his lips. "Well . . ." I started again, my whole body tingly and tight. "Yeah . . . uh-huh."

My heart hammered hard in my chest, while Aerosmith guy's whiskey breath hummed in my ear. "Good answer," he said.

Red Dirt Paradise

"Sorry, man. Didn't know." Josh gave an awkward wave, pursing his lips with a nod, before turning around and walking away.

Aerosmith guy's arm never left my shoulders, even with Josh out of the way, and I trembled when his fingertips brushed my collarbone. "I'm James Cassedy." His voice softened and his green eyes shimmered like emeralds, pulling me in deeper the more I stared. "People call me Cass."

"I'm . . . Austin," I managed to squeak. *Was that* my *voice?*

"Darlin', I think you're about the prettiest thing I've seen around these parts."

Oh, that southern accent is nice.

"Oh, please," Annie spat.

We both turned to see her standing behind us, her arms crossed and face puckered like she'd eaten something sour. *Cruella strikes again.*

"Don't you know those lines don't work on girls like Austin?" she hissed. "Why don't you go on over to those skanks you were talking to before you harassed her?"

Before I could think to say anything, Cass beat me to it. "Hell, Annie, why don't you go stick your nose up every other guy's ass at this party? Leave mine alone, huh?"

Annie narrowed her eyes before storming off. What was her problem?

"Come with me," Cass said with a smile.

He grabbed my hand and led me over to the black Chevy. His hands were rough and callused, while mine were sweating like I'd just ran a half marathon through Galveston in the middle of August. *Why am I so nervous?*

"What're you drinkin'? Will this do?" he asked, handing me a beer.

"Uh . . ." I hesitated before I reached for it. Staring at the unopened can, I tried to think of a way I could back out of drinking it without sounding like a child. When nothing came to mind, I decided it'd be best just to down it. Maybe I'd like it the second time around?

I popped the top and took a small taste, trying to look cool while doing it. And even though it was the smallest little sip, I had to choke it down. It was awful—just like I'd remembered it. Only worse.

Taking the beer from my hand, Cass chuckled. "Here, you ain't gotta drink that."

My cheeks burned on the verge of bursting into flames. "I guess . . . maybe I . . . I'm just not a big drinker." I stumbled to find the right words, trying my hardest not to sound as dumb as I felt.

"Not a thing wrong with that, darlin'." He smiled again, somehow making me feel a little less anxious. "So, you're visiting from Texas, huh?"

"Yeah, I'm visiting my grandparents. How'd you know I live in Texas?"

"I asked Jo about you before I saved you from Josh."

I smiled. "Oh."

"You here for the weekend or all week?"

"I'm here for the summer."

He gazed at me for a few seconds, giving me a look that made me blush. Again. He stared at me like he was burrowing into me, stripping me down and seeing what the naked eye couldn't. I took a short breath as he bit his lip.

"A lot can happen during a summer." The way he said it made me feel as if we somehow already had plans. I smiled, feeling the continued warmth in my cheeks.

"Who're your grandparents?" He took a sip from the can, never taking his eyes from mine.

"Willie and Alice Rose."

"Willie Rose. Yeah, I've heard of him. He farms west of the drive-in, right? Lives in that brick house on the hill?"

"That's him."

"Good to know. Now I know where I'll need to pick you up tomorrow night." He winked at me before lighting another cigarette.

I raised a brow and couldn't think straight for a long second. "We're going somewhere tomorrow night?"

"Oh, you didn't know? We gotta date at the drive-in. It's where I'll put on a little charm and show you what you've been missin' down in H-town for so long." He took another drag. "Darlin', it'll be a night like you ain't ever had."

I stared at him in disbelief. And the more I did, the more I saw. And the more I saw, the more I realized who I was dealing with. Never mind the instant attraction to his dreamy smile and the way he looked when singing Zeppelin. Or how those faded Wranglers hugged him in all the right places. Or how the butterflies hadn't left my stomach since I'd first spotted him. None of that mattered at this point because it was apparent I was only dealing with another Curtis. Another Brad, Davey, and Scott. Another cocky, want-one-thing kind of smooth-talking disappointment. Another guy I'd roll my eyes about when I mentioned him to Lexie and one she'd probably tell me to go out with.

Time to check out.

I slid off the tailgate, feeling almost sick to my stomach. I had to get out of this situation, and fast.

"Wait," Cass said. He dropped his cigarette to the ground. "What's wrong?"

"I, uh . . . I—I better go find Jo." I looked over my shoulder, searching the party, and spotted her standing next to Annie. Annie didn't look happy.

"Did I say somethin' wrong?" He hopped down next to me, and a look of concern mixed with a little shock replaced the confidence that had shown on his face since we met.

"Well . . ." I lowered my gaze, zoning in on his scuffed cowboy boots. *Why can't I just tell him it isn't happening between us and leave?*

"I'm . . ." I looked up and met his eyes, and that same thing happened, where those precious stones drew me in so deep I couldn't think straight. But unfortunately for him, the thought of Curtis putting his hand on my butt an hour after meeting him flashed across my mind.

And that was all it took. *No way I'm doing that again.*

"I'm not that kind of girl," I said. "I gotta go now." I wheeled on my heel, headed toward Jo, but he grabbed my hand.

"Don't go," he said.

I turned to face him but avoided his eyes. I didn't want to get drawn into them again.

"I'm sorry I came off like that," he said. "'Cause that ain't what I want from you."

Yeah, that's what they all say.

"Then what *do* you want?" I asked, not buying it.

He gave me a different kind of smile, and it was one a guy like Curtis could never give. It was honest and innocent and the way his eyes softened with the curve of his lips could've melted anyone within a mile of the barn. I couldn't help but smile back, even though I tried hard not to.

"I wanna take you out to a movie," he said. "I wanna talk to you about things like . . ." He paused and looked down at the cracked concrete before continuing. "Like . . . who's your favorite singer? Who do you look up to? Where's your favorite place to be? Things other people might not know 'cause they ain't ever took the time to try and see what makes you tick." He shrugged and stuffed his hands in his pockets. "I'd also really like to hold your hand."

I was quiet, my shoulders relaxing with every word he spoke. And the guard I'd just built to the sky? It came falling to the ground, tumbling and burning to ashes and embers with his sweet lines and that honeyed smile.

Geez, I can't help it.

"So, will you go out with me?" he asked. "So I can hold your hand?"

I nodded, quicker than planned. "If you promise that's all you want, then I'll go out with you."

"Swear." He chuckled and jerked his head toward the tailgate. "Will you come back over and sit next to me?"

I smiled. "I'll sit next to you."

He sat back down and patted the space beside him. There was a new kind of innocence to him, and it only made him that much more attractive.

"Can I hold your hand?" he asked as I sat down.

"You can hold my hand."

He reached for my hand, then brought it to his lap. "Sometimes I forget my manners. Beer gets to talkin', and I say the wrong things. I gotta work on that. I'm sorry."

"Yeah, I've had a bad run with the past few guys I've been on dates with. I'm on high alert."

"Well, I promise I won't say anything to make you want to leave again."

Good, because I'd much rather stay.

"I think I found me a no-bullshit kinda girl. Am I right?" he asked.

I shrugged. "You could say that."

"I like that, darlin'."

"And as for your questions . . ."

He smiled and squeezed his hand tighter around my own. It was in a protective way. Almost a *loving* way. I stuttered, losing my train of thought in those eyes again.

"Your favorite singer?" he asked. "Who you look up to? Favorite place to be?"

"Right," I said. "Well, I think Waylon Jennings is probably my favorite if I had to pick. I've always looked up to my grandparents, and . . . my favorite place to be is right here."

He brought his opposite hand over and cupped it around mine. He pulled me in a little closer to him and whispered, "Right here?"

Our shoulders were snug up against each other, and we couldn't have gotten any nearer unless I was sitting on his lap. The closeness to him felt good. It felt *right*.

"Well, I meant Oklahoma, but this isn't too bad, either." *Obviously.*

His mouth tugged in a smile. "You know, we got a lot in common already. Waylon's one of my favorites, and my grandpa's my hero. I like Oklahoma, too, but I ain't been many other places to compare it to."

"There's no better place," I assured him.

The more we talked, the more I liked him. I liked the way he gave me his full attention and acted like I was the most interesting person he'd ever met. It was like he'd shut off the world around him because I was the only one who mattered. The way he looked at me made me feel worthy and important, and it was such a change from what I was used to. I could've sat on that tailgate until the morning sun peeked over the grass plains and been more than happy.

"How'd you get so dirty?" I asked curiously, watching him light his third or fourth cigarette of the night.

Lexie would be proud that I hadn't griped about his chain-smoking—not once. The funny thing was, I enjoyed watching him do it. It was like he'd turned a bad habit into a form of art. The way he flicked the ash to the ground, the way he lifted his head and blew his smoke toward the night sky. I enjoyed watching him handle a cigarette, mesmerized by his artistic hands.

"How'd I get so dirty?" Cass blew smoke through a coy smile. "I was workin' on our forty-four fifty. Hose was leakin', and I didn't have a rag."

"A hydraulic hose?"

His eyes darted to mine. "What do you know about hydraulic hoses?"

"I've changed a dry-rotted hose on our forty-four forty before."

He stared at me as if he'd heard me wrong. "You have?"

I laughed at his surprise. "I have."

"Wow."

"Is that a good thing?"

"It damn sure ain't a bad thing."

I smiled, hoping my cheeks would somehow, someway, return to their normal pigment one of these days.

"So, your parents farm?" I asked.

He shook his head, reaching into his ice chest for another can. He popped the top, then quickly reached for my hand again. "My second parents, I guess you could say. Pat and Lonna Jameson. Their son, Larry, is like a brother to me. We plan to take it over one day when Pat retires."

"Farmers never retire," I said, Grandpa on my mind.

"That was the funny part." He smiled and took a drink of his beer. "Since you know so much about hydraulic hoses, I'm guessin' you help him on the farm when you visit?"

"As much as I can."

"You know, I'd never guessed you farmed by the way you look tonight. Kinda caught me off guard there."

"Oh . . . really?" I bit my lip, wanting to tell him this new look wasn't exactly me. But wasn't this look what attracted him to me in the first place? What if it was a turnoff to see me in my dirty jeans and boots, or even my nice jeans and T-shirt like I wore back home? I decided I'd keep my usual look to myself, just in case.

"So, you farm . . . and you like Aerosmith?" I said.

He patted the stained logo on his chest with a grin. "My favorite band. You a fan?"

I nodded. "Oh yeah. I have all their records back home."

He was quiet, staring at me like he hadn't heard me right. "All of them?"

"Yeah."

"What's some of your favorite songs? Favorite album?" He looked at me as if he were testing me.

"Favorite songs? Uh . . . let me think."

He smirked, and I knew he thought I was lying to him.

"'Dream on' is my favorite. I like 'Pandora's Box.' About every song on *Toys In the Attic*. That's a great album. 'Last Child' is good. 'Sweet Emotion' . . ."

His eyes widened, and he shook his head like he was waking up from a dream. "No shit? No shit!"

I shrugged. How could anyone *not* be an Aerosmith fan?

As the night grew on, the more I noticed how much he was drinking. Cass finished off the beer in his cooler and bummed the rest off his friends. And to my surprise, it didn't bother me as much as I thought it would. He kept my full attention and interest—no matter how many pee breaks he took during our conversations.

"Are you ready to go?" I heard Jo say as she tapped my shoulder. I'd been so consumed by Cass in our own little world that I hadn't noticed her walk up to us.

"I guess," I muttered, standing from the tailgate. "Well, it was nice meeting you, Cass."

He stood up, almost falling in the process before balancing himself. All those beers must have caught up to him.

"Hey, don't forget about our date tomorrow. I wanna take you out, darlin'." He leaned in close to my ear and whispered, "So I can hold your hand." He reached for my hand as I laughed under my breath. "Movie starts at eight thirty. Let me pick you up at eight?" His speech may have been slurred, but I still loved the sweetness in his voice. It was as if he couldn't bear the thought I'd turn him down.

I agreed on the time, and we said our goodbyes. Before I turned to follow Jo to her truck, he reached for my hand one more time. He squeezed it, rubbing his thumb in my palm. As he did it, I had the undying urge to leap into his arms. I wanted to kiss him goodbye, to run my hands through all that hair. What would he do if I let myself do something that crazy? *Why am I even thinking like this anyway?*

Jo called my name. I looked at her, then back to Cass. Cass winked at me before he let go of my hand and gave me a soft smile that could've melted a true villain. I waved at him before I turned to follow Jo to her truck, still wondering what a kiss from him would feel like.

I looked around, noticing Annie and Sam were nowhere in sight. I wondered who they'd left with, because obviously they weren't joining in on our ride home. That was probably a good thing, considering Annie's attitude earlier.

When we got into Jo's truck, she quietly chewed her cheek for a moment. She took a deep breath, stalling from turning the key.

"What?" I asked.

She was silent, flicking her fuzzy key ring that matched

the fuzzy dice hanging from her rearview mirror. "So . . ." she said finally. "What'd you think of Cass?"

I smiled, thinking of the way his hand felt when it entangled mine. The way my heart raced when he purposefully brushed up against my shoulder. The smoothness of his voice and the sweetness to it when he called me *darlin'*. That single word dripped from his lips like warm maple syrup.

"He's nice." I chuckled like a grade-schooler after getting kissed on the playground. "I like him."

"I was afraid of that," she said.

"Is that bad?"

"Well . . . he's with Annie."

I looked at her, confused. "He's with Annie?"

What?

"Well, he's not *with* Annie. I mean, he doesn't know he is."

"I don't get it."

"Okay, well, you know how me, Annie, and Sam date around a lot? Well . . . we also have our guys that are off limits to each other. They're basically taken. Off the market. Done deal. No exceptions. Tim is mine, obviously. Sam's is a guy named Keith. And Annie's is Cass."

So that's the reason for Annie's attitude.

"So, Annie isn't *with* Cass," I said. "She just doesn't want anyone else with him?"

"Kinda. But I mean, they go back and forth a lot, too. Plus, Cass is kinda the type who's all over the place. He's wild. Gets with a lot of girls. Big drinker, smooth talker. That kind of thing. He has a bad rep when it comes to that. You know what I mean?"

I knew what she meant. And normally, I wouldn't have pursued the idea. I would've listened to what she had to say about him and left the thought alone. On any other day, a guy with a bad reputation, a number of nasty habits, and an on-and-off romance with Cruella de Vil wouldn't have turned my head.

But on this day, it did.

There was something about Cass that intrigued me. Whether it was the Aerosmith shirt in the crowd of FFA shirts or the smile that crinkled his nose and lit his eyes like wildfire, there was something about him I'd never be able to explain to Jo. *Something*. And because of that something, I wouldn't let Annie claim him like he was her property. I'd go on that date with him tomorrow, and I'd keep my guard down. I'd give him a chance. I'd let him hold my hand.

Once we pulled into her driveway, I thanked her for being honest. I told her goodbye, then hopped in the old Ford. As I started it up, I sat back with a smile on my face as wide as the Oklahoma horizon.

I hadn't come this summer looking for a guy to spend my time thinking about. It was never my intention to give the first guy I saw a flirty smile from across a parking lot, or lose myself in a pair of green eyes on a Chevy tailgate. But sometimes, things just happened.

Boy, I was glad they did.

Chapter 4

I woke up the next morning with the same smile on my face. I was sure I'd slept that way because Cass had been on my mind all night long. I dreamed of his tousled hair and imagined what it would feel like to run my fingers through all those unruly tangles. Every time I thought about his smile or the warmth in his laugh, my heartbeat doubled, and my palms turned a sweaty mess.

"Ready for a sunrise?" Grandpa called from the hallway.

"Be there in a minute," I said.

I rolled out of bed with an extra pep in my step and threw on some work clothes and boots. After pulling my hair up in a ponytail, I rushed to the porch.

"I made you a cup of hot tea with a little extra sugar in it," Grandpa said.

I smiled and took the cup from him. Hot tea was good on any occasion, but it was better when Grandpa made it.

We made ourselves comfortable on the swing and sipped our tea in silence. The early rays of dawn colored the sky with a dull orange, and the first clouds came into sight. The air was still and chilly, locusts continuing their night serenade as if it weren't morning. Grandpa's gray and white speckled Appaloosa, Star, whinnied as she bolted from under a cottonwood tree, trotting with soulful grace through the grassy pasture opposite the porch.

"Sure is pretty out here, isn't it?" Grandpa mused.

"Yeah," I said. "I wish I could see this view every morning."

"If you got to see it every morning, you wouldn't appreciate it as much as you do right now."

"I still wish I could see it. And have a cup of your tea every morning, too."

He chuckled, blowing steadily into his steaming cup. "I *can* make a pretty good cup of tea."

"Grandpa," I said. I tried to take a sip, but it was still too hot. "Thanks for being a farmer."

"Well, I'm happy to oblige . . . but why do you say that?"

"Because if you weren't a farmer, I'd never know what it's like to be one. And I really like being one."

"You always have. You know, when you were two years old, you'd come help me change the sickle sections on the combine. If I ever went to the barn without you, here'd come your mom, bringin' you out. You'd be screamin' your head off 'cause you didn't want me workin' without you."

I'd heard that story a hundred times, but I still loved hearing it. It just proved I'd always had a love for this place, even as a toddler.

"Did . . . my mom like helping you, too?"

He was silent, and my skin prickled while I waited for his response. I took a sip of tea to fight the icy feeling, but it didn't do any good.

"She sure did." There was a deep sadness in his voice, one that seemed to dampen the sunrise. The world appeared darker and sadder at the mention of her.

We were quiet the rest of the morning, swinging and sipping together, staying tucked away in our own little space. The only noise was the creak of the swing and the occasional calf bawling for its momma. We stayed there until our tea was gone and Grandma called us in to eat one of her famous breakfasts.

"Good morning, doll. How was your evening?" Grandma pulled a pan of homemade biscuits out of the oven and put them on the stovetop.

"Good," I said.

"Did you meet anyone we should know about?" She winked at Grandpa, who looked at me curiously from the rim of his Farm Journal mug.

I wanted to tell them about Cass. I wanted to tell them about the boy I'd talked to for hours—the one who made me smile, called me darlin', and asked me on a date. The one with the blonde hair that swayed messily as he sang to Zeppelin, and the one with the greenest eyes I'd ever seen. I wanted to tell them more than anything about the boy with the pretty smile, but Jo's words kept me from it. If he had a bad reputation as being a big drinker and a little wild, what would my grandparents think? Grandma had recently retired from the school, so there was a good possibility she knew him. What if she didn't approve? What if they wouldn't let me go out with him?

I blushed and stuffed a piece of pancake in my mouth,

opting not to tell them quite yet. "Nope," I said with my mouth full.

"Are you sure?" Grandma asked with a suggestive smile. She smothered a spoonful of apricot jam onto a broken biscuit, patiently waiting for my response.

"Well, I . . . I guess I did meet some people. Some of Jo's friends. And . . . she wanted me to go to the drive-in with them tonight, if that's okay."

"Of course it's okay, doll. Have some fun. And by the way, Billy will meet you down at the barn after breakfast." She gave me a wink, and I found it funny she was so anxious for me to meet this Billy guy. He must've really been something for her and Jo both to compliment him. But the real question here was: did he know Cass?

After the pancakes and scrambled eggs were gone, I headed for the barn. The sun was shining bright above, and the cool morning wind blew lightly on my face. The smell of fresh-cut hay filled the air, and it made me long for days spent on a swather.

As I neared the pickup, I could smell strong cologne coming from inside the cab. Billy was already loaded with hay and waiting for me to join him. I reached for the passenger side door and peered inside a rolled-down window.

He was tall from what I could tell—the first sign being how close his head was to the top of the pickup. He had a muscular build with the biggest biceps I'd ever seen on someone his size. His hair was short and ruffled—a pretty chestnut brown. He had big brown eyes to match, along with a strong jaw and a clean-shaven face. I could see why Jo had chosen the word "gorgeous" for his description. It was fitting.

"Hi, I'm Billy," he said. "Jump in, and we'll go feed the heifers." His voice was deep, like Randy Travis's or maybe

Clint Eastwood's. I couldn't believe he was only in high school. He looked so much older than me.

I jumped in the truck and introduced myself. He smiled and shook my hand with a firm grip before pushing in the clutch and starting out the driveway.

"It's good to finally meet you," he said. "Your grandparents brag on you so much, I've been kinda anxious to know you."

I grinned, wondering what they had said about me. Or was he just trying to be nice? Either way, his smile was warm, and there was a kindness in his voice. I could see why Grandma was his number-one fan.

"So, how is your visit going so far?" he asked.

"Good. I met some people last night at the barn. I had a good time." My heart pounded faster as I thought of the way Cass had rubbed my palm. I smiled to myself, my stomach fluttering. The *looks* that boy could give.

"Oh yeah? Who'd you meet?"

"I'm friends with Jo Brewer, and she introduced me to Annie and Sam. There were a few people I met at the barn, but I didn't catch their names."

I didn't know if I should mention Cass or not. What if he had the same things to say about him as Jo did? I debated about it, going back and forth before I decided to go for it. I was too curious not to.

I tried to keep my voice as casual as possible. "I also met Tim . . . and this guy named Cass."

"Oh yeah, I know them well. It's a small town, so it's hard not to know just about everything there is to know about people. Sam's my cousin somehow down the line. Don't care much for Annie, but Jo's cool. I'm good friends with Tim." He paused as he turned down the radio a notch. "Cass is all right."

Well, at least he didn't have anything bad to say about him.

Billy and I spent the morning checking water and fences. Then we pulled the combines out of the barn so we could start preparing them for harvest—something I'd been excited about since I knew I'd be staying the summer. There was nothing I liked more than sitting on a combine and harvesting the crops Grandpa worked so hard to plant. It was rewarding in itself, and I looked forward to it every single summer.

"So, you're a senior this year?" Billy asked, changing out the tube in the grease gun.

"Yeah. Are you?"

"Nope, just graduated. Headed to College Station in the fall."

"You're going to A&M?"

"Yeah. Goin' to play football."

No wonder he's built like Rambo.

"I won't be too far from Houston, will I?" He pumped the grease gun until the veins in his arms bulged.

"Only about an hour," I said, wondering if his comment was meant to be flirty or factual. He was too focused on the grease gun for me to tell.

"What are you majoring in?" I asked, curious what a small-town, farmer-on-the-side jock planned to do after a stint playing college ball.

"I plan to major in political science and minor in pre-law. From there, I'll apply to law school."

Smart and argumentative. Interesting.

He laid the grease gun down on the back combine tire and wiped the sweat from his brow with his soiled T-shirt. I spotted his blocky abs when he did so, but quickly looked away.

"Enough about my future plans," he said, taking off his leather gloves. "Tell me about yourself."

"Well, what do you wanna know?"

"Tell me somethin' about Houston. I've never been." He smiled, and his eyes softened. He looked at me like we'd been friends for a lifetime and he'd missed me while I was gone. He felt familiar somehow.

"Houston's great," I said. "Greenfield's better."

Billy looked surprised, as if that was the last thing he'd expected me to say. "You mean you like Greenfield better than the city?"

"It's just so quiet here. Everything seems so much . . . simpler. It's like I stepped back in time to when things weren't so rushed."

"It is simple here," he agreed. "Kind of old-fashioned, I guess. It's funny . . . I grew up here and can't wait to get out. You grew up somewhere I wish to be, and you'd rather be here. How'd that happen?"

I smiled, thinking about that drive in from the airport. That feeling of being home every time the plane landed in Oklahoma City. *What I'd do to trade places with you, Billy.*

It was hard not to like the brown-eyed farmhand, jock or not. He didn't talk a lot—just enough to keep the conversation going. He was easy to be around and even easier to work with. He was helpful, hardworking, and smart when it came to farming. I could tell by the way he was so careful and detailed when caring for the farm equipment. It reminded me of how Grandpa was. Why hadn't Grandpa hired him before this summer?

Around six o'clock, I said goodbye to Billy and trotted for the house. Preparations for the night began as I jumped in the shower and took more time to get ready than I ever had before. After failing to curl my hair, I resorted to my everyday style—straight, flat, and wondering why I couldn't fix my own hair. My attempt to mimic the makeup I wore the previous night turned out to be a flop, but I went with it anyway. I pulled on my favorite pair of Jordache jeans, the only sandals I'd brought, and a yellow floral blouse that fit tighter than any other shirt I'd packed.

Before the clock read eight, I was sitting on the porch steps waiting nervously. Not wanting to risk Grandma or Grandpa answering the door, I decided it was best to watch for him outside so he wouldn't have a chance to knock.

I combed through my unresponsive hair, pausing when I heard a loud sound coming up the driveway. It was loud for a pickup, but I knew it had to be that black Chevy from last night. Which made it an even bigger shock when a motorcycle came rolling up to the porch.

The chrome exhaust gleamed, even though it was dusk, and the leather was black and clean. The engine roared like a prideful lion, and Cass looked like a dream with it purring between his legs, especially in his tight Wranglers, Led Zeppelin T-shirt, and a beaming smile that proved he was proud of his ride.

He hopped off when he rolled to a stop, then walked over to meet me at the top of the porch steps. He looked cleaned-up, unlike the night before, but his hair still had a greasy look to it. *I'm okay with that.*

He slipped his aviators on the top of his head and checked me out—making it as obvious as he could. I laughed and felt that same heat in my cheeks as I had the previous night.

"Well, don't you shine?" he said with a wink.

My heart pounded faster as I tried to remember how to speak words.

"Guess I forgot to mention I ride a Harley. Hope you don't mind ridin' on the back. Drive-in ain't far from here."

I swallowed nervously. I'd never ridden on one before. Steph's lecture resounded in my head, her voice demanding we take the Ford instead, after questioning my sanity for even considering hopping on the back.

"Sure," I said. *I'm in trouble.*

He must have picked up on my doubt because he carefully put his helmet on me and made sure I was comfortable once I threw a leg over the bike.

"Trust me," he said, buckling my chinstrap. "There ain't nothin' better in this world than the view from behind the handlebars."

He gave me that same look—the look he'd given me the night before—before winking, then he turned and faced the road ahead and dropped the bike into gear.

We sped off, and I scooted as close to him as I could, squeezing my legs tight against his. I wrapped my arms around his stomach and held on, enjoying the feel of his body so close to mine. He was warm and smelled of Ivory soap and Copenhagen—a scent I suddenly found irresistible.

The blood pumped faster through my body as the bike sped up. With each shift of the gears, the rush became more overwhelming and powerful. The wind whipped my face, cool and refreshing, and the feeling somehow calmed my nerves. My head was cleared of all negativity and worry, and my anxious thoughts were left somewhere behind us. There was nothing left but my own peace and the tranquility of the open blacktop road as we rode into the sun. It was then that I fell in love with his motorcycle.

A few minutes later, we pulled into the drive-in, and he steered the bike over to the far side of the parking lot and came to a stop. He picked a spot covered in grass instead of gravel, and we made ourselves comfortable on the soft patch of lawn.

"How was your first ride?" Cass looked at me as if he knew how much I enjoyed it, his smile giving him away.

"I loved it. It's so calming. I felt so . . ."

"Free?" He finished my sentence with the perfect word.

"Yeah. Free."

"Happens to the best of us. Did I mention how pretty you look?"

"Yeah, I think so." A childish giggle escaped my throat, and I tried to hide it with a cough. "You look great, too . . . especially on your bike and all. It's really nice."

He leaned his back against the back tire as a fulsome smile stretched across his face. "It's my pride and joy. Spent my last two summer paychecks on it, so it means a lot to me." His enthusiasm seemed to grow as he continued. "A seventy-seven Harley Ironhead Sportster. She might not be brand-spankin'-new, but she rides like a dream. A real powerhouse with a thousand-cc engine in her. Put in a new four-speed tranny, got her some new shoes. She's a one-kicker badass, bat-outta-hell machine, if you ask the owner." He smiled, and I wished I knew *something* about motorcycles.

All I could think to say was, "I like it."

"I've been told I make a good backrest, just like I'm a good hand-holder. Wanna see for yourself?"

I scooted in his direction, then leaned back against his chest, and he held my hand just like I'd promised he could. I felt his steady heartbeat on my back, which made my own wildly unsteady.

I can get used to this.

The movie started, and with it came more of his confidence. He ran his opposite hand up and down my arm, his fingers gliding over my goose-bumped skin. I was positive

I was blushing, which made me glad it was too dark to tell.

"I'm ready to ask you some questions whenever you feel like answerin' 'em," he said when we were just minutes into the movie.

"I'm ready," I said.

He leaned in close, brushing his lips against my ear before he spoke. "I'll ask and you answer, then I'll give you mine."

"Okay," I breathed.

He traced a finger along my shoulders and moved my hair to fall down my back. It tickled, and I bit my lip to hold in a laugh.

"Let's start with the boring stuff," he said. "What's your favorite class in school?"

"Um. . . English, probably. Only because it comes easier to me than other classes."

"Ag. 'Cause all we do is weld. You ever cheated on a test?"

"Once, in the fifth grade. I got caught and grounded for weeks. I'll never do it again."

He chuckled. "I've cheated way more than once, and I've got caught plenty. You play any sports?"

"Basketball."

"I can see that. You look like a basketball player."

I'd been told that before. That was something all tall, lanky kids were told at least once in their lives.

"Yeah, you look like one, too," I said.

"Me? Play basketball?" He snorted. "I can't make a basket for shit. I play football, though. And I wrestle, even though I hate it."

"Why do you do it if you hate it?"

"Hell, I don't know. Every year I say I'm gonna quit, then Coach rides my ass 'til he talks me into it again." He paused. "But this year I'll probably quit."

I glanced at him as he tight-lipped a smile. "Until Coach talks you into it again?"

He laughed, bumping my shoulder. "See, you're catchin' on to things quick. Now, uh . . . what's your favorite ride at the fair?

"Ferris wheel."

"Cakewalk."

"That's not a ride," I said through laughter.

"It's the ride of a lifetime if you can win one of Ms. Sheri's cakes. What's a memory from when you were a kid that makes you smile?"

I took a second to think about that one. I had a lot of fond memories from when I was a kid, but a couple struck me as favorites. "When we came here to visit my grandparents on the Fourth of July every year, we'd go to town and watch the fireworks. Grandma would always make homemade pineapple ice cream, and we'd take it with us. We'd all sit in our lawn chairs at the park, and sometimes I'd run off to play with Jo. The Fourth of July has always been my favorite holiday."

"I like the Fourth of July, too." He was quiet, thinking to himself for a minute. "I always smile when I think of all the times me and Grandpa would take the horses out and ride all over the place. We'd ride down to the river and pick blackberries, or we'd just ride into town and get a Pepsi from The Grill."

"Memories with grandpas are the best."

"There ain't no comparison," he said, squeezing my hand. "Pepsi or Coke?"

"Coke. Cherry Coke."

"Pepsi. Plain ol' Pepsi. What song do you sing obnoxiously when it comes on the radio?"

"That's easy. 'Heaven' by Bryan Adams."

"'Love Hurts'. Nazareth. Every damn time."
"Oh, that's a good one."
"All right, final one of the night. What did you notice first when you saw me last night?"
I tilted my head up, looking at him as he flashed his smile behind me. "Smile," I said. "Definitely your smile."
He gave me that same smile before reaching down and squeezing my thigh. "Legs."
"You're kidding."
"Nope. You've got killer legs, darlin'."
I'd spent most of my life hating my legs because I felt like they were too skinny. Talk about a major confidence boost.
"Okay, I have one more question I just thought of. Let's say you have a good time on our first date and agree to go on another one with me. Where would you wanna go?"
I think I'd go absolutely anywhere with this boy.
"The skating rink," I said, going with the first thing off the top of my head.
"The skatin' rink? You're sure?"
"Yep," I said. "I haven't been there since I was a kid."
"I ain't been there in years, either. Might be kinda fun to go check it out again sometime. Especially if I have a pretty thing like you on my arm." He wrapped his arms around my stomach, but he did it carefully. I liked how cautious he was about it. It made me feel like he really didn't want to make a bad move and make me uncomfortable.
The movie ended too soon, and we hopped back onto his bike. The night air was cool, and I squeezed him even closer on the way home. We made the way back to my grandparents' house and parked at the bottom of the driveway instead of pulling up to the steps.
"I don't wanna wake 'em up," he said. "I'll walk you up to the door."

I smiled at his courtesy.

We made the walk up the driveway, and he grabbed my hand on the way. He held it tight, our fingers intertwining like the vines that crawled up the house. The moon was high, and the crickets sang to us as we walked toward the porch steps, their steady song sweeter than I'd ever remembered it being.

"I had a real good time tonight, Austin. I'd like to take you out again . . . so I can hold your hand."

"I'd like that." I tried not to sound overly excited, but it wasn't easy. I think I sounded more like a five-year-old girl getting tickets to Disneyland rather than a seventeen-year-old dork getting a second date.

"I'd ask you to hang out this week, but I'll be workin' late nights on the farm. You know how that goes."

I nodded.

"Skatin' rink don't open 'til June, or I'd take you there this weekend. So, instead, would you just wanna come hang out with me at the barn on Friday?"

We made our way to the front porch, where he stood in front of me with his hands in his back pockets. He looked like he was posing for a magazine—a fitting depiction of the perfect cover for *The Rolling Stone*.

"Yes, I would. What time?"

"Pick you up at eight?"

"Sounds great." I shuddered from nerves, thinking a kiss was on the horizon.

Instead, he just chuckled. "Kinda feel like Elvis, darlin'. You're givin' me the shakes." He shook his shoulders and gave me an Elvis-worthy grin. We both laughed before he brushed a light kiss across my cheek and whispered in my ear, "See you Friday, sunshine."

Chapter 5

As harvest neared, Grandpa, Billy, and I spent hours preparing the combines. We changed oil and filters, and cleaned up the machines. Sickle sections were changed, radiators were blown out, and belts replaced. Days were busy, with breaks few and far between. The week seemed to drag on, and I lost patience waiting for the weekend.

Once each workday was over, I'd spend hours going through the clothes I'd brought with me. I'd stare in the mirror, attempting to fix my hair and brush up on my makeup skills. I felt silly, like a little girl playing dress-up at Grandma's house, but I kept doing it. There was a giddiness in my soul that pushed me to try new things and sample a world I wasn't familiar with.

On Friday afternoon, Grandpa told Billy and me to drive

to Geary to grab some engine oil. I knew Cass lived there and wondered if we'd run into him somewhere.

"Do you know the Jamesons?" I asked Billy.

"Yeah. Why do you ask?"

"Cass told me he works for them."

"Oh, so you've been talking to Cass again?" I could've sworn I heard a subtle hint of disappointment in his voice.

"Yeah," I said softly.

"Hmm." Billy shook his head and looked out the window. I didn't press him.

Why is he quiet all of a sudden?

We arrived back at the house around five o'clock, after a trip to the Geary elevator and a hardware store that had next to nothing in stock. Billy hadn't said much after I mentioned Cass, and I was glad there was a decent radio in the truck to tame down the awkward silence on the way home.

"I see you and Billy are getting along," Grandma said as I walked through the door. She smiled and continued beating some sort of batter in a bowl.

"We are," I said, going along with her.

"I have a good feeling about you and him, doll." She walked away, humming a tune and bouncing her hips from side to side.

I shook my head, unable to admit to her I wasn't interested in anything more than a friendship with the farmhand. "Hey, I'm gonna hang out with Jo again tonight." I bit my lip, flushing at the fact I had blatantly lied to her. I couldn't just leave it like that, so I added, "And some other people." That made me feel a little better.

"Ah, I remember those days," Grandma said innocently. She ran a finger along the rim of her orange mixing bowl and tasted the batter with a nostalgic grin. "Friday nights in the big town. Pulling up to Cletus P.'s drugstore for a Coke before zipping down Main Street and meeting up at the diner for a burger and a milkshake. Ending the night with one of Miss Elsie's hot fudge brownies. Oh, the memories."

I smiled while she reminisced. Grandma liked to tell the story of how she fell for Grandpa, and even though I'd heard it a hundred times, I felt like hearing it again. I walked to the table and pulled out a chair, taking a seat as she spooned some more vanilla into the mix.

"How did you and Grandpa meet again?"

She tilted her head back with a giddy chuckle before sharing a part of her heart I would've been grateful to hear a hundred more times.

"Well, me and Shirley Jo Jackson were at the diner eating one Friday night. It was right after school had started back up, and everyone who was anyone was there. The place was packed tight as it could be, and I can remember 'Green Eyes' by Jimmy Dorsey playing on the radio." She smiled to herself before continuing. "Grandpa walked in with a bunch of guys from the football team, and doll, you want to talk about easy on the eyes . . ." She looked over her shoulder at me with her eyes wide and humorous. "Whew. Well, that was your grandad in nineteen forty-one."

I'd seen pictures of Grandpa from his younger years. I understood perfectly.

"Anyway, Shirley Jo saw him come in, and boy, he's all she could talk about. I remember her telling me he'd been stealing peeks at her in choir, and she just *knew* he wanted to go steady. I didn't pay her any mind, though. For one, Shirley thought *everyone* wanted to go steady with her, and for two, she and I were just freshmen. Why would a senior be interested in either one of us?"

I'd also seen a couple pictures of Grandma back in the day. She might've liked to play coy, but she was a genuine knockout. Any guy, no matter their age, was probably chasing her, whether she knew it or not.

"So, Shirley just kept going on and on, and what do you know? Here comes your grandad walking over to us. I thought, good Lord, Shirley's done it this time. She's spent this entire time staring at this poor guy, and now he's come to confront her about it and make us both look like fools."

I laughed as she poured the batter into a bundt pan but left enough of the gooey goodness in it for me to finish off.

"Grandpa came right over to our booth and slid in like he owned the restaurant. He turned to me and said, 'Do you like this song?' Shirley and I kinda looked at each other before I finally said, 'Yes, I do.' And then he said, 'So do I,' and he got up and left."

Grandma started laughing hysterically, and I joined in. I loved that part of the story.

"About five minutes later, he came back over and asked me on a date. Later, he told me he'd been so nervous he'd forgotten my name and had to go ask his buddies what it was before gaining enough courage to come back over. And you wanna talk about someone being pretty perturbed that night . . . Whew, Shirley Jo was *mad*. You know she still calls me up to this day and reminds me of this story? I think she still holds a grudge against me. Of course, I would too if I'd ended up with the man she ended up with. Bert's an ol' devil if I ever saw one."

Grandpa walked in just in time to help me lick the bowl and then plopped down in the chair next to me. "You sharing secrets in here?" he asked, taking a drink from his half-full mug of hot tea.

"Oh, just reminiscing about you and Shirley Jo Jackson." Grandma winked at me while I scooped a big spoonful of batter out for myself.

Grandpa scoffed. "I swear, that woman never could sing a lick. I don't know why she was even *in* choir. The only reason I ever looked at her was because she hurt my ears every time she opened her mouth."

Grandma laughed.

"You goin' out tonight?" Grandpa asked me.

"Yeah, I am."

"You're stayin' away from those boys, aren't ya?" Grandpa's tone was light, but for some reason, I got nervous when he said it. Did he suspect I was sneaking around?

"Mm-hmm," I said. *Convincing.*

He chuckled. "Pass me that spoon, and I'll help you with lickin' this bowl."

I gave him the spoon, thankful he hadn't dug any deeper.

After the bowl was clean, I took a quick shower, partly because I was covered in grease, and partly because it was good for washing away the guilt of keeping Cass a secret.

I went to my bedroom after I was good and cleansed, and before I tackled the mountain of clothes forming on my bed—none of which were good enough to wear—I put on an old record. A certain song had been stuck in my head all day—one that reminded me of Cass and his prized Harley. Steph's old turntable was in the corner of the room, along with some records I'd found in Wal-Mart bargain bins over the years. Paired with a few of Jay's old 45s, I had a pretty impressive stockpile for when I visited.

I filed through the assortment of Doors, Stones, and Zeppelin covers, and came across the very first album Jay had given me. It was Skynyrd's self-titled album with his favorite song on it: "Free Bird." The song was permanently burnt in my head and branded in my mind. Steph always teased that Jay had had that song playing on repeat since '73, but quite honestly, it wasn't a joke. It was still the number-one song on

Red Dirt Paradise

Jay's top-eight list—the other seven songs being the ones on this very album. I smiled to myself, thinking about how he had opened the door for my love of rock music. Grandma had opened it for Willie and Waylon.

I tossed the Skynyrd album aside before finally finding the one I'd been looking for. After pulling it from its sleeve, I dropped the needle on a Montrose vinyl.

Singing to "Bad Motor Scooter," I searched through my closet, unable to find anything I thought looked decent enough for a second date. Why hadn't I packed anything more than tees and tank tops?

When I'd gone through everything I owned a few times, I decided I'd just cut the bottom from one of my T-shirts. I chose a KISS concert tee and went for it, then threw on a pair of cutoff jeans. Annoyed I still hadn't mastered an admirable hairdo, I pulled my hair back and spent the next twenty minutes trying to get my mascara not to look clumpy and cheap.

When it was almost time for Cass to show up, I walked to the front room to wait on him. Thankfully, Grandma and Grandpa were once again in the den, engulfed in an old episode of *Bat Masterson*, and I wouldn't have to worry about them walking out to see me mount a Harley. *Talk about getting gutsy.*

After hearing him pull up, I opened the front door, happy to find his Harley idling just a few feet from the porch steps. He looked good with his hair windblown from his face, wearing tight jeans ripped at the knees and a Black Sabbath shirt. Typical of Cass, he shot me a smile and pulled his aviators to the tip of his nose for a better look. Typical of me, I smiled back while turning a shade of pink.

I took my helmet from his hands and fastened the clasp beneath my chin, then threw my leg over the bike, making myself comfortable behind him. I smiled, feeling like a seasoned biker after just one trip down the road and back. As he revved the engine, I hugged him tight. He must have just left work because he smelled of sweat and diesel—two things that went hand in hand on a farm. I didn't mind at all, happy to be away from Billy's strong cologne.

After a short trip I wished had lasted a lot longer, we arrived at the barn. We walked up to the party, and I spotted Jo and Annie from across the parking lot. Annie looked annoyed and gave us a dirty look, while Jo glanced at her, concerned. Cass put his arm around my waist and gave me a squeeze while I tried to avoid Annie's gaze. The sooner she got over it, the better. I hated awkward encounters, and the next one I had with her would definitely be one.

Cass led us over to a group of guys, where one of them handed him a longneck. He was a tall fellow with curly brown hair and a fuzzy brownish-red beard. His dark Wranglers were covered in cow manure, and he wore a worn-in shirt that read "Shotgun Willie." Since I was a Willie Nelson fan myself, I knew we'd get along just fine.

"So, Cass-man . . . this is her, huh?" he asked, nudging Cass. He spoke out of one side of his mouth when he talked, but that could've been because he had the biggest dip I'd ever seen in his lower lip.

"Yep, this is her. Ain't she somethin'?" Cass smiled and brought me in closer.

I grinned, a sudden rush of confidence blooming in my chest.

"This is Larry, my right-hand man," he said.

Larry nodded, his mouth folding in a smile.

"Where's Heather?" Cass asked him, lighting up a cigarette.

"Hell, I don't know, man. She got pissed off about somethin'." Larry threw his hands up in the air, cursing under his breath. He had a theatrical way about him—the way he spoke with his hands, how he raised his eyebrows and bugged his eyes. It was almost cartoonish. Just watching him could make the saddest person smile.

Cass scoffed, blowing smoke through his nose. "Larry's always pissin' her off somehow."

Larry put his fingers to his temples, shaking his head. "It ain't my fault this time, man. I didn't even know we *had* an anniversary." He walked away, shoving a guy who was walking toward us.

"Where's that sixer you owe me?" the guy asked Cass. He threw his arm over Cass's shoulders and playfully punched him in the gut. He was dirtier than Larry, with grease up to his elbows. His eyes peeked out from under thick brows, and his hair flipped from underneath a warped straw cowboy hat. His jeans had grass stains at the knees, and he wore them tucked inside cowboy boots stitched with purple paisley designs.

"Still at the store," Cass said.

The guy tilted his straw hat to the back of his head and looked me up and down.

I lowered my head in a hurry, avoiding his eyes.

"Who's this?" he demanded.

"Someone you ain't gonna look at like that," Cass said. He said it with a smile, but considering his tone, he wasn't joking.

The guy smirked and patted Cass on the chest. "You always get the good ones, don't ya?" He turned and backed away in Larry's direction. "Don't forget about that sixer."

Cass grumbled under his breath and steered us in the opposite direction. "Keith is fuller than a fuckin' horse's shit."

I smiled, deciding to ignore Keith's comment rather than ask about the other "good ones" that had been before me. Even so, Annie's face flashed in my mind.

We made our way over to Jo, Cass's arm never leaving my shoulders. Annie left before we got there, storming off when she noticed us walking their way. I went and sat by Jo, while Cass hung back and talked to a group of guys a few feet away. Thin Lizzy's "The Boys Are Back In Town" was blaring on somebody's radio, and it fit the scene perfectly.

I watched Cass as he talked to his friends. He seemed to own the center of attention while making jokes and telling stories. People gravitated toward him and left with either a smile on their face or laughing hysterically. Aware I was watching him, he'd look over and wink at me occasionally. He'd run his hands through his greasy hair and flex his lean muscles as he was doing so, making it hard to look away from him.

Seriously hard.

"You really like him, don't you?" Jo asked.

I didn't miss a beat. "Yeah, I do."

She sighed, clicking her heels together like she was Dorothy from *The Wizard of Oz*. "Well, what do you think about Billy?" She asked the question loud enough I was sure Cass had heard her. Then again, that's probably what she was going for.

I shrugged. "Uh . . . he's nice. Seems like a good guy to work with."

"Him and Tim are close. Like, they've been best friends since forever. Tim plans to go to A&M with him after we graduate."

"Yeah, he mentioned that."

"And he's really cute, and smart, and funny . . . he's perfect for you. You should totally give him a shot."

I smiled at her effort. "I like Billy, but just as a friend."

"You're killin' me, girl." She shook her head and reached for another beer. "Well, whenever Cass doesn't work out, give Billy a chance." She lowered her voice as Cass walked up to us.

"Am I interruptin'?" he asked, smiling at Jo and confirming my assumption he'd heard every word that came out of her mouth.

"Not at all," Jo said with a sigh.

"Then I'm gonna borrow my girl from you." He grabbed my hands, pulling me to my feet, then he wrapped my arms around his waist and held my face in his hands. Our mouths were so close, I was sure we were going to have our first kiss in front of the whole party.

"Maybe the barn wasn't the best place to come tonight." He snuck Jo a look, then his eyes moved back to mine.

"Do you have a better place?" My stomach did somersaults as he leaned closer . . . and closer . . .

"I think I do."

"Where?" I let out a breath as he pulled away just a touch. He smiled. "Trust me."

He grabbed my hand, and we ran to his bike, where we hopped on and headed down the asphalt for a few hundred feet. He turned at an intersection, where the road turned to gravel. The full moon spotlighted the road in front of us as all the headlights from the barn disappeared. The cool wind chilled my body, making my arms close in tighter around his warm abs.

We continued down a curvy, narrow road until we arrived at a bridge. The floor was made of rickety wooden planks, and the sides were tall, rusted metal. The smell of creek water and alfalfa filled the night air.

"Come on. You're gonna love this." Cass grabbed my

hand, and we walked to the edge of the bridge. He sat down and dangled his feet off it, then pulled me down to sit in between his legs. As he hugged me close, I felt his warmth surround me.

The moon was full and shone a generous light on the rolling creek in front of us. Fireflies buzzed about the trees and brush below, lighting up the shadowed areas in eager bursts. Occasionally, I heard a fish tail smack the water or a bullfrog croak.

We sat for a long time without saying a word, just enjoying the view, the stillness of the night, and each other's company.

"It's so peaceful here," I said, staring at the moon's reflection on the silky ripples of the water.

"I come here quite a bit. I do some of my best thinkin' here at Fall Bridge." He squeezed me tighter, resting his chin on my shoulder.

"Fall Bridge," I repeated.

"They say if you share a kiss here on this bridge, you'll fall in love."

"Is that so?"

"Yeah, and you have no choice but to fall victim."

I smiled as he softly ran his thumb back and forth over my arm.

"Why's that?" I asked.

"'Cause I'm good lookin' and just so damn irresistible." He moved my hair off my shoulder and lightly bit my neck.

Instead of somersaults, my stomach was now in full back-flip mode. "You're awfully confident, aren't you?" I breathed.

"Tell me I'm wrong."

"I'd . . . be lying if I did."

He grabbed my hips and slid me around until I was facing him, then he caressed my neck and ran his thumb across my lips. "One day, you're gonna love me." Gently, he placed his lips to mine in a kiss that was far better than any I'd ever had before. He moved slowly and deliberately, biding his time as the spell of Fall Bridge was cast upon us. His touch was tender yet persuasive, and I fell head over heels for his romance.

I wrapped my arms around his neck, willingly ready to kiss him like that forever, but things stopped on a dime instead.

He drew away from me and looked into my eyes. "Tell me somethin' about yourself."

"What . . . do you mean?"

"Tell me somethin' about you. Your dreams or what you like to do . . . just anything you haven't told me before."

I thought about it for a moment, not thinking clearly after a kiss like that. It blew all of Peter's hard, sloppy kisses out of the water. "Well, um . . . I . . . I like working."

He threw his head back in laughter. "That ain't exactly what I expected, but I'll take it."

"Well, I mean, I like coming up here and helping my grandpa farm—as weird as that sounds. I like running equipment and working with cattle. Fixing, building . . . I don't know. Just anything like that."

"That's gotta be the sexiest thing I've ever heard." His eyes shone like streetlights in the moonlight. "Anything else?"

"I like photography."

"Like takin' pictures?"

"Yeah."

"What do you like takin' pictures of?"

"Scenery . . . people. Anything that makes for a good picture I guess."

"Well, you're in luck 'cause I happen to be a model."

"Well, I guess you'll have to prove yourself sometime."

"Oh, you bet I will. Do you have a camera?"

"Yeah, I brought my Canon. It used to be my aunt's. She's a professional photographer."

I thought back to the day Steph had let me use the Canon for the first time. It was the year I turned thirteen, and I'd just started going with her to shoots. That day, she'd given me free range with a couple of the models that were there, and she praised my work afterward. We'd done a ton of shoots together since, but that first time was something I'd always remember.

"So, farming and photography run in your family, huh?"

I laughed, realizing that was true. "Yeah, it does, I guess. It's your turn, now. Tell me some things about you."

He sat back against the metal frame of the bridge and rested his hands behind his head. Looking up at the stars, a smile unraveled on his lips before he started to speak. "Don't get me wrong. I like farmin', too. But music is my thing. I sing a little and play some guitar. It's kinda a dream of mine to play in a band. Just take off to California, move into an abandoned apartment off Sunset Boulevard, and join a band of misfits who don't care about nothin' but rock 'n roll." He gazed off into space, letting his mind take him someplace else. His passion for it was as clear as the night sky.

"Music is my escape from reality," he said. "I turn on a song—some good country or rock—and let it take me away to wherever it wants me to go. Whether it's a sad ol' Willie song or a kickass Crüe record, I just let it take hold. I like givin' songs the power to do that to me. The power to change my mood or make it more intense."

With every word he spoke, I was more mesmerized by his love for music. I could hear it in his voice—the feelings that arose from him just talking about it. I fell in love with a certain look in his eyes as he shared part of his soul.

"I'd love to hear you sing," I said, hopeful he'd be willing to share his talent.

"Now?"

"Why not?"

He grinned. "Only if you'll dance with me."

"Okay, only if you sing my favorite song."

He stood up and grabbed my hand, pulling me up with him. "What's your favorite song, sunshine?"

"One of my favorites is 'Good Hearted Woman.' Do you know it?"

"Ha! Of course I know it."

He led me out toward the middle of the bridge and draped one of my arms around his neck, then locked hands with the other.

"Do you know how to two-step?" he asked.

"No, I don't."

"Just follow me. That's all you gotta do. Kinda like the saying 'two steps forward, and one step back.'"

It seemed easy enough, but I tensed right when he led the first step. I wasn't sure how to match his smoothness.

He held me closer, moving his hand to my lower back. "Relax. It's all in your hips. Just move with me. Feel it. Don't force it."

Trying to follow his lead the best I could, I caught on pretty quickly, and it started to come easier.

"You know this song was written about a girl in Texas, don't you?" he asked.

"Really?"

"Well, I don't know that for sure. But I know the best women are in Texas, so I figure I'm right."

He twirled me around, singing my favorite song like he'd written it himself. He was a natural at it, singing a cappella as if he'd practiced that same song for years. His tone was melodic and his words smooth, melting from his mouth like churned butter. He had a voice that could make millions, and one that I could listen to for hours on end.

    Cass moved lightly on his feet, dipping me between verses of the song and spinning me freely across the rotted wood of the bridge. Staring into my eyes, he looked away only if we stumbled upon a loose board. He sang to me as if he were singing to my soul, sending the words somewhere beneath the surface. The emotion—the *passion*—that filled his voice left me breathless, and his slow kisses between words made me wish the night would never end.

Chapter 6

"Hey, Austin, can you hand me that crescent wrench? Austin?"

"Oh, sorry." I handed Billy the wrench, embarrassed he had to bring me back to reality. I was daydreaming again, and he'd noticed.

"How was the barn last night?" he asked as he tightened up a loose nut.

I'd been reliving it all day as we worked beneath the combine. I kept thinking of Cass's kisses, rough hands, and the way he sang the words of that Waylon song. The look he gave me—the one where I felt he was staring into my soul, seeing me in ways nobody else did.

"Looks to me like you had a good time," Billy said.

His words startled me, especially when he didn't give me enough time to answer his question. "Yeah, I had fun."

He stopped what he was doing and looked at me from underneath the header. "If you don't mind my asking, what is it that you like about Cass?"

I stood awkwardly, feeling my cheeks burn from being put on the spot. "Uh . . . well . . . he's nice."

"That's it? He's nice?"

"Well . . . he makes me laugh. He's different from the guys back home." Even if I'd wanted to name all the things I liked about Cass, it didn't matter. Billy's glare made me feel too uneasy to think straight. "I, uh, I guess he just makes me feel different. I'm not sure." I traced circles in the gravel with my boot, never meeting his eyes.

"You're really into him, huh?"

"Yeah," I murmured.

"Okay." He grabbed a different wrench and went back to work.

I let out a sigh of relief and walked to the toolbox for the window cleaner.

When I made my way back to the combine ladder, Billy was waiting for me. He dusted the dirt off his jeans and took off his gloves.

"Look, Austin, I've already made things awkward, so I might as well make them even more awkward. I didn't ask you out right away because I never would've thought you'd meet a guy the first day you got here. I guess I was waitin' for the right moment, and I lost my chance."

I stood in front of him, not knowing what to say or do. I shifted nervously, glad my hands were full. I wouldn't have a clue what to do with them if they weren't.

"I don't exactly know what I expected. I've been workin' with your grandpa for a while now and talkin' to your grandma about you. I see your pictures, I hear stories about you. I guess . . . well, I guess I just thought you'd come down here and work with me and things would just . . . happen." He laughed, and it eased the tension between us. "That's what happens in the movies, isn't it?"

I smiled, appreciating how honest he was being. "Well, truthfully, I wasn't expecting to meet someone so quickly, either. It was a surprise for me, too. Of all the times I've visited, I've never been on a date with anyone here or even talked to another guy. Cass just sort of . . ."

"Happened." Billy pulled his gloves back on.

I nodded.

"Well, I hope it works out." He breathed a sigh of defeat and walked toward the barn.

As I watched Billy walk away, I felt like I'd done something wrong. How had I managed to break someone's heart in my first week in Oklahoma?

I walked into the house around six that evening, still feeling bad about the afternoon. I hoped Grandma had something sweet to eat that might lift my spirits.

"Jo called you around five. She wants you to call her back," she said, taking a maple cream pie out of the oven. Buttered, toasted pecans and warmed syrup filled the room with a sugar-coated scent that made my tastebuds tingle. Grandma always could satisfy a sweet tooth.

I called Jo back, and she answered with an invitation to Annie's house for a party. When I asked, she assured me Annie had gotten over the fact I was seeing Cass, and she wasn't mad about it. I accepted the invitation, but deep down, I still had my doubts about Annie. She didn't seem like the type to forget about something so easily.

I hurried through dinner, making sure to leave room for pie, then rushed upstairs to get ready. Choosing some tight jeans from the pile of clean clothes on the floor, I threw them on and cut another one of my T-shirts. I let my hair fall from my ponytail, shaking out the few bits of straw that had gotten trapped in the tangles, then put on a new eyeshadow I'd found in the bottom of Grandma's makeup drawer.

"Are you going out with Billy?" Grandma asked as I walked into the room.

I chose the seat next to her on the couch, noticing how much she perked up when Billy was mentioned. Her smile was wide and hopeful, her eyes brightening behind her glasses.

"I'm just going out with Jo, Grandma."

"Maybe you'll run into him somewhere. You guys should go to the drive-in some weekend, or maybe the bowling alley. Billy likes to bowl." She nudged me as she poked a needle through her embroidery fabric.

Jo picked me up shortly after, just in time to save me from more of Grandma's matchmaking attempts, and we made the drive to Annie's place.

"Are you *sure* Annie is okay with me coming?" I asked Jo as we made our way through some curvy backroads south of town.

"I'm sure," she said. "If she wasn't, she'd let me know."

"Okay. Just didn't want her hating me when I show up to her house."

"She actually asked me if you were coming with me, and she didn't seem mad at all. I'd say the dust has settled. Knowing Annie, she's got her sights set on someone else."

Annie lived a few miles out of town in a tall, two-story house. It was a gorgeous home that reminded me of some of the houses in our neighborhood back in Houston. Tall pillars decorated the front, with massive windows showing between them. There was white wicker furniture on the porch, and the yard looked professionally landscaped. There was a big rock pond, manicured bushes, and so many flowers in the flowerbeds it looked as if we were entering Greenfield botanical gardens.

When Annie greeted us in the entryway, I looked around and admired the inside of the house. Faux palm trees were on either side of the door, and the walls were covered with brightly colored paintings of oceans, seashells, and white-sand beaches. It felt like we'd just walked into a beach house in the Florida Keys. I studied the art as Annie and Jo talked.

"Here's some beers, or there's wine in the fridge. Help yourselves." Annie handed Jo a bottle, then motioned for us to come out back with her. She gave me a smile that didn't seem like a fake one, which made me believe she was truly over the fact I was seeing Cass. Maybe there *was* someone new in her sights.

The backyard had a pond only a few feet away from the back door. A dock ran about twenty yards into it, and lights were strung along the railing. Lynyrd Skynyrd's "That Smell" was on the stereo, and it was very much appropriate for the time. I could smell marijuana thick in the night air.

Twenty or thirty people were sitting in lawn chairs on the patio, and some were walking along the dock. I scanned the crowd for Cass, but instead saw Billy sitting next to Tim. He was still in his work clothes from earlier, and I swear I could smell his infamous cologne from twenty feet away, even through the skunky smell of weed. He spotted me and smiled, saying something to Tim in the process.

"I heard he opened up to you today," Jo said, acknowledging she'd seen him smiling at me.

"Yeah, a little." I sighed. "It made me feel bad."

"It made you feel bad because you know which guy you should be with."

"No, I just . . . I mean, he's a really nice guy, and I just felt bad for him, I guess."

She laughed and bumped my shoulder. "I have hope you'll come around. Us four could have a lot of fun on double dates, you know."

Billy left his seat and made his way toward us, approaching me with a smile and an extra can of beer.

"Hey, coworker," he said, handing Jo the beer.

She looked at me and mouthed something I couldn't make sense of before leaving us for Tim.

"Can we talk?" Billy asked, looking around as if making sure no one was watching.

"Sure," I said.

"I'm sorry about this afternoon. I didn't mean to make things weird between us. I hope you don't think I'm a creep or something."

"I know you're not a creep. I appreciate your honesty. That took guts."

He laughed under his breath. "Maybe one of these days I'll learn to keep my mouth shut."

"You're fine," I said just as Cass walked in front of us. He appeared out of nowhere, startling Billy and me both.

"Tryin' to make me jealous?" Cass shot me a grin, then looked at Billy. He rocked back on his heels, arms folded across his chest. "Well, hell, Billy, I didn't know you drank."

"I don't . . . usually." Billy lowered his beer. "Tough day at work." He looked at me before taking a step away from us. "See you around."

He walked back to Tim and Jo, and Jo looked disappointed I wasn't by his side.

"Everything okay, darlin'?" Cass asked.

"Yeah, everything's fine." I smiled as he grabbed my hand and led me out onto the dock, where he had two lawn chairs set up with a guitar case in between.

"For you, sunshine." He motioned to one of the chairs, then scooted his own closer to mine before he sat down.

"How long have you been here?" I asked, worried he thought something was going on between me and Billy.

"Long enough to see the way ol' Billy boy looks at you."

My heart dropped to my stomach, and I wondered if I should tell him about the afternoon. "I think he just had a little too much to drink or something."

"There ain't no way in hell he can work beside you every day and not wanna be with you." He leaned in and kissed me before I could tell him he was crazy. "I ain't worried, though. I know who's on your mind throughout the day."

"Who?" I asked, breathless.

"The same guy who has you on his." He kissed me again, this time longer than before, and butterflies two-stepped in my stomach.

"I'm gonna play you a little somethin'." He opened the guitar case and pulled out a black Gibson. It was weathered, revealing years of wear and tear from hours of practice. "Anything in particular you wanna hear?"

"Surprise me."

He smiled and tucked his hair behind his ears, then broke into the first few chords of one of my favorite Creedence Clearwater Revival songs.

As he strummed the chords, I watched his body sway with the rhythm. He closed his eyes, feeling the music as the words to "Have You Ever Seen the Rain" rolled off his tongue like magic. I noticed his voice had a rougher quality to it than it did when he sang to me the first time, and I guessed southern rock was more his element. He seemed more comfortable, shining with confidence while singing with a growl and hitting higher notes.

After a series of CCR songs and a couple Skynyrd numbers, Cass laid his Gibson back in its aged case. He snapped the golden clasps shut and patted the top of it like it was a family pet.

"Amazing," I said, clapping with approval.

"Thanks, darlin'. Lot of hours spent with this damn thing, I'll promise you that."

"Who's your inspiration?"

"Joe Perry for guitar. John Fogerty for the voice. He's been my man since I first heard him sing. I tried to mimic him for so long, a part of me thinks it kinda stuck. I'm proud of that, too."

"I love his voice, and you do sound kinda like him. I hear some Seger in you, too."

A proud smile stretched across Cass's face. "I'd like to think of myself as soundin' a little like Fogerty, a little like Seger, and a lot like James Cassedy."

He grabbed his cigarettes out of his shirt pocket, then reached into his jeans pocket in search of something he didn't find. "Dammit," he growled. "I need a lighter. I need my ice chest, too. I'll be right back. You need anything?"

"I'm okay, thank you."

"A Coke. You need a Coke. I'll get you a Coke. Cherry, if you're lucky." He squeezed my shoulder before walking toward the house.

While he was gone, I opened his guitar case and peeked inside. I ran my hand over the splintered neck and touched the cool wood of the body. I strummed all six strings individually—admiring the tuned sound of each one. "E, B, G,

D, A, E," I said to myself, remembering the guitar lessons Jay had urged me to take in the third grade. I'd only gone to them for a couple months before I gave it up. I couldn't learn a single chord and my fingertips hurt too bad to stick it out.

Cass was gone for more than a few minutes—long enough to make me wonder where he was. Right as I came to the decision that I should go find him, Sam walked onto the dock and took Cass's empty chair.

"Hey, you okay?" she asked, looking uneasy. Her usual bubbly tone was gone, and her cheerful smile was nonexistent.

"Yeah," I said. "Why do you ask?"

"I just noticed Cass left you here by the pond to be with Annie. I wanted to make sure you were okay."

A sinking feeling slowly set in, starting in my chest and ending when it felt like my stomach had bottomed out. When I answered, I tried to keep my voice as steady as I could. "He went to get his ice chest." Disappointment made my voice quiver, and I cleared my throat to try and rid it. "At least . . . that's what he told me."

"Yeah . . ." She pursed her lips. "I don't think his ice chest is why he left. Something's going on between them. They're locked in Annie's room together."

I stared out at the pond for a few seconds, on the verge of frustrated tears. My throat went dry as I realized I'd been played.

"I shouldn't have said anything." Her tone was apologetic, and her eyes full of sympathy. "I'm sorry. I just thought you should know that, like, that's just the type of guy he is. I'm surprised Jo hasn't told you about him. He's such a whore. Everyone knows it."

"She tried to tell me. Guess I should've listened." I left my chair on the dock, too upset to even tell Sam goodbye.

Upset because he'd toyed with me. Upset because I'd fallen for it. But mostly, upset because I should've known.

I should've known.

I walked toward the party in search of a ride home, scanning every face and relieved to find the one I was looking for.

"Nice of you to join the party. Where's Cass?" Jo asked as I took the empty seat to her left. Unfortunately, it was right next to Billy, who looked surprised I was taking it.

"Oh, he . . . he, uh, went inside. I think to get more beer," I stammered, trying to make his lie sound believable.

Jo scoffed. "Should've known."

"Do you mind taking me home?" I asked. "I don't feel very good. I think I'm getting sick or something." I held my stomach, hoping to make my story more convincing.

"Yeah, no problem," Jo said.

"You're okay to drive, right?"

"Yeah, I've barely had anything to drink."

She told Tim goodbye, then grabbed her keys off the table. Billy looked at me as if I was the biggest liar in history and told me to feel better. I told him I would. *Because that's possible right now.*

"So, what's really going on?" Jo asked when we were out of earshot of the guys.

"Nothing. I just don't feel good."

"Yeah, and you're also a liar. A bad one."

I shook my head, sniffing back the sadness in my voice. "Cass told me that he had to get beer from inside. He never came back, and then Sam walks over to me and tells me he's with Annie in her room."

"That jackass," Jo muttered.

We started to drive out of Annie's driveway, but she stopped the truck before pulling onto the blacktop.

"I'm sorry he did that to you, Austin. You're the last

person who deserves that. I'm gonna kick his ass next time I see him."

I forced a pitiful laugh.

"I'm really gonna lay into him," she assured me. "I'll let him know how much of an ass he really is."

"Why did I get so attached to him anyway? I've never been like this with *anyone*. Geez, Jo. Why did he have to do this?" I wiped a tear from my cheek, embarrassed I was crying over something like this. I barely even knew him. Why had I been so stupid?

"Cass just has a way about him," she said. "He says all the right things, makes the best moves, kills a girl with charm. I've seen it happen a lot. I'm telling you, he's no good. You gotta watch guys like him. I learned that the hard way."

"Yeah. Guess I learned the hard way, too." I turned up the radio, not wanting to talk about him anymore.

Why had I let that happen? How could I have fallen for someone so *fast?* I leaned my head back against the headrest and promised myself I'd never fall for someone that fast again.

Jo slammed on her brakes and put her truck in reverse, looking behind her as she backed up. "I don't wanna take you home."

"I . . . I don't wanna go back there," I said. "I'm too embarrassed. I really just wanna go. I don't feel like doing anything else."

She turned down the radio and gave me a signature grin only Jo could give. "This is probably the only summer we'll ever have together. Let's not waste a single night of it. Don't dwell for a second on that dumbass." She turned her truck off and opened her door.

"Where are you going?" I asked.

"To get the boys. We're leaving this stupid party and driving backroads until you forget about what's-his-name."

"Jo—"

"I promise it's better than going home. Just have fun with me this one night. Please?"

I don't know why I even tried to argue. It wasn't like I was going to say no.

"Fine."

"Yes!" she screeched.

"What are you girls doin'?" I turned to see Tim and Billy walking up behind the truck.

"I was just coming to get you guys," Jo said.

"I thought Austin was sick," Billy said.

"She's feeling much better now."

I heard Jo whisper something under her breath before Billy came over to my window.

His voice was low, and I knew he was trying to keep her from hearing. "If you wanna go home, I'll make sure Jo takes you."

I thought about taking him up on his offer. I wasn't in the mood to do much of anything but curl up in bed and regret ever falling for Cass, but then I envisioned him and Annie . . . in her bedroom . . . alone.

"No, it's fine. We can do something if you want to."

His eyes perked up, along with his voice. "You sure?"

"I'm sure."

"I've got my whiskey at Billy's house," Tim said. "And he just bought *National Lampoon's Vacation*. Let's go get drunk and laugh."

Jo walked toward my window and looked at me for approval.

"That works for me," I said.

Billy gave me a smile before leaving for Tim's pickup.

Once Jo got in the driver's side, I looked behind me and scanned the yard. There was no sign of Annie, Cass, or anyone else. The front lawn was lonely, unlike the backyard, where the party was still going on. I looked down at the floorboard, giving up the thought of ever seeing Cass again.

Chapter 7

Billy lived in a small circle drive right down the road from Greenfield High. It was a little two-bedroom home with yellow siding and a basketball goal in the driveway. The inside was dated, looking a lot like the house on the Brady Bunch. The walls were a bright orange, and there was even a deep freezer in the corner that was avocado green, just like the Brady refrigerator. Floral wallpaper covered the walls in the dining room, and a batch of fake daylilies rested in a porcelain vase on the kitchen table.

"It's his aunt's rent house," Jo said. "He gets to stay here for free until he goes to Texas for football. How cool is that?"

"Who wants a Crown and Coke?" Tim yelled from the kitchen.

"I've got beer," Jo said. "Austin doesn't drink."

"Not even after what happened tonight?" Tim said under his breath.

Jo shot him a look.

"All right, then," he said. "I'll just make myself a double."

"Sorry," Jo said after Tim went back to the kitchen.

"It's okay."

She cocked her head and gave me a sympathetic smile. "I can tell you're feeling down about him, but try not to. You can do *so* much better, I promise."

I shrugged, trying not to think about how I'd fallen for a guy so hard he made me cry. Instead, I thought about how Cass sang all those songs to me on the dock. He was so good at playing guitar and expressing himself through that old Gibson. The way he smiled when he picked a song better than the original version, and the fire in his eyes when he talked about his love for it. It was something special. It was honest. It was *real*.

"I promise," Jo said again.

She was right. I *could* do better than someone who left me high and dry for another girl. But for some reason, I didn't want to. I wanted Cass.

"Movie's on!" Billy called.

After Jo grabbed another beer from the fridge, we walked into the small living room that only had a loveseat, a recliner, and an overstuffed dog pillow at the foot of a yellow bricked fireplace. Above the mantle was a giant picture of the Texas A&M stadium, and there was Billy's A&M football jersey tossed over the back of the recliner. The TV played the intro to *National Lampoon's Vacation,* and the smell of buttered popcorn was so heavy in the air it smelled like a concession stand at a theater.

I followed Jo until she split for the recliner to share with Tim, so I headed for the only other spot on the loveseat. Billy smiled as I walked toward him, and for the first time since meeting him, I noticed how ornery he looked.

He reminded me of a freckle-nosed kid about to prank a younger sibling, or maybe a sneaky little boy getting into something he knows he's not supposed to. But at the same time, his face was handsome and full and genuine. It was nice to look at . . . but it still wasn't Cass's.

"I made us some popcorn," Billy said.

He patted the seat next to him, and I took it while reaching for a handful. He gave me a blanket, and I nestled into the opposite side of the sofa, although it was still just a foot or two from him.

Before the movie got off to a good start, Jo and Tim headed for the spare bedroom. They couldn't keep their hands off one another ever since sitting down, and they weren't doing a very good job of hiding it. I was glad when they took it someplace else. It was starting to get awkward.

"More popcorn?" Billy asked as he finished off the bowl. He was so tuned in to the movie, I wasn't sure he'd even noticed we were alone.

"No, thanks," I said.

I'd stopped helping him eat it long before he asked me if I wanted seconds. I'd lost interest in food when my thoughts reverted from Clark and Rusty's beer scene to Cass. Why did he kiss me at Fall Bridge and predict I'd love him one day? Why did he take me on two dates if he was never really interested? Why did he lead me on like that at the party?

Maybe it was because he was the type of guy I usually tried to avoid. He only wanted a piece of action, and I was taking too long to give it to him. Maybe at the party he got tired of waiting, and whenever he saw Annie, he lost interest in chasing me.

Or maybe it was because Annie was so pretty. He'd taken one look at her all dressed up and decided he'd rather have a beauty queen. After all, her face was clear of teenage acne, she could bat her eyelashes like Marilyn Monroe, and her body was anything but a pencil like mine. She might have been a little rude at times, but maybe Cass didn't care. He was attracted to her beauty—the kind he'd never see when looking at me.

"Austin?" Billy said.

I shifted my eyes from the TV to his and watched as he blinked nervously.

"Yeah?"

"I want you to know something," he said. "What Cass did to you . . . it wasn't right. I know you liked him, and you were probably hoping for a better outcome, but he's just that type of guy. You didn't do anything wrong, and it's not that you aren't beautiful."

He paused, his smile timid. I smiled back, and he seemed to relax a little.

"You're so beautiful. You're smart, you're a hard worker, and you can read cattle like no one's business."

I laughed under my breath, thinking of how cattle seemed more at ease and willing to do what they were supposed to do when I was around. When Billy tried to herd anything, they did the opposite.

"Thanks," I said. "That's really nice of you to say."

"Well, I know you're feeling bad about it, and I thought you needed to hear that. He's been this way since I've known him. And I've known the guy for a long time."

I sighed. "I guess I should've listened to Jo."

"Well, Jo's right about a lot of things, you know."

His mouth twitched with a grin, and I saw him in a different light the second I was willing to.

Billy was attractive. He was *really* attractive.

I'd known it since I'd met him, but for some reason, he was even more so now. Besides that, he was a good person. He was nice, honest, and the type of guy everyone wanted me to be with. Actually, he was the *exact* guy everyone wanted me to be with.

A giggle escaped from the hallway, followed by Tim's back smacking against the wall. He stumbled into the room and fell into his recliner, while Jo jumped in beside him.

"Tim had a little too much whiskey." She laughed as he held up a middle finger to the sky.

"No such thing as too much Crown," he said.

"I think throwing up is a sign of it."

Billy groaned. "Did he miss the toilet again?"

"Just got a little on the floor this time," Jo said. "So, I'm proud of him. At least he *almost* made it."

Billy shook his head like he was annoyed with both of them. Not only for Tim throwing up, but because they'd interrupted a moment between us.

Within minutes, a hardy snore came from Tim. I looked over, and Jo had fallen asleep, too. The movie was almost over, and I could sense Billy getting restless. He stole looks my way, and he'd scooted a little closer since the beginning of the movie.

Would he try to make a move on me? I wouldn't think he'd try to kiss me after a night like I'd had. *Surely* he wouldn't. I wasn't ready to move on already. I didn't *want* to move on already. But at the same time, Cass wasn't happening. That ship had crashed, burned, sank, and buried itself. I was sure of it. Right?

With a subtle move, Billy put his arm over the back of the couch and gave me a hopeful grin. I bit my lip nervously, and Cass's Copenhagen smile flashed in my mind. *That smile.*

Billy scooted closer to me, and by now, he was right up against me. He lowered his arm to my shoulders and gave me a little squeeze. He was warm, and it felt good in the cool house. Even wrapped in a blanket, I'd still been chilly throughout the movie. But not anymore. Billy was warm. Billy was safe.

But Billy isn't Cass.

As the movie's end credits rolled, I gave up. I was tired, confused, exhausted. It had to be close to one or two in the morning, and my eyes were heavy. I stopped fighting it because it wasn't worth it, and I rested my head on Billy's shoulder, pushing Cass to the back of my mind and trying to focus on the present. Not the past. Cass was the past.

As I started to fade to sleep, a knock at the door shook the whole house. I jumped from dreams to reality as a startled Billy stared back at me.

Jo looked around the room, rubbing her eyes. "Who the hell is that?"

Billy looked at his watch before answering. "Oh," he said coolly. "It's my brother. I told him he could stay here tonight if he wanted."

Jo jumped from the chair when she saw him get up. "I'll get it. No need to interrupt Austin's dreams." She winked at me as Billy sat back down.

I hugged the blanket around me a little tighter as Billy scooted in close to me. He threw his arm over me, and I hunkered down, laying my head back on his shoulder. I closed my eyes, smelling his cologne when I took a breath. Thank goodness it had worn off and wasn't as strong as it was in the mornings, but it was still there. I made a mental note to tell him sometime soon that I preferred his natural scent over smelly perfume any day. Maybe I'd fake a sneeze and just tell him I was allergic to it.

A voice I never thought I'd hear again sounded from the kitchen. "What the fuck?"

My heartbeat picked up a million miles a minute as I shot off Billy's shoulder, stumbling to unwrap myself from the blanket. "Cass?" I said.

He stood with his fists clenched, staring at Billy.

"What are you doing here?" Billy demanded, walking in front of me.

"I came to talk to Austin." Cass looked at me, but I was too shocked to say anything.

"You don't deserve to talk to her after what you did," Billy said. His voice seemed even deeper than usual, and there was a low grumble to it.

"I ain't done a fuckin' thing. Annie set me up."

Jo walked into the kitchen with her arms crossed and her face as red as a tomato. "Oh, please. We all know what happened at the party. You shouldn't be here."

Cass didn't acknowledge her. He looked at me, ignoring everyone around him. "Can I talk to you alone?"

Before I could answer, Jo cut in again. "No, you may not talk to her alone! You've done enough already, and you're not going to mess with her mind anymore."

"Please, Austin. Just talk to me," Cass pleaded.

"I don't think that's a good idea." Billy took a few steps toward Cass, and Cass clenched his jaw.

"Watch it," Cass said.

"No, you watch it. Get outta my house before—"

Billy took another step toward him, but that was all he did before Cass struck a kitchen barstool and toppled it over. It hit the floor with a boom before he met Billy in the middle of the living room. They were both equal in height, and Billy was a lot more muscular, but Cass seemed to tower over him like he was the bigger man. He nosed up to Billy, forcing him to take a couple steps back.

"Before you *what?*" Cass growled. His eyes were sharp as blades, and his glare could've cut Billy into crumbs.

"It's okay," I said.

Billy turned to look at me, but Cass never moved his eyes from Billy.

"I'll talk to him," I said. "It's okay. Really."

Billy hunched his shoulders and looked to the floor as I walked away from him. It was as if he knew he'd already lost the fight.

I turned toward the front door and heard Cass's footsteps behind me. Before I was outside, he started to explain himself.

"Austin, I wasn't alone with Annie in her room or whatever bullshit Sam told you." He talked fast, barely taking a breath as he explained himself. "I walked in the kitchen for my beer, and she was in there. She said she needed to talk to me about somethin' important, and for some damn reason, I let her. Nothin' happened but her makin' up shit about Larry and Heather and anything to keep me in there long enough for Sam to play her little game."

Before he could even finish, a heaping helping of guilt ran its course through my veins. If this was all true, Cass had done nothing wrong. I was the one who'd messed up by coming here.

"I left to go find you," he continued, "and you were gone. I didn't know where you went. I searched the party, asked Sam, and she said you left with Jo but were comin' back. I waited for a long time, and when you didn't show, I had a feelin' somethin' was up. They set me up, Austin. I swear, you gotta believe me."

My stomach churned.

"I wouldn't just leave you like that," he said. "I'd never try to hook up with Annie. You gotta believe me."

I opened my mouth to speak, but Jo was right behind us before I could say anything.

"Why should we believe you?" she asked. She stood in the doorway like an overprotective parent and tapped her foot impatiently.

"Because it's the truth. You don't think this is somethin' those two would make up just to fuck with me? You know them a whole lot better than I do, and I can see that."

She was silent for a second as she glared at him. "If that was the case, what took you so long to get here?"

"I went to Austin's place and waited there for a while, then I went to your place. Then I went to Tim's. Then I went all over this fuckin' town until I thought about comin' here. Hell, I shoulda known."

Jo's eyes were wide, but she didn't say anything. She looked at me, and for a second, I thought she was feeling as guilty as I was.

Cass grabbed my hands. "Do you believe me now?"

I nodded.

He brought me closer to him and cupped his hands around my face. "You don't want Billy, do you?"

"No," I said, shaking my head. "I just want you."

"Good, 'cause I just want you." He kissed me, and I fell into his apology like nothing had ever happened between us. All was forgiven as our lips grew inseparable.

Jo cleared her throat dramatically, so we ended the kiss sooner than I'd have liked.

"I'm not done with you," she said, pointing her finger at Cass. She walked from the top step and met us at the bottom, jabbing her finger in his chest and narrowing her eyes.

"You hurt her in *any* kind of way, and I will physically assault you. Understand?"

He grabbed her finger and lowered it from his chest. "Yes, ma'am. And if you keep pushin' Billy down her throat, I will physically assault *him*."

Cass looked toward the house, but Billy hadn't stepped outside. He wasn't even in the doorway.

"Fine," Jo huffed. "I'll quit."

Cass turned to me and ran his fingers up my arm. "Come with me."

"She's supposed to be with me tonight," Jo said firmly.

"Well, you ain't stayin' here, are you?"

Before I had a chance to answer him, Jo said, "Well, that was the plan."

"I hope it ain't *still* the plan," he said.

Jo rolled her eyes. "Seriously . . ."

"Fuck, it's bad enough she's gotta work with the guy. You think I'm happy about her spendin' the night with him?"

"I'm not staying here." I looked at Jo. "Let's just go to your house." I wanted to tell her I'd prefer Cass take me home, but I knew that would hurt her feelings.

"Fine," she said. "We'll do that."

"Can I see you tomorrow?" Cass asked. "I wanna take you out again. I want it to just be us."

"Yeah, we can do something. I wanna see you."

He smiled. "Meet me at the Geary co-op at eight?"

"I can do that."

"I'll show you around my neck of the woods." He gave me a long goodbye kiss and finished off with a tight hug.

Jo turned and walked back inside, probably to tell a sleeping Tim goodbye. When she was inside with the door closed behind her, I spewed my guilt like a shaken can of soda.

"Cass, I'm sorry about Billy. I . . . I thought we were done and you liked Annie. I don't like him like that, I was just hurt and . . . and I thought I lost you—"

He laid another kiss on me, pulling my hips into his. "You didn't lose me. It ain't your fault."

"But it *is* my fault."

"No, it ain't. This never would've happened if Annie and Sam hadn't done what they did."

I hugged him tighter, regretting ever cozying up to Billy. "I'm so sorry," I said again. "I really am. I'm really just the worst."

He chuckled, smoothing my hair. "How about we just forget about everything that happened after I left the dock, okay? None of it matters." He smiled, and I soaked up every bit of the sincerity reflected in his green eyes.

"Trust me," Cass said. "All you gotta do is trust me, and everything'll be all right."

Chapter 8

I drove with the windows down, letting the wind hit me like an angry fist. It wasn't near the pleasure I got on the motorcycle, but it would have to do until I could take my spot on the back of Cass's Harley again. The sun lowered in the sky in preparation for another classic Oklahoma sunset. It would hopefully be a good one since Cass and I would be sharing it.

I pulled up to the Geary co-op and parked by the scales in the front. It seemed lonely without all the old farmers going to and from the door, coffee in hand, and a proud smile after selling their wheat crop—or a scowl, depending on the unpredictable market.

After a few minutes and a couple nervous looks in the rearview mirror, I saw a brown Dodge pull up beside me. It was louder than Cass's motorcycle and had a body hanging halfway out the passenger side window. I wasn't surprised to see it was Cass, a wild look on his face and holding a beer. Mötley Crüe roared from the speakers, and both he and Larry sang like they weren't in the middle of a small-town neighborhood.

Cass crawled out the rolled-down window before grabbing his guitar and a case of beer from the truck bed. He put them in the bed of mine, belting lyrics from "Livewire."

He jumped into the passenger-side seat, flashing a smile. He smelled of alcohol and smoke, but I grabbed him and gave him a kiss anyway.

"What was that for?" he asked, licking his lips.

"I just couldn't wait."

He smiled and kissed me again.

I pulled out of the co-op as he gave me directions. We drove to the end of town, passing endless rows of white-sided houses with mowed lawns, American flags snapping in the wind, and the occasional cow dog running about the yard. We passed a sign that read "Welcome to Geary! There ain't much here, but we're proud of what is" before rolling through two lonely intersections and driving down a half-mile-long potholed street. We found our way onto a gravel road, crossed another decrepit bridge, then pulled into an open-grass field.

"I like your hat," I said, noticing Ozzy's logo on the front.

"There's a hell of a story behind this hat." Cass laughed and took it off, putting it on his knee to showcase. "Blizzard of Ozz Tour of eighty-one. He came to Tulsa, and I was hell-bent on goin'. I mean, fuck, it's Ozzy! So, I tell Larry about it, and we plan on goin'. I tell him not to ask his parents because I know they won't let us go. And, of course, he asks 'em."

"I'm gonna guess they said no?"

He slapped his knee. "Huge hell no. But that didn't

matter 'cause we were goin' anyway. It's fuckin' Ozzy Osbourne! The plan was, we were just gonna sneak off with some seniors, but they bailed on the day of the concert. So, we did the only thing two freshmen with no license or car or parents' permission would do. We stole Pat's truck."

My mouth fell open as I imagined Cass and Larry driving three hours away in a stolen truck. I clapped in admiration. I mean, he was right—it was Ozzy.

"Larry was allowed to drive it around, but never past County Line Road. You can do the math, but Tulsa is a few hundred miles past County Line Road. Don't ask me how, but that rusted-out flatbed made it all the way to Tulsa town that night. I got to see Ozzy do some of the craziest shit I've ever seen and watch Randy Rhoads kill every note he played on his polka-dotted flyin' V. Left with this hat, and now you're lookin' at it."

"What kind of trouble did you get into?" I asked. "I would've been grounded for a decade if I even *thought* about pulling something like that."

"Oh, we were in deep shit. Larry couldn't hang out with me all summer, and Pat made us clean out some grain bins full of rotten seed. I don't know how many times I threw up doin' that." He smiled mischievously. "But it was worth it."

I parked the truck on a dead-end oil field road that overlooked the tiny town of Geary. The sun was setting at the perfect time, so we watched it from my tailgate. He brought the unopened case of beer to his side, then grabbed one for himself. When he didn't offer me one, I asked for it. He looked at me, surprised, and handed me the one he'd just opened. I took a sip, thinking maybe the third time would be the charm, but I gave it back to him.

"Never mind," I said, shuddering.

He laughed, taking a big drink.

"So," I began, "you and Larry have been friends for a while?"

"Oh yeah. We grew up together here in Geary."

"Do you go to school here in Geary? Or in Greenfield?"

"Geary. We just hang out with the people from Greenfield a lot. Towns are so close, we all kinda just know each other."

"A little different from Houston. I don't know most of the people I go to school with."

"Hard to imagine. I think I know every person who's ever graduated from Geary."

He guzzled the remainder of the beer, then swapped the empty can for a full one. I wondered how long it would take him to polish off the whole case. He'd probably be done within an hour at this pace.

"So, tell me somethin'. How'd you end up so far away from me? Houston?"

"My uncle's job. We used to live in Oklahoma City, but we moved there before I even started school."

"Do you like livin' in the city?"

"I don't mind it, I guess, but I'd rather live here. It feels more like home than Houston does."

"Why don't you move back?"

"My Aunt Steph would never go for that."

"What about your parents?"

I hesitated, just like I always did when someone asked me about my parents. Something about that question always tied my tongue in knots.

"Shit, I'm sorry," he said, noticing my pause.

"No, it's okay. My dad lives in Dallas . . . I think. He, well . . . he's just not in my life. He never has been." It felt like I was speaking too quickly, and I tried to slow down my thoughts for what came next. "My mom passed away when I was two."

"I'm sorry I made you talk about it," he said. "Dammit, I shouldn't have said anything."

"I don't mind talking about it, I just hardly ever do. I don't talk about her much to my grandparents or Steph. It makes them sad every time I bring her up and makes me feel bad."

"Well, you can tell me anything," he said, putting his arm around my waist and pulling me closer. "I hope you know that."

"Same goes for you." I looked up at him, but he looked away quickly.

"So, uh, do you get along with your aunt and uncle?" he asked.

I couldn't tell for sure what it was about his manner, but something had changed about him. There was something going on in his head. Something he was holding back.

"Yeah, I do. They're the best. We're different, though . . . about a lot of things."

"How?"

"Well, Steph, for instance. I mean, we're pretty much opposite, except when it comes to photography." I stopped, not sure if he'd care to hear more.

Cass hugged my waist again, and his closeness reassured me he was a good listener.

"She's pretty set in her ways," I continued. "She likes to be pampered. She'd shop for a living if that were an actual career. She might be a little high maintenance." I laughed, thinking of all the times she'd assured me she wasn't high maintenance, only to prove she was, without a doubt, high maintenance.

"I can see how you're opposite, then."

"I guess I'm more like . . ." I sighed, almost regretting I'd even started this conversation.

"You're more like who?"

I chewed my cheek, smoothing the thighs of my jeans. "Well, people say I'm just like my mom. They say I act like her, and I look just like her. I don't really know for sure, though. I mean I've seen some pictures, but . . ."

"If she was anything like you, she was one hell of a cool chick."

I laughed, hiding the grief that filled my heart. I wanted to say more about my mom. I hated I never got to talk about her to anyone, but doing so was so foreign to me that it was hard. I didn't even know what to say about her.

"Remember the first time we met, and you asked me about my favorite place to be?"

"Yeah. You said here in Oklahoma."

I nodded. "I love it here. I mean, I love the simplicity of things, the quietness. I love spending time with my grandparents and helping on the farm. But the main reason I like coming here is because . . . well . . . I feel closer to my mom. I just . . . I can feel her here with me." I placed my hand over my heart, knowing my mom would always have a piece of it. Just like Oklahoma would.

Cass grabbed my hand and kissed it, then held it in his lap. "Have you ever told anyone that before?"

I shook my head. "Never."

He looked at me with sympathetic eyes and a knowing heart I knew housed its own secrets. "It'd be nice if life was fair, but I'm right there with you knowin' that it ain't."

"I guess I shouldn't dwell on it. It's something I can't change."

"But it's okay to talk about it."

The way he said that made me smile. Because it *was*

okay to talk about it. No matter how hard that was to do sometimes.

"Tell me about you," I said, wanting him to let me in. I could feel his tension, his jumpiness when I asked him to open up. There was something he had buried behind his everyday smiles and laughter.

"There, uh . . . I mean, there ain't a whole lot about me that's interesting. You know about everything there is to know."

I smiled and kissed his cheek. As much as I wanted him to open up, I didn't want to pry either.

Cass grabbed another beer and took a swig before picking up his guitar. He turned his body to lean on the side of the bed, then strummed a few chords before playing an Eagles song.

After another flawless cover, he smiled. I stared at his fingers as if they held some kind of power, awestruck by the fact he could play a song like "Hotel California" and somehow make it sound better than any version I'd ever heard.

"I can't believe how good you are at that," I said. "You play like some kind of professional. You just amaze me every time you pick that thing up."

He smiled and shook his head. "I ain't no professional, darlin'."

"You sound like one."

He shrugged, picking the strings one by one. "Lotta practice. Guess I just love it."

Cass played a melody I didn't recognize, blowing through chords with flying fingers, then wrapped up his solo before moving straight into a Waylon tune. He played it slow, his voice deep and rich with country soul. When he closed his eyes, I could feel Waylon's message bleeding through his guitar. His rhythm was perfect, his tone soft and even. I leaned my back against the truck bed opposite him and watched him perform as if he were on a stage in front of millions and I was just a lucky fan in the front row.

Once he finished, I had to wipe away a tear. It wasn't every day somebody played a song like "Come With Me" as if they'd written it for me.

"That was beautiful, Cass. My favorite out of all the songs you've played for me."

He didn't say a word, just stared at his guitar for a long time. We sat in silence as the sun settled below the next hill and twilight left shadows around us.

Cass's voice was low, and he seemed to struggle with saying the words. "I. . . I wanna tell you somethin'."

"Okay," I said softly.

"There's a reason I'm good at guitar, and it ain't just because I love it." He looked up for the first time since he'd stopped playing. The darkness made it hard to make out his face, so I scooted closer to him.

"It's more than that," he said. "It's somewhere I can lay all the pain . . . all the bullshit. It's my escape that keeps me sane long enough to get to the next day." He rubbed the neck of his guitar with his hand as if he were talking to the brass strings instead of me. "I jam every time I feel like I'm about to lose it . . . every time I can't shake the memories. I gotta habit of bottlin' up all the bad shit, and it eats me alive a lot of the time. Drives me fuckin' mad." He took a deep breath, as if to calm himself from his own words. "But the madder I get, the more I play. The *better* I play. When I channel my insanity into these six strings . . ."

He played the intro to "Stairway to Heaven" in a spellbinding, entrancing kind of way. "That's when things start to happen . . . the *magic* starts to happen."

He sang the first verses in almost a whisper, giving off a trippy, distant vibe. I listened, mesmerized. Hypnotized.

He stopped singing soon after he'd started, and lifted his head to stare out into the velvety night. His eyes never met mine, and the sounds from his guitar became hushed. He grazed the strings so lightly they barely made a sound.

"Seems bad times inspire me more than the good," he said softly.

He ended the Zeppelin tune and quickly went to strumming Bob Dylan's "Knockin' on Heaven's Door." He wrapped it up before singing any words, then lowered his guitar back into its case. "I don't know if I should tell you," he said with a sigh.

"Why not?"

He shook his head, smoothing his whiskers and taking time to answer. "Might make you feel different about me. Might make you feel weird . . . scared. I don't know."

I smiled, placing a hand on his knee. "Nothing you say will make me think different of you. You can tell me anything. Remember?"

He nodded, smiling beneath a nervous face. "I wanna tell you, darlin'. I want you to know me." He cleared his throat, drank the rest of his beer, then smashed the can under his boot. He pursed his lips, letting seconds pass between us. I knew he was having a debate in his head whether he should tell me or not—going back and forth about it, weighing it silently. So, I didn't rush him. I sat quietly and waited for him to make up his mind, hoping he'd decide to share.

"Guess I'll start with Jim . . . my dad." He reached for another beer, looking at the can as if it held the answers.

"I never knew him 'til he got outta prison. I was ten when he got out. We lived with my Grandpa Bill until one day Mom packed us up and we moved in with him."

He took a drink, swallowing hard before continuing. "I hated him from the beginning. For one, he wasn't Grandpa. He was the exact opposite—a real bastard with a fuckin' bad attitude and shit temper." Cass paused, fidgeting with a loose thread that hung from the knee of his jeans. "He'd make me do things for him like bring him beers or pour his whiskey. Three ice cubes and filled to the rim—no spills, or it'd be my ass. I was ten years old for fuck's sake. But did that matter to him?"

He shook his head as memories flashed through his mind so clearly I could almost see them.

"He'd cuss me out for no reason, slap me around for stupid shit. I remember one time right after he got outta prison, he came home, and I was watchin' an old Western—somethin' I always did with Grandpa. He grabbed me up by the neck of my shirt and said, 'You ain't a fuckin' cowboy,' then threw me down on the ground. I busted my head open on the coffee table, but he didn't give a shit. Just walked in the kitchen while Mom hauled me to the bathroom to clean me up."

He paused and looked away from me while I sat frozen and unable to say anything. I touched his arm when I could move again, and he looked back in my direction.

"The more he drank, especially when he drank whiskey, the braver he got. He started hittin' Mom. Hard." He took a deep breath, clenching his fists. His voice was shaky, and I knew he was forcing himself to tell the story. It was something that didn't come easy.

"I'd watch it when I was little and not know what to do or how to help her. But when I got older, I started to fight back. He didn't hold back when I stepped in, either. I'd go to school with bruises, split lips, black eyes. People would question me. I'd just tell 'em I like fightin' other kids. I looked the part, so teachers believed me. I kept the secret for a long time . . . until Larry walked in on a fight one day. That was, uh . . . that was a pretty bad one. After that, he made me tell his parents, Pat and Lonna. I sugarcoated it—just told 'em enough so it got Larry off my back. Then they wanted me to move in with them, but I wouldn't do it. Not with Mom still bein' there with him."

Tears pricked my eyes, and my heart ached for him like it had never ached for another person. I couldn't imagine the pain he'd gone through as a kid—the pain he still dealt with today. I didn't know what to say, so I just held his hand as a tear rolled down my cheek.

"I don't mean to make you feel bad, and I don't want you to feel sorry for me. I just want you to know me like no one else does."

I nodded, though questions ran through my brain, one after the other. "Does he still . . . ?"

"He gets mouthy, but it ain't got outta hand in a while. He knows I'll kick his ass if he touches Mom. I ain't a kid anymore. I'm the bigger man with the harder punches."

He paused, the silence stretching on, and it seemed to calm him. After a few more seconds, he moved closer to me and put his arms around my waist. His body wasn't shaking like it had been, and he seemed a lot more relaxed than he was before.

How could he be so stable when talking about such a thing, when I was on the verge of losing it just listening to him?

"So, you took the pain out with music." I looked at his guitar, realizing it was more of a savior than a painted piece of wood with strings.

"I listened to my first Aerosmith record when I was eleven. *Toys in the Attic*. You said it was a great album . . . well, it's my favorite to this day. The minute that needle dropped, I wanted to be just like Joe Perry. Grandpa gave me his guitar when I asked for it, and he taught me a few chords. I ain't went a day without playin' it since."

I hugged him, holding him as tightly as I could. His sleeve was wet when I let him go.

"Why didn't you ever tell anyone?" I asked. "Teachers or friends . . . your grandpa?"

Cass shrugged. "I don't have that answer, really. When somethin' like that happens, it's . . . it's like you're too scared to speak. I didn't trust anyone with it. I didn't know what he'd do if he found out I told. Some things are just better left in the dark where no one can see."

I nodded, trying to understand something I couldn't. "You didn't deserve that. You don't deserve to have a dad like that."

"Yeah, but that's what I got."

"Why didn't your mom just leave?"

"Don't have the answer to that, either."

I bit my lip, feeling as though I'd said the wrong thing. "I'm . . . sure it wasn't easy for you to tell me about that part of your life."

"I needed you to know that about me. I ain't ever told anyone about it, but I had to make you know that I'm serious about you."

I wiped a tear from my cheek. "I won't ever tell anyone. It's safe with me."

"I know it is."

I threw my arms around his neck, wanting to hug away the hurt. Instead, he went in for a solid kiss. But it wasn't *just* a kiss, it was the most emotional kiss I'd ever had in my life—one that put those famous kisses in the movies to shame.

Cass pulled away but held my face in his hands. "I ain't

perfect. That's why Jo was so protective of you last night. She knows how I am when it comes to Annie and other girls." He put his forehead to mine, and I wrapped my hands around the back of his neck.

"But it's different with you. Ever since I saw you at the barn and we hung out a few times . . . *Man*. It just feels right. Me and you . . . we just fit."

Even though I was still teary from his story, I smiled. "I feel the same way. Something about this just feels different. Real. You know?"

He chuckled. "I mean, the *minute* you said you liked Aerosmith, I was in."

I laughed, wiping the mascara from under my eyes. There was no way it wasn't smeared all over the place. "You only like me because I like Aerosmith. Great."

"That ain't the only reason. There's a lot of 'em, darlin'. You're a good girl."

"Ah, the good girl image." I rolled my eyes at that. Lexie always said I was a goody two-shoes, and it got under my skin. Not that I thought I was *bad*, I just didn't like the title.

"I like it, though," he said. "And what I *really* like is you put me in my place when we first met. You weren't about the bullshit, and you let me know it. It's also cool you didn't give a shit when other people warned you about me. You still gave me a chance. Even though you're way cooler than me."

I laughed hard at that one. "You think *I'm* cooler than *you*? What?"

He smirked. "Not many chicks'll let me cruise 'em around on the bike."

I scoffed. "That's a little hard to believe, Cass."

"I'm serious."

"Well, not many guys are cool enough to even *have* a bike

like that. And not to mention the fact you're basically David Lee Roth in Wranglers."

"David Lee Roth? Way off. Way, way, way, *way* off!" He gave me a bear hug, laying me down in the truck bed. "Way the hell off, woman."

"Close enough."

He laughed, nuzzling into my neck.

I tangled his hair in my hands before he popped his head up.

"You sure you don't want Billy?"

"I'm sure!"

He laughed, while I regretted the previous night all over again.

"I promise there's no feelings there," I said as I sat up. "I was just so jealous of the thought of you and Annie together. I was hurt. But I'm sorry you had to see us like that. I should've just gone home after the party."

"You know how to make an ol' boy jealous, darlin'. That's all there is to it."

"Enough of that." I crawled on his lap, wrapping my legs around him. Pushing the hair out of his face, I kissed him. "We weren't supposed to bring that night up again, as I recall."

"Shit, you're right." He grinned. "Last night never happened."

From the corner of my eye, his guitar caught my attention. I took a good look at it, but this time with a new perspective. It had a different meaning now. It wasn't just something he played to pass the time. It meant way more than that to him. And now it meant way more to me.

"Play me something else," I said as I crawled out of his lap.

Cass gave me a long kiss before he grabbed it out of its case. He smiled to himself while picking strings, changing chords so smoothly it looked effortless. We sat there for a long time without either of us saying anything, him strumming lightly and me soaking up the way he moved so fluid with the music. I could've sat there all night and listened to him, even if he just plucked away on random chords. It was beautiful no matter the melody.

When he started to play a rhythm I recognized as "You Ask Me To" by Waylon, I watched him with more admiration for his talent. I thought about how something good had come from something so bad, how he had turned his feelings of anger and helplessness into something so sweet that he could share with me. As he played with a faint smile on his face, I wondered how he could do it. How could he be okay after everything he'd told me about his past? How could someone who went through what he had, smile at all after reliving that pain? How could someone be that strong?

I'd never been allowed into anybody's world like that, and I couldn't believe he'd opened that door for me to step into. He shared his past so he could prove to me he wanted me in his future. He'd laid everything out on the table, and now I knew him better than anyone else did. Maybe more than anyone else ever would. If that were the case, nothing could've made me happier.

Chapter 9

It was another ninety-something-degree afternoon, but a light breeze made the heat tolerable. I sat my camera down in the passenger seat of the Ford, next to Cass's guitar case. The night before, he'd told me to put the guitar in my truck and take it to a place on some of Pat and Lonna's land that would make a perfect backdrop for our photo shoot.

I decided on having a photo shoot after he made the comment for the second time that he was a good model. I told him I was no believer until I saw it with my own eyes. He said he was in. I said name the place.

I followed the detailed directions he'd scribbled on a piece of notebook paper, and after about twenty minutes of driving, arrived at my destination. The spot where he wanted me to meet him was over a cattle guard and a few hundred feet off a red dirt road. It was hidden back in a group of cottonwood trees, where a large red rock embankment stood about thirty or forty feet off the ground. In front of it was the creek, which wound its way through the green pasture like a snake. The water was clear as tap water, rolling over rocks of every size and color on its way downstream. The spot was perfect—a quaint little work of art tucked away in a secret corner of Oklahoma.

Cass was already waiting on me, his bike parked in front of the water. His denim button-up shirt and clean blue jeans were a change from his usual grease-stained attire, and I blushed from pure pleasure.

"Hello, darlin'," he called from his bike.

As I walked toward him, my camera in one hand and his guitar in the other, a blue heeler greeted me with a happy bark and wet kisses.

"Down, Belle. Sorry, that's Lonna's dog. She followed me down here from their house. They live just up the road."

"No, it's okay," I said, giving her a friendly pat on the head. "She might look good in our photo shoot. I'm glad she followed you."

It was cooler down here with the rugged oak trees blocking the sun and casting shadows that danced on the stream. I was relieved to have some cover for the pictures, hoping the lighting worked in my favor. Not that it had to be perfect. Look who the model was.

"Okay, I'm ready. Do your thing, and I'll snap you while you do it," I called to him. I wanted to see what he had before I started barking orders Steph-style.

Within the first few minutes, Cass proved he could please a camera. He ran his fingers through his hair at all the right times and posed like he'd modeled all his life. Occasionally, he'd turn his face toward the camera and show me the same flashy grin that caught my attention the night I'd met him.

He did a few poses leaning on the handlebars and a few leaning back on the seat. He pulled out a cigarette and let it hang from his lips, looking like the next rebel without a cause.

"All right. Now I want you to lean on your bike, both legs facing me," I said. "Grab your guitar, and play me something."

He followed my instruction, strumming the first few chords of my favorite Mellencamp song.

I peered over the lens, watching him sing about Jack and Diane and sway with the beat. Sweat glistened on his cheekbones and rolled down his temples, making a hot summer evening steamier.

"Mind taking your shirt off?" I smiled when he looked pleased I'd asked.

"Well now, sunshine, I wasn't plannin' on gettin' naked out here. But if you insist . . ."

He unbuttoned his shirt, every freed button revealing more of his bare chest and rippled abs. An impressive farmer's tan and a small tattoo on his left pec caught my attention.

Cass dropped his shirt to the ground, then ran his hands through his hair like a T-birds greaser. He curved his body, full on thrusting on his bike, then bit his lip and looked into the camera straight on. I lost my balance as I watched him satisfy me through the lens, and I thought I might fall flat on my face.

Keep your cool, Austin. Keep your cool.

"Uh . . . just . . . keep doing that," I said.

He ran his hand from his hair, down to his chest, over his abs, and grabbed his crotch. He threw his head back and closed his eyes, teasing me with his every move.

"What's . . . what's the tattoo of?" I asked, trying to think about something besides his half-naked body.

"Ridin' with the wind. It's a Hendrix lyric. You like it?"

I wasn't a fan of tattoos, but I loved one on him. Especially one that had to do with Jimi Hendrix. "Yeah, I do. Do you want more of them?"

"Maybe your name somewhere."

"You wouldn't get a tattoo of my name." I smiled, imagining Austin in black letters across his shoulder. I didn't hate the idea.

"I would if you wanted me to."

Cass rose from his Harley and walked toward me, his eyes wild. I sat my camera on the ground as he grabbed me by the shoulders and cast me against the nearest cottonwood. He pressed his Copenhagen lips hard against mine, digging his fingers into my sides. I grabbed his forearms, which were drenched with sweat, and held on as I lost control. He bit my bottom lip then pulled away, moving down to my neck. He ran his tongue from my collarbone to my jawbone, then bit my ear.

"Dammit, Belle," Cass said under his breath. He pulled away from me and lightly booted her out of the way. She'd been jumping on him the entire time, I'd just forced myself to ignore her.

He went back to my neck, only to stop again a few seconds later. Belle was barking, and this time she was jumping on my leg and wedging her plump body between us.

"You've gotta be shittin' me," Cass mumbled.

"I think she's jealous."

"She can't stand not gettin' all the attention." He gave me one more kiss, then knelt down to pet her. "Crazy dog," he said. He groaned, rubbing his forehead. "We gotta take a rain check, as bad as I don't wanna. I told Lonna we'd make it for supper. You don't mind joinin' me, do you?"

"I'd love to." I smiled, happy to get to meet the two

people in Cass's life that were always looking out for him, according to his stories.

I opened the passenger-side door of the Ford and let Belle hitch a ride. Cass started his bike and pulled out in front of me, leading the way.

Taking a quick glance in the rearview mirror, I made sure my makeup wasn't smeared. My mascara was a little runny from the summer heat, and I wiped it away before smoothing my brows. My cheeks were a deep red, and I was thankful it was a little drive to their house. I needed some time to cool down. Because how hot was *that?*

We arrived at a single-story house just down the road from the creek. It was made of red rock and had dark wooden shutters, giving the home an old western touch. There were two big barns filled with equipment sitting on either side of the house, along with a beaming Corvette in the driveway.

I stepped out of my truck and walked over to the shiny white classic, wondering if Cass was allowed to take it for a spin.

"Nice, ain't it?" he said, knocking his knuckles on the hood. "Sixty-nine Stingray. Lonna's pride and joy."

I trailed him up the porch steps, and he opened the front door to the house. Delicious smells hit us head-on, making my mouth water. I was such a sucker for good southern meals.

I followed him through the doorway, studying several framed pictures that lined the hallway wall. There were two of Cass—one recent and one from what looked like a few years back. In the more recent one, he and Larry were saddled on horses and making silly faces into the camera. Snow-capped mountains and tall evergreen trees were in the background.

"Is Larry here?" I asked.

"Nah, he's out with Heather tonight."

"Is that Heather?" I pointed to another picture of Larry standing next to a small-framed girl with curls that fell effortlessly over her shoulders. Her dimples were perfect deep-set dots on either side of her smile, and the ocean in the background brought out her blue-green eyes.

"Yeah, that's her. You'll like her. She's a good girl, too." He winked, giving me a spank.

"Cass!" I looked around to make sure no one saw that.

But we were caught.

"You must be Austin," said a petite lady with a southern accent as thick as her fiery red hair.

I felt my cheeks ablaze.

She gave Cass a little grin before bringing me in for a hug. "Nothing beats an ornery boy like this one, huh?" she said in my ear.

I laughed nervously as she held me tight and patted my back like she'd known me all my life. My tension eased after a few of her kindhearted pats, and I smiled when she gave me one last little squeeze before pulling away. I loved her already.

"Nice to meet you," I said.

I watched her as she returned my smile, admiring the pretty way she had about her. Her cheekbones were high and distinct, like perfect circles as red as ripened cherries. Her face was round and cheerful and pleasant, bursting with a certain niceness and warmth that made you want to get lost in deep conversation with her for hours. It was a face you never forget—one that sticks in your mind no matter how long it's been and brings a sense of peace and nostalgia just remembering it.

"It's certainly nice to meet you, too, dear. James has told

us so much about you. We're so glad to have you in our home for supper."

I smiled, flattered by that. He liked me well enough to share with these kind people how much he really cared about me. *Me.*

But guilt snatched that feeling away as quickly as a pickpocket when I remembered I hadn't told a single soul about him. I hadn't mentioned him to my grandparents, Steph, or even Lexie. In fact, I'd lied to every one of them about him. This proved I shouldn't put it off any longer. I needed to tell someone. No matter what the outcome might be.

We followed her into the dining room, where a large table was set with four plates. A handsome man with a sharp jawline and silver-streaked hair sat at the head of the table, reading a newspaper.

He laid the paper down and stood to shake my hand. "Nice to meet you, miss. Heard a lot about you."

"You have?" I glanced at Cass, who was beaming.

"I have. Only good things." Pat smiled, and his soft eyes seemed to assure me he was telling the truth.

We sat down, where Lonna brought out chicken fried steak, mashed potatoes and gravy, homemade bread, and corn on the cob. She was a true southern cook, no doubt.

As we cleaned our plates, conversation flowed like we'd known each other for years. They were such kind people, their grace filling the room with pure comfort and happiness. I was thankful Cass had a second family in his life—one that genuinely cared for him. At least whenever things were bad at home, he had a retreat here with Larry's parents.

"I hear you're Willie's granddaughter. Is that right?" Pat asked, smoothing an unruly sideburn with his grease-stained fingers.

"That's right."

"I overheard him talkin' about you at the co-op the other day. Sounds like you're a hard worker."

I smiled. "I try to help out the best I can."

"He mentioned you helped him in the field?"

"As much as I can. I don't visit a lot, but when I do, I'm usually on a tractor somewhere."

He glanced at Cass. "That's a mighty fine young lady there, Cass. You better keep her around."

Cass squeezed my knee and grinned. "She ain't goin' nowhere."

"James just goes on and on about you, sweetheart," Lonna said, pointing her fork toward Cass.

The way she called him by his first name made me smile. It was such a motherly thing to do and only made me respect her more.

"You know he's never brought a girl around before," she said.

I looked at Cass, expecting him to be embarrassed, but he just smiled and said, "They're right."

After dinner, we had a piece of fantastic apple pie and some homemade ice cream. The pie was almost as good as Grandma's, and that in itself was impressive.

We thanked them for dinner, then said our goodbyes as Cass walked me to the door.

"I'm stayin' here tonight. I gotta get up in the mornin' and bale hay." He leaned against the doorway and lowered his voice. "I had fun today. Too bad Belle ruined the good part." He laughed and moved in closer to steal a kiss.

"It's all right," I whispered. "We can pick back up another time."

"I'll hold you to it. I'll call you whenever I get a chance. The next couple of weeks'll be busy, but I'll make time."

I gave him my grandparents' number, and he gave me

another kiss—one that soon turned into another, and yet another. He stepped outside with me, never unlocking his lips from mine, and fumbled to close the door behind him. He held my face and pressed me up against the side of the house. My heart raced as he laid into me, kissing me like he was never going to see me again. A few minutes passed before he pulled back. We were both breathing heavy, and I could tell he was wishing for more than a make-out session. He wasn't the only one.

"Shit," he said under his breath. "I can't take it." He looked into my eyes for a few seconds before giving me one last kiss. It was slower and sweeter than before, lingering even after he pulled away.

It was in that moment, on a front porch of a farmhouse in Oklahoma, that I fell in love for the first time.

Chapter 10

"So, are we gonna talk about the other night?" Billy asked as he filled the combine with coolant.

We'd gone about our Monday, mostly in silence, and the awkwardness grew more painful every second.

"Yeah, I guess we should," I murmured. I tinkered with the radiator, acting as though I was cleaning straw from it. Anything to keep my eyes from his.

"Well, you go first," he said. "What'd Cass have to say?"

"He said it was all a misunderstanding. He and Annie never happened. Sam just made it seem like something had."

He scoffed. "A misunderstanding?"

"Yeah." I threw a clump of straw on the ground to make it seem like I was really working at it.

"I don't believe it." There was a difference in his voice—a darker tone that was out of character for him. It was strange.

"I do." My voice was a mere whisper compared to his.

"What exactly happened, then? What did they talk about for so long that Sam had time to trick you, you find a ride, and then us take our time leaving the party?"

"I . . . I don't know exactly what they talked about," I started. "All I know is that I overreacted and left the party when I shouldn't have."

"So, he turned it around on you?"

"No, that's not it. He never made me feel bad about leaving. It was just a misunderstanding on both our parts. That's all."

Billy shook his head and leaned against the air filter. "I know how he is, Austin. I know what kind of guy he is. He isn't who he's pretending to be."

I clenched my jaw, losing patience with him. Billy had no idea what kind of guy Cass was.

No one really knew.

"You might think you know him," I said, trying to soften the edge in my voice. "But you don't." Turning my back to him, I crawled down the ladder, skipping the bottom two steps and jumping to my feet.

"I didn't mean to make you mad," Billy called from the top of the combine.

I walked to the fuel tank and shut off the prehistoric pump, and Billy hurried off the ladder to confront me.

"I don't want you to hate me because I'm honest," he said.

"I don't hate you. I just don't wanna talk about it. There's things you don't know about him."

"And there's things you don't know about me, but I guarantee you I wouldn't have let Annie talk to me for a second while you were waiting around outside."

I stared down at my boots, trying to think of something to say, but there was nothing I could say back to that.

"I thought there was something between us the other night," he said. "I felt it, and I know you felt it, too."

"I . . . I was hurt. I should've never even gone to your house. I should've just had Jo take me home in the first place."

"So, that's it, huh? We just act like it never happened and you give him another chance?"

"This isn't his second chance. He's still on his first."

He took a deep breath and stared at the ground. He kicked the gravel with his boot before nodding. "Okay. I can't make you stop talking to him, but I'll warn you again. Cass'll mess up. I know it'll happen."

"I have faith in him . . . but I'll still be careful."

"It's just a matter of time, Austin. Doesn't matter how careful you are."

He frowned and shook his head before walking to his pickup. I knew I'd hurt him, and that was the last thing I wanted to do.

"Billy," I called.

He turned around on his heel but kept walking backward.

"Thanks for what you said at your house," I said. "It was really nice of you to cheer me up . . . and just be there for me."

"No problem. I'll be around whenever you need me. And that includes whenever he messes up."

The sun beat down on my tired muscles as I topped off the fuel tank with pink diesel. My tank top and jeans were doused in oil, my sunburned shoulders browning by the second.

The air was filled with hopes of a successful wheat harvest and wheat dust as thick as smoke from a forest fire. Combines rolled through surrounding fields with hungry augers and hurried reels. Harvest had arrived.

We cut a sample mid-afternoon, and it tested dry enough, so the time had come to start cutting wheat. As I drove the combine, I looked out the windshield at the never-ending fields of gold. The wheat was thick and tall, the heads long, and the berries full and plentiful.

I couldn't see the other combine Grandpa drove because it was a quarter of a mile downfield from me and there was a line of trees and a hill between us. But I knew there was a wholesome smile on the farmer who sat in the driver's seat.

I pictured Cass doing the same thing I was doing, just a few miles away. His clothes were just as stained as mine, soiled with oil from busted hoses and dirt from digging out a plugged header. His hair was probably dripping wet from working too hard in the heat, and the line from his farmer's tan was getting more pronounced every day. His whiskers were speckled with stray bits of wheat straw and chaff, and his bump of Copenhagen was noticeably larger than usual due to the extra stress from this time of year. He was tired and dragging from late nights and early mornings. Beer was on his breath, and a wilted cigarette was tucked behind his ear. Curse words were spoken more frequently, and there were probably a few fights between him, Larry, and Pat. Harvest time brought out crankiness and a loss of patience in even the nicest folks.

Cass.

I missed him. It'd been a long week, and I missed his

kisses. His smile. Did he go through the workdays thinking about *my* smile? My lips? Did he crave my company and reminisce about the past few weeks we'd shared together? Was I the only girl he wanted to spend a Saturday night with?

For me, he had taken front and center on a stage that had always been bare. It felt odd, but at the same time, it felt right, like it was always supposed to be this way. I was falling for him, and it was happening so fast I couldn't slow down. Then again, I didn't want to slow down. I wanted to take this ride as fast as it would go. I wanted to laugh until tears wet my cheeks and kiss until it led to more. I wanted to rebel against good decisions and see the world from the back of a motorcycle. I wanted to be with him and find myself in the process.

My smile fell thinking of the future. How would things be after the summer was over and I found myself back in the maddening rush of Houston? How could I go so long without being with Cass? Without seeing his smile or hearing him play songs for me? *Why* couldn't I just move in with my grandparents for my senior year? I longed to spend the remainder of my high school career in a classroom in Greenfield. I'd give anything to do it. But I knew what Steph's answer would be if I ever asked.

"You're not moving back to that dried up, shit-hole town. Dammit, Austin, you're going to give me a mental breakdown," she'd say.

Steph hated this town, and she never outright told me why she did. I assumed it was the whole when-I-turn-eighteen-I'm-moving-out-and-never-coming-back kind of thing, but it could've been for other reasons. Losing her little sister could've been one. Or maybe it was the ex-boyfriend she'd mentioned in passing. I'm not sure what happened between them, but maybe it gave her a bad taste in her mouth toward her hometown. I'd never asked. Maybe I would in the future.

I thought about Cass again, and the hard truth to the matter meant a long-distance relationship was in the works. Would he be willing to be in a relationship with someone over eight hours away? Was I moving too fast to even be thinking about this? Of course I was. No question.

But was I the only one thinking about it?

That question would have to remain unanswered until the wheat was in the elevator and the combines stored back in the barns.

Harvest entailed long hours and tiring work. The crop had to be harvested and out of the field as soon as it was ripened. I knew I'd be glued to a combine seat until it was over—the only breaks coming when it rained.

Unfortunately, rain wasn't in the forecast, so neither was Cass.

Chapter 11

Long hours turned into long days. It was Sunday or maybe Monday—the days ran together during this time of the year. It'd been over a week since I'd last seen or talked to Cass, and I missed him more than I probably should have.

I came home one night around nine, which was earlier than usual. We'd finished up a field and decided to go home instead of moving the equipment in the dark.

"Doll, you had a missed call from someone named James. He said he knew you would be working but to give him a call whenever you got home. Would you like to tell me about him?" Grandma stood by the sink, eyeing me like she knew I was hiding something from her.

Grandpa walked in right behind me and waited by the door for an answer.

This was it. The perfect opportunity to tell them both about Cass had finally presented itself.

Grandma's hand went on her hip, and she looked impatient. Grandpa pushed his glasses up the bridge of his nose and leaned a hand on the back of the recliner. They waited.

We all waited.

"James?" I said finally. I bit my lip and picked at a hangnail that really wasn't a hangnail until I made it a painful one.

Grandpa sniffed, side-eyeing Grandma in the silence.

I cleared my throat. "James is . . . a friend. Really, there's nothing to really tell . . . really."

That sounded suspicious even to *my* ears.

"James who?" Grandma asked. "I'm sure we know him if he's from around here."

"Uh . . ." The honest answer was on the tip of my tongue, so close it was the next word in line to come out of my mouth. "I . . . don't know. I guess I'll have to ask him."

I couldn't do it. Something inside me told me it wasn't a good idea to tell them just yet. I didn't know why the feeling was so unshakeable, but I couldn't bring myself to say it.

"Is it Wilcox?" Grandma pressed. "There was a James Wilcox around your age. When I was still at the school, he'd come by and chat with me and the other secretary sometimes between classes. He was such a nice boy."

"Yeah . . ." I shrugged. "I don't know. Maybe."

I *hated* lying.

"Hmm. Well, when you find out, let us know," Grandpa said. "I'm a little curious now."

"Sure thing," I said, backing away toward the telephone.

Grandpa walked toward the bathroom, and Grandma headed back to the kitchen, so I knew I was safe.

I picked up the rotary phone and dialed the number Grandma had written down.

Lonna answered. "Hello?"

I was relieved Cass hadn't left his home phone number.

"Hi, Lonna. It's Austin. I'm returning Cass's phone call."

"Oh, yes, he's right here. Come see us again."

I agreed to visit, and then the phone was handed to someone I'd missed over the long week.

"Hey, darlin'. How's it goin'?"

It was nice hearing his voice. It gave me the rush I'd been missing.

"Good," I said. "I've been busy in the field. I'm sure you have, too."

"Yep, it's a bumper crop this year. Moisture did us right in the spring. When am I gonna see you again?"

"I hope soon. If everything goes smoothly, we should be done by the end of the week."

"Pat hired on some custom cutters this year, so with our two combines, we should be done by Friday. And that's a good thing because I have a surprise for you."

"What is it?"

"Hell, it wouldn't be much of a surprise if I told you, darlin'."

I laughed, twirling the phone cord around my finger. "Can you at least give me a hint?"

"It's tickets to a concert, but I ain't tellin' you who it is. It's Saturday night. You think you can come with me?"

"Yeah, we should be done by then. I'll let you know if we aren't, but it should work out."

I loved concerts, although I hadn't been to many that were by choice. Lexie had dragged me to a number of them in the past, but most were artists she preferred—Cyndi Lauper, Wham!, Culture Club. One time, she had to bribe me with radio rights for a whole month just to accompany her to some concert in Tomball. In the end, the hour-long show was worth it. Waylon got to play nonstop in her car all that June.

"Alright, well, call me whenever you guys are finished cuttin' wheat," he said.

I could hear the smile in his voice as he spoke.

I hung up the phone and helped Grandma with the dishes. She'd brought food to the field every day since harvest started, so I felt I needed to repay her by drying plates. Thankfully, she never asked about my phone conversation or any more questions about my secret friend.

I made myself a quick cup of hot tea—a ritual before bedtime—and headed for my room. I closed my door and sat on my bed, flipping through channels before settling on *Happy Days*. There was nothing like watching a night full of Fonzie on a static TV.

"Austin."

I jumped three feet off my bed, spilling my tea all over my quilt.

"Damn, I didn't mean to scare you, sunshine."

"Cass?" I sat down my now empty cup and walked toward the window. Cass was on the other side, though I could barely make him out in the dark. "What are you doing here? How did you . . .?"

"I was just in the neighborhood. Thought I'd drop by."

I opened the screen, which took me a couple tries, and smiled down at him. "How did you get here so fast? I swear I just hung up the phone two minutes ago."

"The bike has an extra gear for when I'm missin' you. Come on. It's a pretty night."

I pulled my work boots on and climbed out the window. It wasn't a big window, but I managed to squeeze myself through and into his arms.

I looked up at the night sky and realized what he meant.

Red Dirt Paradise

Every star above us seemed twice as big and ten times as bright. There wasn't a cloud anywhere in sight, and if I hadn't known any better, I'd have guessed the shiny jewels were only a few feet above us.

He grabbed my hand and led me out in the backyard, toward the wheat field we had just finished harvesting. The old blue wheat truck was parked a few yards into the field, and I nudged him in that direction. Using the hood for stargazing would be perfect.

"What made you want to come all the way out here to see me?" I asked.

He crawled onto the hood and reached for my hand to help lift me up. "I was just thinkin' that a week was long enough. I couldn't wait for another one."

"Well, I'm glad you came. I missed you."

Smiling, Cass reached for something in the front pocket of his T-shirt. "I missed you, too, darlin'. Picked you somethin' on my way to your window." He pulled out a single red rose with a short stem and full bloom, then handed it to me.

"One of Grandma's roses," I said with a smile. I put it to my nose, taking in the sweet smell, then laid it on the hood. "Roses always remind me of the farm. They remind me of home."

"I'd have picked you more, couple dozen or so, but figured your grandma might notice if I did that."

"This one is perfect all on its own," I assured him.

We laid our backs against the windshield and stared up above us. The Milky Way was so bright and the dippers so clear, I felt as though we were standing among them instead of light-years away.

He grabbed my hand, lacing my fingers between his. They fit perfectly together, like puzzle pieces.

"Do you ever look at somethin' so beautiful that it makes you forget all the bad stuff in life?"

"Yes," I answered. "I know what you mean."

"I ain't talkin' about the sky, darlin'."

I turned my head to face his, knowing his eyes were never on the stars. "Neither was I."

He brushed his hand across my cheek and laughed under his breath. The way he was looking at me—like he wanted every part of me—made me jump the gun. I kissed him before he could kiss me, and I don't think he expected that. He laid into me harder than he ever had, pushing me back onto the hood. He rolled on top of me, neither of us taking a breath from our fevered kisses. His hand went under my shirt and touched my hips, moving up to my ribs and inching even higher. He forced his body against mine, making me wish there weren't clothes between us.

To my dismay, he stopped and pulled back before flashing his famous smile.

He brushed my hair out of my face and slid his thumb over my bottom lip. "I come out here to look at the stars with you and look what happens."

"I'm not complaining."

"You know you ain't just another girl, right? I mean it when I say you're damn special to me, Austin. You're the only girl who's ever meant somethin' to me."

"Promise?"

"I promise." He rolled onto his back, and I laid my head on his arm.

"Do you trust me?" he asked.

"I trust you."

He raised up to look at me, then moved a piece of hair from my face and smiled. "This is the Austin I like. No makeup, little grease on your shirt, work jeans, and dirty boots. You're prettier this way than any other way."

I cocked my head. "Really?"

"Hell yeah."

"But . . . well, I thought since you met me when I was all dressed up, that meant you were attracted to that . . . not this."

"Listen, you're beautiful all dolled up. And yeah, of course I'm attracted to that, but you're more attractive when you're just yourself. This is what you look like when no one's around, who you're comfortable bein'. And that's what I like."

A weight was lifted off my shoulders when he spoke those words. I'd tried my hardest to look a certain way since our first date. I'd worried about my hair, my makeup, what I wore, and how I looked the last few weeks more than I had in my entire life. I'd stressed about being around him, hoping I could compare to Annie and Jo and Sam and all the other girls who looked like they belonged in Hollywood rather than Greenfield. And now, knowing he preferred me the way I really was, it meant my act was over. I could be myself again. Thank goodness I wouldn't have to cut off another T-shirt.

He kissed the top of my head before we lay motionless for a long while. He was so still I thought he'd fallen asleep.

"My grandpa always liked lookin' at the stars." His voice was almost a whisper as he pointed to the sky. "I can remember summers when we'd lay in the bed of his pickup and stare at 'em for hours. He'd tell me stories about the Old West . . . probably stories he made up as he went. He was good at that." He chuckled under his breath, and I could hear the love in his laughter. "'Tell me a story, Grandpa,' I'd always say to him. And he'd tell a hell of a doozy every time."

"Tell me more about him." I looked up at the smile on his face, falling in love with the starry look in his eyes.

"He was . . . somethin'. Always grinnin'. Never complained about a damn thing. He was a man who was just happy to be here doin' what he loved. Workin' with cattle, workin' with the land."

"That's where you get it from?"

"Yeah, I get a lot from my grandpa. I get a lot from him, learned a lot from him. To me, there'll never be a greater man or a better teacher. He was everything to me."

"What happened to him?" I asked softly.

"He had a heart attack last November."

I laid my arm across his chest, feeling his heartache.

"I was supposed to be with him that night. I'd told him I was stayin' with him, but I ended up goin' to Kansas with Larry to look at a baler. I still hate myself for goin'. Not that I knew he wouldn't live to see another day, I just . . . I hate that I didn't get to say goodbye, ya know? I hate that I didn't get to give him a hug, or . . . or tell him how much he meant to me. It's just shit knowin' so much was left unsaid."

I squeezed him tightly, knowing the wound from losing his grandpa was still fresh. It might've been last fall when he'd passed, but that wasn't enough time to even begin to heal.

The thought of what life would be like without my own grandpa crossed my mind. I quickly pushed the intrusive idea out of my head, unable to face something like that. I couldn't imagine it. I wouldn't let myself imagine it. Because a world without Grandpa meant a world where my heart would never be as whole as it was when he was in it.

"Man, I'd give anything to spend just one more day with him," Cass said lightly. "Just sit in the tractor with him . . . listen to him talk about his high school days, or his old milk cows, or how his mom used to make the best fried chicken. Hell, I'd be okay sittin' there and not even sayin' anything. Just as long as we could sing together when ol' Johnny Cash came on the radio." He laughed, but there was a strain in his voice. I knew there was a knot that had settled in the back of his throat, and I squeezed his hand in hopes to comfort him.

"Grandpa had the best voice," he continued. "Real deep with this sorta rumble to it. Kinda like Pat's ol' Peterbilt Cabover, you could tell those pipes from a mile away. You know he was in a barbershop quartet in high school?" He leaned up to look at me with a proud grin before settling back against the windshield. "Best one that school ever had, I guarantee it."

Hearing the way Cass talked about his grandpa made me smile. I imagined the two of them sitting on a rusty tailgate somewhere staring up at the stars and laughing at each other's stories. He must have felt so lost without him.

"Losin' him was hard on me," he said. "Whenever you lose someone who means so much to you, it's hard to get up the next mornin'. And the next. You know what I mean, though. You've lost someone just as important to you."

"It's not the same thing you went through. I don't remember her. The person I lost is more of an idea in my mind rather than a memory. I hate that, but that's how it is. I can't imagine what you went through with your grandpa."

"Like I said before, life ain't fair. Whatever happens, happens. All that's left are memories worth more than gold." Cass wrapped both of his arms around me, holding me close to him. "You might not remember your mom, but it doesn't hurt any less. You missed out on a lot of stuff. You're left wonderin' about her instead of rememberin' about her. It's tough, I know it has to be. What happened to her?"

"She was in a car accident."

"Shit. I'm sorry."

"It's okay."

"Seems like we have enough heartache to go around, don't we? We sound like a damn country song over here."

"We're sitting on the hood of a wheat truck in the middle of a field, looking up at the stars, and telling sad stories. I'd say we are the definition of a country song."

I rested on his shoulder for quite a while longer before we decided it was time to go. The night was getting chilly and neither of us knew how late it was, so we made our way back to the house. He boosted me up when we got back to the little window, and I crawled on through.

We kissed goodbye, and I watched him walk to the very end of the driveway until he disappeared in the night shadows of the oak trees. I heard his Harley fire up, and I listened until the only thing I could hear was the steady tick of the clock on my wall. I lay back onto my bed, staring at the ceiling and reliving every second of the evening.

It was perfect.

And in his own rough around the edges, unpredictable, gritty kind of way, *he* was perfect.

And well worth the cold, wet spot of spilled tea at the foot of my bed.

Chapter 12

It was Saturday night, and Grandpa had just taken the last load of wheat to town that morning. I was glad to be finished and excited to see Cass for the first time since our night under the stars.

Billy took my spot on the tractor for the evening so I could get ready, and I took advantage of the extra time I had to fix up. I knew I'd never figure out a curling iron, so I vouched for wavy hair by way of braids. I dressed in my cut-offs and a yellow tank top, curled my lashes, then smoothed on the red lipstick I borrowed from Grandma. It was labeled "Rockin' Red," so I figured it'd work pretty well for the occasion.

As I finished off the bottle of Aqua Net, I heard a vehicle outside my window. I rushed to grab my wallet, a hair tie, and a disposable camera, then headed for the door.

Lonna's white Corvette idled in the driveway as I made my way down the front porch steps. I was shocked Cass had talked her into borrowing it for the night, and even more impressed when I saw him step out of it. After all, a guy wearing an Aerosmith shirt was next to the best-looking thing I could think of.

He met me at the passenger's side door and gave me a kiss before opening it for me. I melted in his arms, taking in his warmth and the gentle way he held me close.

"It's a little bit of a drive, so I figured I'd park the Harley for the night."

"I can't believe Lonna let you borrow her car." I slid into the tan seat and ran my hand over the soft leather. It smelled brand-new, not a crease, wrinkle, or speck of dirt anywhere to be found.

"She likes you. That's the only reason." He sat down in the driver's seat and dropped the car into first gear, but not before revving the engine.

"I hear you like Aerosmith," he said. "Ready to see them live?"

Aerosmith.

Aerosmith.

I felt as if I were in a daze—in some kind of rock 'n roll dream—as we followed a crowd of rowdy fans through the doors of the venue. Everyone around us was talking, laughing, drinking, and passing joints as if we'd known each other for years.

"Why aren't you smokin'?" a lanky guy with a matted

mullet and a faded Beatles shirt asked. He looked at me, and when I couldn't come up with an answer, he looked at Cass.

"She don't smoke." Cass took the joint from him and inhaled before handing it back to him.

"Come on," said mullet man. "Aerosmith is up there just poundin' on shit. We're all here together, man. All of us are friends tonight. We came through that door as one, we smoke as one, and we leave as one . . . one big crowd of just . . . people who love the music, man. People who drive to our houses and turn on our record machines and just rock. We just sit and smoke and wish we could be here—right here in this moment, man. Right here where we're standin'. The music starts tonight. Weed brings the people together, man. Weed and music and beautiful ladies like you. Here."

He handed me the joint, and to my own surprise, I reached for it. I wasn't sure why. Was it the atmosphere or motivation from his interesting speech? Maybe it was because I thought Cass would like it if I tried it. Maybe it was my own rebellion against the "good girl" label.

I held it between my fingers, staring at it for what seemed like too long. The smell was strong, and I wrinkled my nose in disapproval. It wasn't long before I regretted taking it in the first place.

"Not today, man. Enjoy the show," Cass said, grabbing the joint and handing it back to him. Then, Cass led me toward the stage and away from the group of people we'd walked in with.

I squeezed his hand. "Thank you for that."

"Not a problem, darlin'."

"I bet you think I'm lame, don't you?"

"Not at all. I told you I like how you're a good girl."

"I thought you might just be saying that."

He shook his head. "I ain't ever dated a woman who turned her nose up to smoke or booze. I like it."

"You do?"

"Hell yeah. I do enough of it for the both of us. It's nice knowin' I found me someone a lot smarter than I am."

The venue was set up on a hill with the stage at the bottom. We fought our way toward the front and ended up settling for a spot in the crowd about twenty feet from the stage. People were packed in shoulder to shoulder, admiring Ted Nugent, who was opening. His presence dominated the stage as he ran from one side to the other. For a minute, I thought we were in the middle of a jungle somewhere—his loincloth being the first clue.

Nugent played his guitar with a vengeance, hitting the strings hard and steady. The crowd roared, worshipping the wild animal of a man who stalked the stage with his weapon of choice: a Gibson.

Cass bobbed his head and sang along, his eyes as bright as Fourth of July sparklers. As I watched him, I noticed some of the surrounding girls couldn't take their eyes off him, either. Some were even pointing at him and whispering to their friends.

"I think you're the center of attention, and you don't even know it," I said, keeping my eyes glued on a blonde who kept inching her way closer to us.

"What?" He looked around, noticing all the googly eyes. He raised a brow, then looked back at me. "You jealous?"

"No," I said, looking back at the blonde who had managed to squirm her way right beside us. She paid me no mind and looked at Cass like he was hers for the taking.

"You sure?"

I narrowed my eyes as I watched her scoot even closer. "Well, she acts like I'm not even here."

He laughed, then leaned in close to my ear. "Show 'er she ain't got a chance."

The blonde purposefully brushed her shoulder against his, and that was enough to make me take his advice.

I grabbed him by the belt loops and brought him in close to me. I wrapped my arms tight around his neck and gave him a long, sultry kiss. He slid his hands into the back pockets of my jeans and pulled me into him, and I bit his bottom lip as I pulled away. He smiled and brought me back in, kissing me even harder. And apparently, that did it, because the blonde was soon out of sight.

Nothing like a good confidence boost to start out the show.

About that time, the band we all came to see walked on stage. And if you weren't looking at the stage, you still knew they'd come on by the screams that left every person's throat.

Steven Tyler's voice pierced the smoky night air, proving he could sing better live than on any record or cassette. His energy and stage presence were incredible and matched by the band that backed him. They opened to "Sweet Emotion," and I remembered it was Cass's favorite song. He sang as loud as he possibly could, matching Tyler note for note. He held both arms high, signing horns and banging his head to the beat.

His smile said it all. He was in his element. Music was his thing. Aerosmith was his band.

I joined in and sang along to every song I knew. My singing voice was below average, but I sang anyway. The music and atmosphere were perfect, and I couldn't remember another time I'd had so much fun singing and dancing and laughing.

"You havin' a good time?" Cass asked after a few more songs. He took out a couple lighters from his front pocket and handed me one, and we raised them high for my favorite power ballad.

I smiled and kissed his cheek. "The best. I'm so glad you brought me."

"Why wouldn't I wanna bring my sexy girlfriend to see my favorite band?" He looked at me as if to make sure I'd heard the specific title he'd just used.

"Girlfriend?" I said with a smile.

"I don't want it any other way. Do you?"

I shook my head and gave him a reassuring kiss, and he brought me to stand in front of him instead of beside him. He draped an arm over my shoulder and waved his lighter in the hazy night air as Aerosmith played "Dream On."

I wondered how a night like this could be any better. After all, what surpassed an Aerosmith concert with a boy who could've been a poster child for the band? A boy who thought I was sexy? A boy who was now my boyfriend?

I'd never considered myself much more than an awkwardly built blonde who was flat in all the wrong places, but the way he looked at me—the way he touched me, kissed me, and held me like I was the only one who mattered—made me feel different. I had more confidence in myself than I'd ever had before.

Cass's eyes never left Joe Perry. Even when other members of the band were the center of attention, his eyes were still in Perry's direction. He seemed to study him, watching his blurred fingers as they flew along the neck of his guitar. He sang every word of every song as if he were imagining himself singing on stage instead of Tyler—as if it were just Cass and Perry performing to an audience.

Even a man who was standing next to us said, "Dude can sing."

I said to the man, "You should hear him play guitar."

Red Dirt Paradise

Cass belted out the lyrics with a throaty growl, not realizing he was being listened to. I was left amazed at how well he could sing this style of rock.

My mind drifted as I wondered how hard it would be to persuade him to pursue a singing career, even after he told me his plan was to farm. The day he realized his talent was bigger than any wheat field or John Deere tractor in Blaine County would be the day he could make enough money to buy any wheat field or John Deere tractor in Blaine County.

After an awesome set list and three hours of the greatest rock performance I'd ever seen, Aerosmith bowed, leaving us wanting more. Regrettably, we headed toward the doors, ears ringing and souls on fire for rock 'n roll.

"That was so kick-*ass!*" Cass yelled as he opened the door of the Corvette for me.

"That was . . ." I couldn't even find the right words to describe it. "Can you believe Steven Tyler? I mean, he sounds better in person!"

"Damn right he does. And what about Joe? He can play the *fuck* out of a guitar. He makes me wanna go home and practice for hours. The inspiration that man can give is just wicked."

He crawled into the driver's seat, put his hands on the steering wheel, and just sat there for a second. "I can't believe I just witnessed that." He slowly shook his head with a smile. "Aerosmith. *Aerosmith.* My band. My heroes. My fuckin' *boys.* Holy shit . . . I'm just . . . I'm in shock. Did that really just happen? *Come on!"*

I laughed. "They were awesome . . . and you weren't bad, either. You had a little audience of your own, you know."

"Hell, I was just tryin' to impress you." He let out another verse of "Last Child," where he threw in a high-pitched shriek.

"Cass, you need to pursue that," I said. "I'm not kidding."

"Yeah, right." He put the car in first gear, then shrugged. "Maybe it'll just be my side job apart from takin' care of you."

"You think you need to take care of me?"

We pulled out of the parking lot as I reached for his hand.

"Only if you'll let me, darlin'." Cass tucked his hair behind his ear and turned down the Foghat song playing on the radio. "You know, I've been thinkin' a lot lately. I know we ain't got but the summer together, but I wanna be with you after that. What do you think?"

I looked over at him as he drove us home. His eyes seemed so bright, flickering like candlelight in the dark.

"I wanna be with you, too," I said. "I don't want this to end."

"So, you're tellin' me you ain't gonna run off with an Aggie when you get back?"

"No, you can count on that." I figured he was referring to Billy as the Aggie since he was going to Texas A&M. I didn't even acknowledge it. Billy was the last person on my mind.

"How often do you visit your grandparents?" he asked, messing with the radio.

"I'll be back for Christmas. We usually stay a week or so."

"Christmas? That's a long time without you. I'll ride down there a couple times before then."

"Cass, you're not riding your bike all the way to Houston. Are you crazy?"

"Figured you knew the answer to that by now."

"Well, don't be *that* crazy."

"I'll miss you too much to wait that long. Hell, a week was pushin' it."

"Maybe I can talk Steph into letting me visit for fall break." I nodded to myself. "Yeah, that's what I'll do. So maybe I can catch a football game."

"It'd be cool if you could come watch me play. That way, I can show you off."

"And we can call each other and write until then. It's only for a year. Then, after I graduate, I can move here for college. I mean, I was considering it anyway."

He looked at me half-heartedly as future plans ran through my mind too fast to try and stop them. After it was too late, I realized what I'd said. I felt a pang of embarrassment, knowing I'd probably come off too strong. *Way to go, Austin.*

"You ain't goin' to any college for me. You go to the school you wanna go to, and we'll figure it out from there." He smiled, side-eyeing me. "If you're gonna be a famous photographer who takes pictures of half-naked men, then you gotta go to a good school."

I laughed, sloughing off the sudden heartache I had of not seeing him for months at a time. "I guess that's something we can figure out when the time comes."

"That's right."

I leaned across the console and brushed a kiss across his whiskers. I stayed there smiling at him for a long time and taking in the moment, admiring him in his post-Aerosmith buzz. His left arm draped lazily over the steering wheel, his body relaxed and leaning toward me. His hair was tangled and knotty, greasily pushed away from his face in cool rocker fashion. The outline of a small bump of Copenhagen rested in his lip, where a smile danced—probably from visions of Joe Perry still playing in his head.

I swore to myself I'd always remember him this way. When I had to leave for Houston and all I could do was think back on the best summer of my life, I'd flash back to this moment. I'd think of him right here, right now.

This was the Cass I'd dream about.

After we'd made our way through the busiest part of the city, Cass left the interstate and jumped on the historic Route 66. He pushed in Side One of his Springsteen cassette and fast-forwarded through the songs until "Born to Run" sounded through the speakers. Then, he carefully checked both side mirrors and the rearview mirror. Twice.

"You wanna see what this three-fifty is made of?" he asked. He downshifted until we were at a dead stop, idling in the middle of the isolated road.

I looked cautiously in front and behind us, thinking I might see some headlights in the distance, but only the inky blackness of the night surrounded us.

He revved the engine.

I threw a smile his way and turned up the volume. The sound of the drums, the guitars, the saxophone, the bells, they all blended together with the roar and rage and fire of the engine. Mixed with Cass's singing, there was a kind of electricity and desire that bolted through me, taking me on a crazy ride even though the car was at a stand-still.

"You ready?" he asked.

"Ready." I gripped the door in one hand and the console in the other.

"You sure?" He revved it again, the whole car vibrating and rattling from the muscle under the hood. He checked his mirrors one last time, white-knuckling the steering wheel.

"I'm ready," I said again.

"Say it louder."

"I'm ready," I yelled this time.

"Louder," he shouted over the motor.

"I'm ready!"

He punched the clutch to the floorboard and slammed the gearshift into place. Alongside Springsteen, he said, "One, two, three, four!"

The tires spun out on the asphalt and both of us were thrown back against the leather seats. He sang at the top of his lungs as the car lurched forward and we sped down the patchy paved road going faster and faster and faster. My stomach leaped into my chest as he kept the pedal floored, never missing a note of the song. He looked over at me, his eyes fiery and wild as he sang the part about loving with all the madness in his soul. I knew what he sang were only lyrics—words written by someone else about someone else—but in that moment, it didn't feel that way. Those lyrics meant something to me. I knew they meant something to him, too.

He backed off the gas until we were driving the speed limit, both of us still singing and laughing. My arms were above my head as if we'd just dropped from the highest track of a roller coaster, free-falling into the great unknown. But when he reached up and grabbed my hand, his touch brought me back down to ground-level.

The song faded with Springsteen's "whoa's" and after the tape ran out, there was only the thrumming sound of the engine that was left. I looked over at him, he looked over at me, and there was something between us that wasn't there before. It was a feeling that caught in my throat and would've sparked tears if I'd let it. It filled Lonna's Corvette and gave me goosebumps, my heart swelling in my chest as I watched him grin at me in his charming way.

"You ever go that fast before?" he asked.

"No way." I put my hand on my stomach, still feeling the ticklish flutters of butterflies from the speed.

"Kinda scary the first time, huh?"

I shrugged. "Kinda. But . . . kind of amazing, too."

He was quiet for a moment, clutching my hand in the silence. When he shifted in his seat, I looked his way and noticed him take a hard swallow. His eyes darted from the road to the speedometer and back again, before he cleared his throat.

"You ever felt like this with anyone else?"

"No," I answered. "Have you?"

"No." He shook his head. "No way."

"Kinda scary the first time. . . right?"

He laughed under his breath, easing off the gas. "Kinda. Kind of amazing though, too."

"Yeah." I let out a breath. "It is."

He ejected the cassette, then dug around in the map pockets for a different one. After he switched them out, he rolled down his window. I did the same.

The breeze blew through the car, swooshing through the cab and tangling our hair. I dangled my arm out the window, feeling the brisk wind as it cut smoothly through my fingers. I leaned my head back, closed my eyes, and breathed in the dry, summery June air.

"I hope it's always like this with me and you," I said, thinking aloud. I wasn't even sure if he'd heard me or not.

Cass was quiet, running his fingertips gently up my arm. He rested his hand on my shoulder, and I leaned my cheek against his knuckles.

"It will be," he said, giving me a squeeze. "It'll always be this way. Trust me."

Chapter 13

"You know, Austin, I really thought we were going somewhere. I really liked the guy." Even through the phone, I could sense Lexie's glum at the mention of Gunner. I could almost feel the sadness that engulfed her when she spoke—her voice weak, breaking every few words. And just hearing it was odd, since Lexie was never that way. She was all about flings and having fun and not settling with anyone. The grass was always greener with her, but now things seemed different.

"So, he just up and left the party?" I asked. "Without saying goodbye or anything?"

"Yeah. Just left, right there. When I asked him if he wanted to come to our Fourth of July, it's like a light went off in his head—like it suddenly made sense to him how much I liked him or something. I guess I scared him. So he left."

Red Dirt Paradise

Lexie asking a guy to a family Fourth of July get-together? That was even stranger. What happened to her while I was gone?

"Wow," I said. "I can't believe he did that. He could've at least told you bye!"

"Tell me about it. You know, I should've known he'd do this. He did the same thing to Danielle freshman year, remember? I thought she was just weird, but turns out he's a total ass."

"Well, now you won't waste any more time on him, I guess. Ugh. I hate that it didn't work out."

"Yeah, and thanks to you, I'm having to suffer alone."

"I'm sorry about that, too."

"Yeah, whatever. I'm sure you're much happier in Oklahoma. What are you doing there to pass the time? Growing things? Milking things?"

I hesitated and looked over my shoulder. Grandma was in the kitchen wiping down the counter, and Grandpa was in the den watching *The Rifleman*. If I told her about Cass, which I wanted to, there was a chance they'd hear me. Especially Grandma. I thought about switching phones and using the one upstairs, but what if Grandma decided to eavesdrop? Would she do that? Probably not. But what if she did?

"Working," I finally said. "I hang out with Jo some, but I mostly work."

"No boys? I kind of figured you'd have found you a hillbilly by now."

I laughed under my breath. "No hillbillies for me."

"Well, isn't that just boring?"

Oh, if she only knew what I was keeping from her.

"Reba McEntire told me I was cute once."

Cass and I walked hand in hand, strolling the banks of the South Canadian River. The full moon was high, casting its light across the dirty water littered with broken tree limbs and the occasional beer can.

I laughed at another one of his silly stories. "She did not."

"I swear. You can ask Larry and Keith. I have two witnesses."

"Where did you see her at?"

"A dance hall called the Country Palace about ten minutes from here."

"So, she just came right up to you at a dance hall and told you that you were cute?"

"Pretty much. We were standin' at the back by the bar. I couldn't see over Larry's frizz ball, which ain't nothin' new. I had a few beers in me, so told him to put me on his shoulders. And he did. After the show, she came through the crowd and said she had to meet the guy goofy enough to do somethin' like that. Then she said I was cute."

I laughed, not only at his story, but at the smug smile spread across his face.

"All because of Larry's frizz ball," I joked.

"It's a pain in the ass, I'm tellin' you."

We walked toward the firelight coming from the other side of the bridge. The party was still going strong as people danced around a hot June bonfire and finished off packs of beer and cigarettes.

"What time do you have to be home?" Cass asked, throwing his arm around my shoulders.

"I'm supposed to be staying with Jo, but Jo's staying with Tim tonight. So . . . I guess I don't really have to be anywhere."

"Really, now." Cass slid his hand down my back and touched my hips before slipping his warm fingertips inside the waistband of my jean shorts. "Just so happens I'll be stayin' with my buddy, Mike, tonight," he said. "It also just so happens he's got a guest bed."

"Is that some kind of an invite?" I ran my hand under his shirt, touching the bare muscles of his back.

He stopped and swept me up in a long kiss. "That's damn sure an invite. Let's find Mike, and we'll get outta here."

"You find Mike, and I'll find Jo and tell her I'm leaving with you."

Cass nodded and left to walk through the crowd of people while I did the same, looking for Jo and Tim. When I couldn't find either one, I searched for someone I at least recognized. It wasn't long before I came across not one, but two people I knew fairly well: Annie and Sam.

They were both standing beside the bonfire, which was only a couple feet from where I stood. They were talking to a girl in a short blue sundress and feathered hair, but the chatter quickly came to an end once Annie's eyes found mine through the crackling flames of the fire.

I stood awkwardly, flushing in the firelight. I was close enough to Annie to see her nose flare as she stared at me, and I took a swallow when she twisted her glossy pink lips into a grimace. She blew smoke out of the corner of her mouth before lifting a middle finger my way and mouthing the word "whore." My jaw dropped as she tilted her head toward the sky, letting out a cackle that sounded over the noise of the party. Sam covered her mouth, and her body heaved to match Annie's laughter, as I stood alone and embarrassed.

I missed Lexie. If she were here, she would've stood up for me. Just like that time in sixth grade when Cara Conner made fun of my hair, and Lexie threw her up against the lockers and threatened her. It was a little over-the-top for the crime, but I hadn't left Lexie's side since. She'd always been there for me, and she would've found a set of lockers somewhere close.

"Hey, you lost?" a gruff voice boomed from behind me. I turned slowly toward the sound as someone touched my arm. He was a taller guy with shaggy hair like Cass. His dark eyes went with his tanned skin and Sam Elliott-styled mustache.

"Oh, no, I'm not lost," I replied, my voice quiet and brittle.

Why did I let Annie get to me? Why did I even care that she felt the need to flip me the bird and call me names? I had done nothing wrong. I hadn't broken up a relationship or had some kind of an affair. She wasn't with Cass when he pursued me. She'd even called him an asshole! Yet here she was acting like I'd personally done something to deserve her insults and middle finger.

"I can keep you company if you'd like." The guy's mouth quirked in a smile, and he handed me can of beer. He swayed from side to side, squinting as he tried to focus on me.

"No . . . no, I'm okay. I've gotta go. Thanks anyway." I started to walk around him, in the opposite direction of the girls, when he stepped in front of me. His mouth was so close to mine I could smell his liquored breath. I took a step back when he grabbed my arm.

"Where you think you're goin'?" He smiled again, but this time it wasn't friendly. He looked at me as if I were something to satisfy his hunger—the way a predator looks at his less fortunate prey. He squeezed my arm until it hurt and barked out a laugh when I couldn't free myself. "Why do you look so scared? I ain't hurtin' you," he said, tightening his grip.

"Ow! That *does* hurt!" I tried to move away from him, but it didn't do any good.

"I just want to get to know you."

My heart pounded in my ears. *Where is Cass?*

"I have a boyfriend," I said, managing to keep my voice steady.

"He don't have to know." He took a step away from the party, dragging me with him.

From the corner of my eye, I saw the girl in the blue dress step forward. "Hey, let her go!" she shouted.

I glanced their way, hoping Annie and Sam would offer help, but all I got was a hit below the belt as I watched Sam duck her head like she didn't see and a witchy smile unravel itself on Annie's face.

The guy ignored the girl in the dress, taking another step away from everyone.

My adrenaline pulsed.

I ripped my arm from his grip as hard as I could and lost my balance, stumbling and landing right beside the fire. I rolled away from it just as I saw Cass racing toward me.

"Hey!" he yelled, forcing people out of his way. "Are you okay?" He rushed to my side, kneeling to help me to my feet.

"Yeah, I'm fine," I answered, rubbing the raised red marks the guy had imprinted on my arm.

Cass's face turned from worried to livid in a split second as he turned and pushed the guy who'd grabbed me. "What the fuck were you doin' grabbin' her like that?"

The guy tried to back away, but Cass grabbed him by the shirt collar and threw him up against a Chevy pickup parked a few feet away. The guy spluttered something I couldn't understand as Cass hurled him against the truck repeatedly. "Cass," the guy said, barely audible. "I didn't know she was your chick . . . I—I swear. You weren't around. I—I didn't know, man. I'm sorry. I'm sorry!"

"You ever so much as fuckin' *look* at her again, you know what'll happen to you, don't you?"

"I got it. I got it, man! I'm sorry."

Cass tightened his grip on the guy's collar until he gasped for air. "I don't think you do."

"I swear I do," he struggled to say, grabbing at Cass's hands. "Please. I got it!"

With a quick fist, Cass reared back and punched him in the face. The guy fell to the ground, cupping his hands around a bloodied, busted nose.

"You broke my nose, man!"

"Yeah, be glad that's all I broke." Cass left the guy rolling and whining on the ground as he came my way. I looked around us and noticed every eye staring. The crowd was silent except for the few drunks who were chanting Cass's name.

"Let me see your arm." He ran his hands over the marks, shaking his head. "That stupid son of a bitch." He turned back toward the guy. "We ain't done yet, fucker!"

"No," I grabbed Cass's shirttail, pulling him back toward me. "It's okay, really. I'm fine. Let's just go."

He tensed his jaw. "What if I wasn't around and that shit happened? What if you'd fallen in the fire?"

"But you were, and I didn't. Let's just go. Please?" I felt Annie's eyes like laser beams on my back. I knew she was judging Cass for defending me, and I could sense her hatred without even looking her way.

"That was totally uncalled for." There it was. Annie's two cents about the situation. I knew it was coming, I just didn't know when.

Cass shot her a look but quickly chose to ignore her. "If

that's what you want, we'll just go," he said, putting his arm around me and guiding me away from the party—away from the drama.

I took one last look at Annie and Sam, who were quietly sharing secrets amongst each other, and a certain sadness set within my soul. I'd already forgotten the fear of being grabbed by a stranger, dragged a few steps, and falling near a fire. It was the hurt caused by the girls' cattiness that stung like an angry hornet.

"Has Annie always been that way?" I asked Cass as we neared the truck.

He stopped, furrowing his brows. "What'd she do to you?"

I shook my head. "Nothing. Just kinda catty, you know."

He grit his teeth. "She said something, didn't she? What'd she say?"

"Nothing, really." I thought of the way she'd mouthed that particular word and laughed at me when I was in trouble. I looked to the ground, feeling helpless. *Pathetic,* almost. And I wouldn't tell him what she did because of it.

He took a deep breath and brought me in close. "Don't pay her any mind. There ain't a lot of people that like Annie, and there's a good reason for that. You just gotta ignore her like I do."

I laid my head against his chest, thinking of how he'd been on and off with Annie for long enough she "claimed" him. The thought of it put a foul taste in my mouth.

"Why were you with her?" I said it without thinking and regretted it immediately. My face was hot as I pulled away from him, and I quickly backtracked because I knew why he was probably with her, and I didn't want an explanation about what happened behind closed bedroom doors. "Don't answer that," I said, taking a step toward the truck. "I don't know why I just said that."

"Wait," he said, pulling me back into him. "It's okay to ask questions. I ain't tryin' to hide nothin' from you."

I swallowed, looking to the ground once again.

"It's a damn good question, honestly, 'cause hell, I ain't real sure what I saw in her."

I laid my arms across my stomach, feeling sick for getting into a conversation about his past love life. "Yeah, Jo told me you two were on and off a lot . . . but it's none of my business, really."

"My business is your business now." He rubbed his whiskers, taking his time to answer like he wasn't sure what to say. "Me and Annie . . . yeah, we ran around together in the past. But I kinda ran around a lot in the past."

"Oh, geez," I said, under my breath.

"Hey, I ain't gonna act like I didn't. But I told you before that none of those girls mattered to me. None of 'em did. Annie included. Annie bein' at the top of that list." He lifted my chin toward him, and for some reason, I felt like crying.

"I promise you, darlin', you're the only one I've ever cared about like this. Don't you trust me?"

I nodded, feeling silly for needing to be reassured. "I trust you."

He smiled. "Good. Now let's get outta here."

"Wait." I looked back at the party. "What about Mike? Are we not taking him with us?"

He scoffed. "Not after I broke the fucker's nose."

Chapter 14

"So, since Mike's place is out of the question, where do we go from here?" I asked, turning onto the highway.

Cass thought about it while pinching some Copenhagen between his fingers. "We can go to Pat and Lonna's," he said. "I got my own room over there."

"Pat and Lonna's?" I shot him a look from behind the wheel of the truck.

He grinned like he was daring me to agree to it. "There's a lock on my door. I ain't ever seen 'em up after ten."

"No way," I said. I cringed at the shame I'd feel if Pat or Lonna walked in on us. "We can't do that. That's crazy."

He chuckled. "Come on. It'll be fun. We just gotta be quiet." He moved his empty beer box that was between us and slid over to the middle seat.

"And what if we get caught?"

"We ain't gonna get caught."

"But what if we do?"

"Well, we'll just tell 'em we're workin' on a science project."

"A science project? It's summer. And I don't even go to school here."

"Well then, we better think of a better excuse." He put his arm around me, sweeping my hair from my neck. "Head that way," he said. He gave me a kiss on the cheek, then moved his lips along my jawline. I buried my free hand in all his hair and held my breath as he moved toward my ear.

"Can't we just . . . sleep in here?" I asked, breathless.

"We could . . . I guess," he said between kisses. "Just find a place to park, and I'll lay you down on this bench seat for our first time. Or . . . we could make it a little more interesting."

My eyes nearly popped out of my head. Anxiety bubbled like hot oil in my stomach, rising until it tickled the back of my throat.

Did he just say "our first time?"

"So, you . . . you really wanna go there?" I asked, trying to hold back the jitters from finding their way to my voice. "To Pat and Lonna's, I mean?"

"Yeah, take a left up here. It's the back way to their house. We'll park in the field and walk up there. Crawl through my window, and we're in business. What do you think?"

I slowed the truck, creeping up to the intersection. My thoughts raced as I tried to decide what to do. I drummed my fingertips on the steering wheel and bit my lip, taking some time before I came up with an answer. Could I really do something like that?

Me?

Red Dirt Paradise

The radio was low, but I could hear "Feel Like Makin' Love" by Bad Company playing.

Cass turned it up, a rebel grin on his face. "How's that for motivation?" He started singing the words to me, and I knew right then which way I was going to turn.

I cranked the wheel to the left and punched the gas.

"Hell yeah, baby!" he yelled. He slammed his hand on the dash. "We're doin' this?"

I smiled, singing the chorus. "We're doin' this."

"But what if we get caught?" he asked.

"We won't get caught." I said it with confidence, despite the nerves that almost choked me.

He scooted closer to me and squeezed my knee, then slowly ran his callused hand along the inside of my thigh. He inched his fingers into my shorts, outlining the hem of my panties. "You think you can keep from screamin'?" he whispered in my ear.

I couldn't breathe. Forgetting to watch where I was going, I ended up with two tires off the road. I swerved back to the blacktop after almost losing control, my hands gripping the steering wheel so tight they hurt.

He laughed as he pulled his hand away. "I don't know if you can."

"I don't . . . know if I can, either," I answered truthfully.

"Turn right here," he said suddenly.

"Here?" I slammed on the brakes, turning in the direction he told me to. The road looked like a driveway, gray rocked with weeds growing in between the tire tracks, and we were nowhere near Pat and Lonna's.

"Where are we going?" I asked.

"This is where we're stayin'."

"Huh?"

"We're stayin' here with my buddy, Shawn."

I looked at him, confused.

"Shit, I'd never sneak you over to Pat's." He reached for his spit can. "He'd have my ass, and I'd be out of a job."

I let out a sigh of relief, relaxing my shoulders from being so tense they were near my ears.

"You were really gonna let me sneak you in?" He eyed me, bringing his spit can to his lips.

"I was planning on it."

He laughed, throwing his head back. "Shit, I ain't got the balls to do somethin' like that. Badass that you were for it, though."

I smiled, proud of myself for agreeing to something like that. Would I have actually gone through with it? Maybe. If he'd kept singing to me? I definitely would've.

"So, who lives here? Shawn?" I asked.

"Yeah, I work for him some. Keep goin' down this road, and we'll drive right up to his place."

I did as he said, and within a couple seconds we came across a white-sided trailer house, the outside of it looking aged and worn through the glow of my headlights. Every light in the home looked to be on and every window open, and there was a small junkyard of vehicles to the west of it.

"I can't believe you were gonna let me sneak you in," he said again as we stepped out of the truck. "Man, I can't wait to tell Larry about this."

We walked toward the door of the trailer, making our way through pigweeds and Johnson grass. But before I knew it, a man wearing overalls with no shirt shouted at us from his doorway.

"Stop, or I'll shoot your ass!" He kicked open his screen door and pumped his shotgun.

I froze while Cass walked in his direction like nothing had happened.

Red Dirt Paradise

"He's just fuckin' with us," Cass said. "He ain't gonna shoot us."

I watched him sprint toward the door as I backed away. *What is he thinking?*

"Well, I ought to, with you pullin' in here at damn near midnight," the man said.

Cass flipped the guy's straw cowboy hat off his head and whispered something to him. He put his gun down, and when I decided it was safe to walk to his door, I did it slowly.

"Sorry there, miss. I wasn't really goin' to shoot you," he said, smiling and holding out his hand. "I'm Shawn."

"It's . . . okay," I said. "Austin."

Cass chuckled. "We're crashin' here tonight. Is Tish up?"

"Yeah," answered Shawn. "She's in the bedroom. I'll go get her."

Cass led us into a small kitchen decorated with vases full of faux sunflowers and crowded rooster decor. It reminded me of a kitchen that would've been on a sitcom.

We sat down at a small card table, where poker chips were piled high next to empty beer bottles.

"Want somethin' to drink?" Shawn asked, walking into the kitchen. He'd put on a shirt under his overalls and combed his wavy brown hair to one side. And unlike the pump of his shotgun seconds earlier, his smile was welcoming.

"Water is fine," I said. "Thank you."

He reached in the cabinet for a plastic cup, checking inside of it before holding it under the faucet.

"Oh, no," said a woman from the corner of the room. Her dark hair fell in a loose bun, and her smeared mascara suggested she'd been sleeping before we barged in.

"Why don't you give me some warning before you bring company with you, Cass? The house is a wreck, and I look just about as bad. You'd think a bunch of hogs lived in here with us."

"Looks good in here to me," Cass said.

"I'm Tish. How—" She stopped mid-sentence, staring at me with eyes as big as the poker chips stacked in front of me. She pushed her glasses closer to her face, as if she couldn't believe I was in her house.

"Uh, everything okay? Too much wine tonight, darlin'?" Cass asked, patting her back.

She looked at him, then back at me. "What did you say your name was?"

"Austin," I replied.

She didn't say a word—just held her hand over her mouth and made me feel like I shouldn't have been there.

"I'm sorry," I said. "We shouldn't have bugged you guys this late." I stood from my chair, mad that Cass had something against sleeping in the truck.

"No, no. Oh my gosh," Tish said quickly. "It's okay! I don't mind that you guys came at all. I'm so sorry." She pushed her glasses on the top of her head and wiped her eyes.

"Tish, what the hell are you doin'? Are you *cryin'?*" Shawn asked, looking about as confused as me and Cass.

"You look just like her. I mean, it's like I'm standing here looking at Sandy." Tish wiped another tear from her eye as I plopped back down in my seat. Cass came to sit next to me and rubbed my back soothingly.

"You knew my mom?" I asked, leaning into Cass's touch. This was the last thing I'd ever expected.

"Yes. Your mom and I were best friends. We grew up together. Sorry for the tears. This probably makes you feel pretty uncomfortable." Tish took the seat beside me, wrapping her robe around her tiny body. "Are you two friends?" she asked, directing the question to Cass.

"She's my girl."

"Your girl? You guys are . . . *together?*" She looked startled by his response, glancing from me and back to him.

"Is there somethin' wrong with that?" he asked.

"Uh . . . no . . . well, I'm surprised. Just a little surprised. I mean, well, you've just never been serious before, and then you come in here with Austin, and it's just mind-blowing, really. I just feel like I'm sitting here . . . you guys . . . together . . . and . . . You know what? Never mind. I'm rambling. It's the wine."

"How about you and I go drink in the livin' room and leave these two ladies to their wine, huh?" Shawn looked at Cass, and he nodded in agreement.

"You should probably just have water, Tish," Cass said, squeezing her shoulder.

"Been tellin' her that for years," Shawn muttered.

"Oh, go on," she said, rolling her eyes.

Cass and Shawn went into the living room and turned up the TV so loud that I knew our conversation couldn't be heard.

Tish kept the questions coming just as fast as I could get them answered. We talked about Steph and Jay, my grandparents, and Houston. We talked about school and colleges I was looking into. She asked about my friends back home and what I did for pastimes. We talked of music, movies—everything two old friends would talk about. Her eyes were starry while she spoke to me, as if she'd been missing me for years.

"So, you were best friends with my mom?" I asked her after we'd only talked about my own life for an hour.

"We were really close growing up. Inseparable in high school. I would come over to your grandparents' house all the time and play with you when you were little. Gosh, that seems like so long ago."

I smiled, trying to remember her face in a few faded memories.

"When she passed away, it was so hard on me. It was hard on all of us—our friends, your family. She was really special. You remind me so much of her."

"Thank you. I get that a lot. Enough to make me think I could've been her twin."

"Oh, honey, there's no denying it. You are *definitely* Sandy's twin. Your freckles, the hair. You guys even have the same smile. Your eyes . . . Just not a lot you didn't get from her." Tish smiled, putting the poker chips back in a black case sitting next to the table. "I hope you don't mind me asking if your father ever came back into the picture?"

I shook my head. "I saw him once when I was in grade school. He came to Houston for something and somehow got ahold of Steph. We met at a park for a few minutes, and I never saw him again."

"That sounds like Vince. Drop in long enough to make things awkward, then leave."

"It *was* awkward meeting him. I do remember that." In my mind's eye, I could see my dad as he sat across from me on that old concrete bench in a lonesome Houston park. He was handsome, even with his receding hairline and round tortoise-shell prescription glasses. Fidgety and nervous, he cracked his knuckles too often and bounced his leg until he was nearly winded. His eyes rarely met mine, and when they did, no emotion was behind them. He was just a stranger to me, as I was to him, with no ounce of love between the two of us—at least not the kind a father and daughter were supposed to share.

"I don't even know why he wanted to meet up," I said.

"There's no telling. Maybe he was thinking of your mom and just wanted to meet you. He always liked your mom, although I'm glad that relationship never worked out. It's better that you were brought up with Stephanie and Jay. Much, much better."

I nodded, needing a change in subject. "Tell me something about my mom. I never get to hear stories about her."

"Oh, I love telling stories about Sandy." Tish smiled and leaned back in her chair. "Well, there was this one time in high school when your mom was dating a guy named Rich Faulkner. He was a stud athlete and about as good lookin' as they get . . . but he was also a pro at breaking hearts. I dated him before he got ahold of your mom, and he did me in just as bad. Anyway, his dad had built him a little shed to the side of their house, where everyone would hang out on Friday nights. One night after a football game, your mom had this bright idea of spying on him to figure out if he was cheating on her. We walked a half a mile in the dark to his house, then army-crawled across his parents' back yard to spy on him." She looked up at the ceiling, letting out a hearty laugh. "Honestly, I can't even remember if we caught him doing anything. We were giggling so hard, I don't think we could've heard him even if he was."

I laughed, enjoying a story coming from someone who was once so close to her. It was nice to hear a happy memory of my mom.

"I miss her every day. Every single day," she said, looking to the ground.

My heart hurt for her as I imagined what it would be like to lose a best friend. And seeing the pain that clouded Tish's eyes, I knew the loss of my mom still affected her. Much like it still affected me.

"So, how did you meet Cass?" she asked, changing the

subject. She smoothed her hands over her face as if to wipe away the sadness, and then she smiled as she waited for my answer.

"I met him in town the day I got here."

She leaned closer and lowered her voice. "He's pretty cute, isn't he?"

She nudged me, and I laughed, thinking about the way he looked through my camera lens during our photo shoot.

"Yeah, and he knows it, too."

Tish laughed and looked toward the living room. "Cass is a good guy. Lord knows that boy is ornery, but he's got a good heart."

"Yeah, he does. I love that about him." I couldn't help but smile just talking about him. I hadn't gotten to do that with someone who admired him like I did.

"He's been working for Shawn on and off for a few years now. He's never mentioned a girl before, and he's sure never brought one over here. I can tell you're pretty special to him."

I remembered the night in Grandpa's field when he'd told me those words exactly. "He's special to me, too. I really like him." I laughed under my breath. "I *really* like him."

"He really likes you, too," she said. "The way he looks at you proves that. I think you two will be together for a long time." She stood up, wrapping her faded robe tight around her. "And if a problem does arise . . ." She hesitated, hugging herself like she was suddenly chilled. Her face seemed tenser as she avoided my gaze, looking nervously off to the side. "Well . . ." She nodded her head as if to reassure herself. "You'll get through it."

I was quiet, eyeing her carefully. What did she mean, "If a problem does arise"?

"All I'm saying is young love can be hard sometimes." She said it quickly after seeing my reaction. "And it's getting late, so I better leave you two alone." Her smile was back on her face before I had time to analyze any further.

I stood, and she swept me up in a hug.

"It was so nice to see you, Austin." Tish squeezed me tightly, and any worries I had about her odd comment quickly vanished in her arms.

"Come back anytime. Even if Cass isn't with you, I'd love to see you again." She held on to me for a long time, and when she pulled back, there was a tear falling down her cheek.

"I will," I said, loving the idea of having someone like Tish to talk to. Especially about my mom.

"There's a guest bedroom down the hallway that you guys are welcome to sleep in."

Shawn came in from the kitchen, shaking his head. "Austin might sleep in there, but you ain't gonna wake that boy up for shit." He looked at Tish. "And I got a feelin' he's gonna hate you for talkin' so long he fell asleep."

Tish shrugged. "He'll get over it." She gave me a wink, then followed Shawn into the bedroom and closed the door behind her.

I walked into the living room and looked at Cass as he snored in the recliner. His shirt was off, his pants were unbuttoned, and he had a beer still in his hand. I tried to wake him, but he wouldn't budge. If anything, he snored louder. When I finally gave up, I kissed him on the cheek and covered him with a flannel blanket that was thrown across the loveseat. I smiled, knowing he'd kick himself when he woke up in the morning. Our first night together, and he got the chair while I got the couch.

Chapter 15

"Grandma?" I said over the steady hum of the dryer. I peeked into the laundry room, but she was nowhere to be found.

"Hmm." I walked back into the kitchen and scanned the fridge door. Usually, there was a note left under a magnet if she had to leave for errands, but there were none anywhere I could see.

"Grandma?" I walked through the hallway toward her sewing room. She was sometimes so knee-deep in quilting that she was oblivious to anything else going on in the world. That was probably where she was hiding.

I opened the door, expecting her to be threading a needle or cutting fabric, but her chair was empty. I paused, hanging out in the doorway and enjoying the feel of the room. The white lace curtains were pushed to the side, letting in a soft orange hue that flooded through the age-old windows. The evening sun shared its warmth with the small space that was used to patch jeans and cross-stitch on lazy days.

The same space my mother used to sleep in.

I stepped inside, taking in the familiar scent that hung light and fresh in the air. It'd always smelled this way. I remembered it from when I was a kid. It was the smell of clean linen, from Grandma's material, mixed with a sort of perfume that dusted every corner. It was a sweet vanilla kind of smell, which was odd considering it wasn't the kind Grandma ever spritzed on her wrists. I always told myself it was my mom who kept the room smelling like it once did fifteen years before.

I walked toward the cutting table, where a small oval-shaped portrait of my mom rested on an antique side table. It was her senior portrait, and the only one of her that was framed in the whole house. Steph's was on the other side of the room, making the two pictures the only evidence they'd grown up in this home.

"What are you doing, doll?" Grandma called from behind me. I turned to see her standing in the hallway, wiping her hands on a blue checkered tea towel.

I picked up the picture of my mom and stared at it for a minute, smiling at the way her eyes lit up the black-and-white portrait.

"I was looking for you," I said. "Then I got sidetracked."

"Oh, I was in the back patio watering plants." She walked up next to me and looked at the photo she'd probably stared at a million times before. "You look so much like her. Goodness me, it's almost scary."

I rubbed the dust off the glass with my thumb, smiling at how the scent in the room seemed stronger now.

"I wish we had some more pictures for you to look at," she said. "That damned fire really cost us."

Ten or twelve years ago, there was an electrical fire that burnt up the garage and part of the kitchen. All of the family photos—all of my mom and Steph's keepsakes, all the family heirlooms, and my grandpa's old 1930 Ford Coupe—went up in smoke. I was little when it happened and didn't understand the impact it had on the family, but I can still remember seeing the charred remains and hearing Grandma cry so hard she couldn't catch her breath.

"At least we have that one album from when she was a kid," I said, hoping to make Grandma see some light after thinking of those heart-wrenching flames. "And we have this picture."

Grandma patted my back as she cleared her throat. "Well," she said, stopping her sadness with a halt. "I'm going to the garden to pick some tomatoes. You can come help me if you'd like."

I put the picture back down in its place, taking one last look at it.

"Grandma?" I said as she headed for the door.

She stopped and turned to look at me.

"Can you teach me how to sew?" I'd been craving some one-on-one time with her. I'd gotten plenty with Grandpa while working together every day, but I'd been missing some with her. Spending some moments over a sewing machine from the comfort of my mom's old bedroom seemed the perfect opportunity to bond.

She smiled, throwing the tea towel over her shoulder. "We'll start this evening."

I took one last look at my mom's photo before following her out the door and slipping away with her to the garden.

Chapter 16

I combed through the tangles in my hair, determined to teach myself how to curl it. I'd tried all summer without any luck, but this time, I'd make it happen. Even if Cass couldn't care less about whether my hair was curly or straight, I wanted to figure out how this thing worked. I checked the iron. It was hot, so I sectioned a lock to conquer.

"Since when do you curl your hair?" Lexie's voice called from the hallway.

I jumped, slamming the iron down on the counter. "Lexie? You scared me! What in the world are you doing here?"

She moaned, slipping the duffel bag off her shoulder and letting it fall to the ground like a bag of concrete. "Fred and Marge are dragging me across the country to visit some relative I've never heard of. I'm not happy about it. Obviously."

"But why are you *here*?"

"They dropped me off for the night while they stay with some of their friends."

"Your parents have friends out here?"

"Somewhere . . . I can't remember the name of the place. It's something I can't even pronounce, thanks to all these weird town names. I need a translator to read a map in this state."

"How long are you staying? How did you know how to get here? I'm a little lost here, Lex."

"Just for tonight. We're leaving sometime in the morning. Steph gave us directions and wanted me to surprise you, so . . . surprise!" She stepped into the bathroom, eyeing the curling iron and makeup strewn across the countertop. "Who are you, and what have you done with Austin?"

"Uh . . . I'm glad you're here, actually. I need some help." I pointed the iron in her direction, giving her a hopeful look.

"I'll ask this again. Since when do you curl your hair?" She put her hands on her hips like I was doing something to royally upset her.

I hesitated, knowing she was going to throw a fit when she heard what I'd been keeping from her.

"Well . . ." I smiled, unable to hide the pride that came from being Cass's girlfriend. "Since I have a boyfriend."

"You *what?*" she screeched, throwing her arms in the air.

"Shh! Not so loud," I whispered. "Sorry, I didn't—"

"You have a boyfriend, and you didn't even tell me?"

"I was going to—"

"What was all that shit on the phone about 'Oh, all I do is work, and I never do anything else'? But you found time to have a *boyfriend?*"

"Shh," I said again, peeping around the doorframe to make sure Grandma wasn't in earshot.

"What are you—"

"Keep it down, Lexie!" I hissed. "My grandparents don't know."

"Well, we'd better start a club together since we're all out of the loop on this one!"

"I wanted to tell you," I said, "but every time we talk on the phone, they're always close enough to overhear me. I just didn't want them to ask me questions."

"Why wouldn't you just tell them? Does Steph know?"

"No. I . . . I just haven't told them yet."

"Why? Is he a serial killer or something? An old man? Is he married?"

I crossed my arms, jutting out my hip to rest against the counter. "You have some high expectations of me, don't you?"

"Just tell me everything." She shut the door, snapping the lock with a loud click. She turned and leaned against the door, her lips so tight they were a white line.

"Okay, well . . . his name is Cass."

"Cass?" She ducked her chin, raising a brow like I'd pulled the name out of thin air.

"James Cassedy, but people call him Cass." I smiled, thinking of how he'd told me that same line the first time we'd met. Butterflies tickled my insides thinking about that night with him at the barn. The way he looked with his leg propped up on that Chevy tailgate. His smirky smile, his Robert Plant vibes. Everything about that moment seemed like a clip from a rock 'n roll music video.

"He's so cute, Lex," I continued. "Like, real good-looking. Like, the best-looking guy I've ever seen." I started to rush the words like I was on a time limit, too excited not to gush. "He's perfect. Really genuine, you know? He makes me laugh, he's sweet, and he's fun to be around. Oh, and he plays the guitar, and he can sing like—like you wouldn't *believe* how good he can sing. He's got this cool rock 'n—"

"Whoa." The corners of her mouth turned up, revealing an all-knowing smile. "Someone is in love."

I was quiet, avoiding her eyes.

She gasped. "You *are!*"

"It's too early to tell." I looked away from her, biting my lip. I didn't want her knowing I'd fallen for Cass so fast, but I knew my cheeks would give me away.

"Maybe for you to tell, but not for me. Your face says it all without having to say a thing."

I brushed her off and grabbed the curling iron, acting as if I knew what I was doing.

"Give it here," she said, sliding a strand of my hair around the iron. "You're taking me to meet him as soon as I'm done."

"I told him I'd meet him at the barn in an hour, so you're in luck."

"The barn?" She sputtered a laugh. "Hillbillies."

"It's not really a barn. They just call it that. It's really just a parking lot we all hang out in."

In a horrid, fake southern accent, she said, "Whatever you say, sugar."

Lexie finished curling my hair before freshening up herself. She redid her makeup, teased her hair, sprayed enough Aqua Net to fog up the bathroom, then changed into a pair of Gloria Vanderbilt jeans and a deep V-neck top.

"Does this shirt bring out my eyes?" she asked flipping her hair away from her puffed-out chest.

"Uh, yeah. That's the first thing I noticed."

"Hillbillies like boobs, too, ya know."

I rolled my eyes and threw on a tank top and jean shorts.

We started down the road toward the barn, driving into a

sunset I was sure would catch her eye. When all she did was flip through the radio stations and groan about the bumpy road, I decided there was no point in even suggesting she appreciate it.

"How are you doing after the whole Gunner thing?" I asked. "Are you doing better?"

She scoffed and turned her head to stare out the window. "I'm fine. It's not a big deal."

In Lexie's world, that meant she was *not* fine, and it *was* a big deal.

"Is there not a decent radio in here?" she asked.

"It's got some static issues."

She went through all the stations two or three times before settling on one playing Madonna's "Like a Virgin." She leaned over and stared at me.

"What?" I asked, nervous my makeup didn't look as good as I thought it did. I looked in the rear-view mirror one more time, making sure I was put together.

"Is Austin Rose still a virgin?"

"Really?"

"Is that a yes?"

"Yes, Lexie," I murmured.

"Well, it's not like you'd tell me if you weren't."

"I would've already told you if I wasn't."

"Is he a good kisser?"

"Definitely."

"Better than Pete?"

I snorted at the comparison. "Way better than Pete. A lot more patient, too." I shook my head, thinking of all the times Peter the Petter wouldn't stop . . . petting. Even when he knew I wasn't ready to take the next step with him, there he'd be.

Petting.

She lay against the seat, putting her bare feet on the dusty dashboard. "The hillbilly who stole Austin's heart. I just can't *wait* to have the honor of meeting him."

I pulled into the barn, parking beside Jo's truck. There was a lighter crowd tonight, and I didn't spot Cass's bike anywhere.

"This is where everyone hangs out?" Lexie asked, looking less than enthused to be joining me.

"What's wrong with it?"

She stared at the crowd in front of her as if they were all from another planet. I grew impatient as she slammed the door behind her.

"Hey!" I called to Jo, Tim, and a couple guys in Geary wrestling shirts. "This is Lexie. Lexie, this is Jo."

Lexie smiled while all of them, including Tim, sized her up. She beamed when she noticed their stares.

"Nice to meet you," Jo said. "I didn't know you were coming to town. I should've warned the boys."

Lexie smiled, scoping out the parking lot. "We were *all* a little surprised by my visit."

We sat on the tailgate while Jo went on a search for beer. Lexie crossed her legs, twirling her dark hair around a red fingernail. The boys from around the parking lot continued to steal glances at her, probably trying to gain enough liquid courage to come up and talk to her.

"So, where's Cass?" Lexie asked, tossing her stiff hair over her shoulder.

"He's not here yet. You'll know when he pulls up."

"How will I know? You haven't told me anything about him. What does he look like?"

"You'll see." I smiled when I heard a motorcycle in the distance. "There he is," I said when a black Harley with a shaggy blond pulled up across the parking lot from us.

"Where?"

"He's on the bike."

She glanced at Cass, who was dismounting the Harley, and laughed. "Yeah, right. Where is he?"

"That's him." I bit my lip, hopeful she'd be impressed.

"No way."

"That's Cass."

"The guy who looks like he just robbed a bank?"

I frowned, offended by the look of disgust on her face. "Seriously, where is he?"

"That's him!"

She looked at him again, cocking her head to the side like a confused puppy. "You're serious?"

"Yeah, why is that so hard to believe?"

"Because, Austin, he looks like he just escaped the Mayberry Jail."

"Lexie!"

"No wonder you kept him a secret."

Before I could defend him, Cass strolled up next to me and put his arm around my shoulders. "Hey, sunshine. Who's this?"

"Lexie," I muttered, too mad to offer up why or how she was here.

"Lexie?" He held out his hand, squeezing me closer to his side. "Nice to meet you. Hear you two are pretty good friends."

Lexie stared at his hand as if she'd just witnessed him pull it out of sewage. "I'm sunshine's best friend," she said. "As in, bodyguard. As in, if you touch her wrong, I'll chop your balls off."

He dropped his hand, and I nearly died of embarrassment. "Lexie," I said through my teeth.

"It's okay, darlin'." Cass rubbed my back and threw a

devilish grin her way. "It's nice to know my woman has a bodyguard with a pair of her own."

"Watch it," Lexie snarled.

"Sounds like you could use a beer. I'll get a few." Before he left, he brought me into his arms and kissed me long and hard. I smiled when I heard Lexie's disapproving groan. He offered her another grin before turning toward the party and squeezed my butt as he left.

"I don't like him," she spat when he was out of sight.

I threw my arms up in protest. "You don't even know him."

"I know him enough to not like him. Steph is going to *kill* you."

"I don't care. He makes me happy. Isn't that all that matters?"

"He makes you happy?"

"Yeah. He does."

She looked at me in disbelief. "How can you be happy with *that*?"

I grit my teeth as tears burned my eyes.

"What's goin' on? You okay?" Cass walked up with a couple beers and shot a look to Lexie.

She glared back.

"What'd you say?" Cass asked, looking at her for an explanation.

"It's fine," I muttered. "It was nothing."

"You gotta problem with me?" Cass asked her.

Lexie's glare never budged, and neither did her attitude. "I just don't know you."

I could tell she wanted to say more but held it back. At this point, I'm not sure why she bothered to hold anything back.

"You could get to know me right now if you'd stop bein'

so snooty." Cass handed her a beer, and she snatched it from him like him touching it was contamination.

"I'll drink your beer, but I'd rather not get to know you."

I shook my head, at a loss for words. Lexie could be hard to get along with sometimes. She could be a handful and often a little much, but she was never this downright *rude*.

"Well, well, well . . . who do we have here?" Keith, the guy who wore purple paisley boots and Cass had described as being "fuller than a horse's shit" walked up to join our awkward gathering. He smiled Lexie's way, and I watched as his eyes slid smoothly down her face, to her bulging chest, then to her legs. "Baby, those jeans are *tight*," he said, blowing a cloud of smoke from his rolled-up joint. "It may take me a little bit to get 'em off."

Lexie's eyes bugged, and her mouth dropped. Cass laughed under his breath. I didn't know *what* to think.

Keith bit his lower lip lustfully, and I could see the anger radiating off Lexie as she inhaled slowly. "If you think," she said, emphasizing every word, "I'd *ever* let a hillbilly like you take these jeans off, you are out of your fucking redneck mind."

Keith grinned. "You're right. I'll let you take 'em off for me. It'll be faster that way."

Lexie's eyes narrowed to tiny slits. "You think you're just *so* cute, don't you?"

Keith shrugged. "Maybe."

She sized him up just like he'd done to her moments before, then slowly shook her head. "You and that misshapen cowboy hat." She looked at his feet, and her face twisted with disgust. "And those *awful* boots. You look like you just crawled in from the woods somewhere."

"Least it don't look like I'm tryin' to keep up with the people from *Dynasty*."

"Well, I'd rather look like a Carrington than a Clampett."

Keith took a drink from his beer. "Who did your make-up? Boy George?"

Lexie crossed her arms. "When was the last time you showered? Or do you bumpkins still bathe in creeks around here?"

"We call it the waterin' hole."

"Well, you should use it every now and then."

He smashed his hat down on his head and poured his southern accent on thick. "Well, Maw says we ain't got to but ever couple weeks!"

She scoffed. "Hillbilly."

"Snob."

"Hayseed."

"Brat."

"Hick."

"Yuppie."

"How much moonshine do you make on the weekends?"

"How much does your daddy put in your trust fund?"

Lexie was silent. Keith was, too, until he ducked his head and let out a chuckle. When he looked back at Lexie, she was smiling at him. But it wasn't just *a* smile. It was *the* smile.

Lexie was giving him the look.

Keith waved the joint toward her. "You wanna hit? We grow our own around here. Comes from the riverbanks. We call it river weed."

"That's original," she said, reaching for the joint.

"Ah," Keith said, snatching it out of reach. "Gotta have a beer with me first."

Lexie rolled her eyes. "Of course you'd say that." She kept up her act, but I knew better.

"Come check out my Trans Am. Smoke rolls better with the seats laid back."

He winked at her, and she tried to look annoyed. It fell flat. I could tell it from here to Fort Worth she was into him.

Keith led the way to his silver Trans Am, and Lexie followed close behind. She didn't turn to acknowledge me when leaving or take her time in following him. She didn't even protest when Keith fell in step beside her and put his hand on her lower back. She just walked beside him, as if she hadn't just spent their entire encounter insulting everything from his hat to his smell.

"Uh, what just happened?" I asked Cass, watching Keith open the passenger-side door for her.

"Think Lexie just found herself a hillbilly," he answered as she stepped inside without a hint of a pause.

Chapter 17

"Lexie's a little firecracker, ain't she?" Larry said, passing a beer to Cass.

"That's her," I said, glancing across the parking lot toward Keith's car.

They were still sitting in there, and something told me they weren't just talking. I couldn't believe it. Lexie? With someone like *Keith*?

"What did she say earlier that bothered you?" Cass asked, taking my mind off the unimaginable.

I shook my head. "Oh, just Lexie being Lexie. I usually ignore her when she acts like that. I guess it got to me tonight."

"She took one look at me and disapproved, huh?"

"That doesn't matter. Don't take her judgment to heart. I sure don't."

"How are you two friends, anyway? She kinda seems like a pain in the ass."

I took a deep breath, thinking of the Cara Conner incident. Where was *that* Lexie? The Lexie that always had my back? The Lexie that always supported me?

"Well, Steph and her mom are best friends, so we kinda grew up together. She and her mom even lived with us while her parents were separated a few years ago. And Lexie . . . she's always been there for me in the past."

"Well, she is protective, I guess. In a rude, shitty kinda way."

I agreed with him on that.

"You think they moved to the back seat yet?" Larry asked, packing his can of snuff.

"I'd put a ten and my Skynyrd tape on it," Cass said, lighting a cigarette.

"Austin, we have a problem."

I looked behind me and saw that Jo was leaning over the bed of the Dodge. "What is it?" I asked her.

"It's Sam."

Suddenly, I remembered Sam had a thing for Keith. And now Keith was possibly naked in his back seat with my best friend.

Uh-oh.

I crawled over the side of the bed and landed next to her. "Is she here?" I asked, dusting off the butt of my shorts.

"She and Annie just pulled up. This isn't good."

I looked over my shoulder, noticing Annie's Camaro across the lot. I saw her and Sam's figures through the windows, and the sight of them brought up all those feelings they'd caused me to have at Annie's party and at the bonfire. A sharp pain struck my gut when I thought of the way Annie flipped me off and called me a whore, and the way they both laughed about it. I thought of the way Sam had looked so sympathetic about Cass leaving me at Annie's party when she knew he never actually did. I'd lost all confidence in myself and thought I wasn't good enough for Cass. Because of her. Because of them.

"Now that I think about it," I said, trying to fight off every bad feeling they'd caused me to have since meeting them. "You know, I think it'll be okay." I leaned against the truck. "Sam might get mad, but if she and Keith aren't actually together, I don't think there's *really* a problem. Is there?"

"Sam's in love with the guy." She pursed her lips. "And . . . well, she can be kinda crazy when it comes to Keith. I know she probably deserves to catch him with another girl after what she and Annie did to you at her party, but I just don't want there to be a fight. You know?"

If you knew what they did at the bonfire, you might think differently.

I thought about filling her in on the events of that particular night but decided against it. It wasn't worth it to continue the drama with those two, which was why I'd go get Lexie and save any more from happening. Plus, the last thing I wanted was to have to pull Lexie off Sam in a catfight over someone like Keith. There was no need in causing a scene over a guy with pick-up lines that trashy. Although, they had obviously worked.

"You keep Annie and Sam distracted," I said. "I'll go get Lexie."

Jo agreed and hurried over to Annie's car. I told Cass what was going on, then headed toward Keith's Trans Am, which was conveniently parked beside a rusted, bulky VW bus. As long as Annie and Sam stayed in or near their car, they wouldn't see the Trans Am or who was in it.

When I approached the window, I half-expected it to be

foggy and the passenger seat empty. Luckily, that wasn't the case because I could see Lexie sitting right where I'd hoped she'd be. *Thank goodness.* At least I wouldn't have to persuade her to put her jeans back on.

Lexie rolled down the window, and through a cloud of smoke, smiled at me. She reached for the stereo and turned down Eric Clapton's "Cocaine" low enough we could at least hear one another talk. "You wanna get in and try this stuff?" she asked.

"No," I said through a cough. "We gotta go."

"Go?" she said. "I'm kinda busy here." She raised her brows and jerked her head toward Keith.

He winked at me.

"Yeah, well . . ." I chewed my lip, trying to think of an excuse. "Larry wants to take us around town. In his Dodge. Now." *That's the best I can do?*

Keith brought the joint near Lexie's mouth, and she took a hit while he held it for her.

"I'm having *way* too much fun with Keith here, Austin."

I leaned in closer and ducked my head into the window.

"Hey, hey," Keith said. "Paws off the paint, baby."

I pulled my hands away from the door. "Sorry."

Lexie burst into laughter. "God, Keith, you're hilarious."

I rolled my eyes. "Lexie, please. Come on, let's go."

She shook her head. "I don't think so."

I looked over the top of the Trans Am, making sure nobody was walking our way. The coast was clear.

"This wouldn't have anything to do with Sam pullin' in, would it?" Keith asked before taking one last drag. He then tossed the roach out the window and took a peek in his side mirror.

"Sam?" Lexie said. "Who's he, and why do we care that he's here?"

"*Samantha* is a chick," Keith said. "And she thinks she owns me."

"Oh, so you have a girlfriend?" Lexie sounded amused. She grabbed another beer from the beer box in the back, as if she still had no intention of leaving her seat.

"No, ma'am." Keith motioned his arms like he was making the "safe" signal in baseball. "I only got the hots for you, baby." He then laid his hand on her thigh and smiled at her.

"Then why would she think she owns you?" Lexie popped the top, still not showing much concern.

Keith tapped a finger on his chin. "Beats me."

"All of them think like that," I murmured.

"Yeah, Austin knows a thing or two about *that*," Keith snickered. "Annie's thought she owned Cass since freshman year. Poor fucker."

"Annie?" Lexie said.

"She's one of Jo's friends," I said. "I think she's still kinda jealous of Cass and me."

Keith howled with laughter. "Kinda?"

"Hmm," Lexie said, seemingly unconcerned about it. "Sounds like Austin won't be the only one causing some jealousy tonight, then."

I checked over the top of the car again. Nothing. "Well, I still think we should go. A confrontation isn't really worth it, is it?"

Keith threw his arm around Lexie. "Hell, I don't know why you care so damn much about Sam anyway. It ain't like she was lookin' out for you when she done what she did to you."

"Wait, what'd she do?" Lexie asked, immediately alert. She shot a look to Keith like she demanded an explanation, pronto.

"Oh, she told Austin that Cass was shaggin' Annie at a

party. It was bullshit though, 'cause Cass ain't touched anyone since Austin came to town. Her and Annie just set him up for the hell of it." Keith looked at me. "Worked, too, didn't it? Heard you left the party all upset and Cass had to run you down to explain things."

"Did that really happen?" Lexie snapped.

I looked away. "Yeah, it did, unfortunately."

"I guarantee you those girls were laughin' their asses off all night about it." Keith sneered. "They do that kind of shit all the time."

"Those *bitches*." I could see Lexie's want for revenge shining in her bloodshot eyes.

"Lexie, calm down," I said. "Every—"

"That's what they are," Keith interrupted. "Bitches."

"Well, then," Lexie said, crossing her legs and getting a little more comfortable. "I'll just be sitting my big ass right here in this seat until the bitch wants to come pull me out. Doesn't bother me a bit. Does it bother you, Keith?"

"Nope," he said.

"Then that's that."

"It wasn't a big deal," I said under my breath, knowing that it was.

"It *is* a big deal, Austin. You can't just let people walk all over you. You have to stand up and fight back every now and then. Right, Keith?"

"Right!" he yelled, throwing his fist in the air.

"Austin?"

I snapped my head toward Sam, who'd quietly walked up beside me.

"What are you doing?" she asked. She couldn't see who was sitting in the car, so I was stuck having to explain why I was there.

"Uh . . ." Not sure what I was supposed to do, I looked

at Jo, who was standing behind Sam. Jo bit her lip but didn't say a word. She didn't know what to do, either.

"Well?" Annie said. She walked up beside Sam and crossed her arms. "What? Was Cass not enough for you? Had to come over here and try your luck with Keith, too?"

Wrong time for that, Annie.

Keith's car door swung open, and Lexie flew out like there was a fire under the waxy blue leather. "All right, you bitches."

I just put my head down. There was nothing I could do at this point. Because like Larry said, Lexie was a firecracker. You light her fuse, you're gonna see some hotheaded sparks.

"I heard about the mean-girl shit you pulled with Austin at a party. Good thing it worked, huh?" She looked at Annie. I'm not sure how she knew it was Annie, but she knew.

"Yep," Lexie said, "good thing Cass fell for your little game and went running back to you, leaving Austin. Right? How are you two doing now? Has he bought you a ring yet?"

"Lexie, come on," I said.

"No, Austin. They need to hear this."

Annie rolled her eyes, and Sam stood with her jaw clenched, peeking around Lexie and trying to see if Keith was in the car.

"Just because you two are obsessed with these guys doesn't mean you *own* them. Take a hint every now and then, and move on." She looked at Annie. "If Cass wanted to be with you, don't you think he would've left Austin that night to chase after *you?*" She looked at Sam. "And don't you think if Keith wanted you, he would've kept his hands off my—"

"Okay!" I shouted.

Sam moved toward Lexie and grabbed her by the shoulders so quick I couldn't react. She tried to push her down, but Lexie wasn't going anywhere.

"Whoa! Whoa!" Cass grabbed Sam about the same time Keith appeared and grabbed Lexie, and the fight was over before it even started.

"Let go of me!" Sam yelled. She tried to wiggle free from Cass, but he had too good of a grip around her.

"Let's just take a little breather, Sammy," Cass said, carrying her away.

Annie followed them, while Jo stayed with us.

"They're not gonna do that shit to you and get away with it," Lexie said. "And that little Annie isn't gonna run her mouth around me, either."

"Let's just go home," I said edgily enough she didn't argue.

Keith let go of her, and she straightened her shirt. I turned and walked back toward the Ford, hearing Lexie's footsteps as she followed close behind.

Chapter 18

"You can't be mad at me for sticking up for you." It was the first thing Lexie had said since we got in the truck. Besides the clicking sound her nails made on her empty beer can, there had been silence.

"I'm not mad you stuck up for me, Lexie."

"Good, because I can't stand that they did that to you."

"You can't stand that they tried to break up me and Cass? That's funny, because you made it clear you don't even *like* Cass. So, what's the big deal with them trying to break us up?"

She shifted in her seat. "It's not that I don't *like* Cass." She flicked the tab on her beer until it got annoying.

"Well, please enlighten me on how exactly you *do* feel about him, then. Because it sure seemed to me like you don't much care for him."

She turned her head to look out the window, just like she'd done earlier that evening. "I'm jealous," she mumbled.

"What?"

"I'm jealous," she said again.

"Jealous?"

"Yeah." She took a deep breath and tore the tab off, dropping it inside the can. She was quiet a few more seconds before clearing her throat. "I mean . . . Gunner . . . he left me." Her voice cracked when she said his name, and my heart went from cold to empathetic when I saw the sadness that overcame her.

I'd never heard Lexie cry before. Even when her parents had separated, she hadn't shed a tear. When she'd torn her ACL during a middle-school basketball game, when she'd wrecked her mom's car after prom last year, the time Sheryl Moss told everyone she'd slept with our math teacher for a good grade. None of those times resulted in a cry from Lexie.

Gunner changed that dry streak.

"I come here after my heart's been completely shit on, Austin, and—and you're all happy and in love. I just . . . I'm jealous of that. I'm jealous of you and Cass. Usually, it's me who gets the guy while you turn them all down. It just sucks." She held her hands over her eyes in an attempt to stop the tears, but it didn't seem to work. "I loved him, Austin. I loved the guy, and he didn't love me back."

I scooted to the middle seat and swung my arm over her shoulders. She laid her head against mine, wiping her tears.

"I had no idea you felt this way," I said. "I'm so sorry things didn't work out. I really am. I wish he wasn't such a jerk."

"I wish he wasn't, either."

"But you'll find another guy who's way better than him.

One who actually treats you right and loves you for all the right reasons. It'll happen one day, I promise."

"I can find other guys. That's not the problem. The problem is, I won't want them like I wanted Gunner. I really, really wanted this to happen between us."

I thought about how I'd felt when I thought Cass had rejected me. It was the worst feeling imaginable, and I wouldn't wish that on anyone. Especially Lexie.

"I'm sorry," I said again. "I wish there was something more I could do."

"I just need to get over it and stop being such a baby. It's time for me to move on from him."

"Well . . . what about Keith?"

"No way." She sniffed, and that was the end of the waterworks.

"But you gave him the look. I thought you were into him?"

"I mean, intrigued maybe. He made me laugh, but that's it. Didn't you see how he wore his jeans tucked inside those hideous cowboy boots? I mean, come on. I can't go from someone like Gunner to someone like Keith. That doesn't make any sense."

"Hey, I'm definitely not saying I think you should be with him. I mean, his pick-up lines were a little much for me."

"Baby, those jeans are *tight,*" she said, in her best version of Keith.

"He's ridiculous," I said, laughing along with her.

"Yeah, he is. Terrible kisser, too. Not that I really expected much more from him." She sat up and looked at me, and there was the classic look of regret written on her face. "I'm sorry I was such a bitch about Cass."

I smiled. "It's okay. Now that I know why you were being like that, I get it."

"I asked Keith about Cass when we were in his car. He made it clear I was in the wrong about him. Sounds like Cass is a catch. I'm glad you found someone like him."

"What'd he say about him?" I asked, too curious not to know.

"He said you're all Cass ever talks about and that he really cares about you. Coming from a guy like Keith, I know that's saying a lot right there."

There was a tap on the driver's side window. When I turned to see who it was, Cass was standing outside the glass.

"He's cute, right?" I said, looking back at Lexie.

"Well, I've never been into the whole long hair, Harley boy, dirty rock star thing . . ."

Cass brought his arms up to rest above the window, and his Copenhagen grin spread across his face like he knew what we were talking about.

"But I have to admit, his Mötley Crüe-meets-*The Dukes of Hazzard* vibe is somehow hard to look away from."

I scooted back over to the driver's seat and rolled down the glass.

"How's the bodyguard?" Cass asked, smiling at Lexie.

Lexie laughed under her breath. "I'm fine."

"Hell, one thing's for certain," he said. "I ain't ever gotta worry about Austin when she's around you. Somethin' happens a little sideways, I know you'll take care of her for me."

"I'll always have her back," she said. "And I owe you an apology. Sorry for the way I treated you earlier. I was just . . ."

"Havin' a bad day?"

"Yeah, that's it. Just had a bad day."

"Ah, it ain't no big deal." He smiled and reached in the truck for my hand.

"From what I know so far," she said, "I think you're a pretty good guy. Austin's lucky to have someone like you."

Cass smiled and leaned in, putting his lips on mine. His Copenhagen kiss might've been salty, but there was a sweetness to it I'd splurge on every second if I could.

"Austin's a lotta things, but lucky ain't one of 'em," he said, never taking his eyes from mine. "But, as for me?" He looked at Lexie. "I've been one lucky son of a bitch all summer long."

Chapter 19

"Where are you taking me?" I asked Cass, fighting my way through wild sunflowers and native grass as tall as our waists.

"You'll see," he said. "Almost there, darlin'."

When he made his way to the top of the red dirt hill, he turned and smiled at me. He held out his hand and waited for me to catch up.

When I came to stand beside him, I stared down at a clearing with fresh-cut grass that was the perfect shade of July green. Red, yellow, and blue speckled wildflowers surrounded the area and butterflies floated easily above all the painted blooms.

And then there was the view.

It was like looking at a still from an award-winning movie or the front cover of a classic novel. Three, maybe four surrounding towns were in eyesight as we stood on what felt like a mountaintop.

I had a feeling this fireworks show would be one I'd never forget.

A blanket and picnic basket were laid out under a big oak tree standing in the middle of the clearing. It was the perfect setup, and I hated that I hadn't brought my camera.

"Cass . . ." I stood open-mouthed and at a loss for the right words to show how much it meant to me. "You . . . you did all this for . . . me?"

"Anything for you, sunshine."

"You took the time to mow, pack dinner, and bring it all the way up here just to turn around and have to come right back for me?"

"You make it sound like you ain't worth it. I don't want you to feel like that."

He held my hand, and we walked toward the towering oak. On the way, he knelt and picked some Indian blankets and gave them to me.

I smiled down at the bouquet of firewheels, admiring their orangey-red centers and bright yellow tips. The blooms were small, the stems dainty. The Oklahoma wind had done a number on the petals and some of the blooms had already had their moments in the sun and were now wilted and shriveled. But most of the blooms were full and vibrant and very much alive, and I marveled at their subtle beauty.

"My grandma used to tell me a story about how when she was a little girl she'd go visit her own grandma, who lived way out in the country somewhere around here. There was a field behind her grandma's house that was full of Indian blankets, and she'd spend all day out there just playing, dancing, and running through them. Her grandma told her the flowers were magical."

I looked up, meeting his eyes. They were greener and deeper than ever.

"I've always believed that," I said.

He smiled, rubbing one of the petals between his fingers. "I believe it, too."

He grabbed my hand again and led me to the spot under the tree where the blanket was spread. We sat down, and he unpacked the picnic basket, revealing chicken legs, rolls, and two slices of cheesecake tucked inside.

"I made it myself," he said.

I took a bite out of a buttered roll. "You did?"

"No, Lonna did, but I put it in the picnic basket."

"Well, that's just as good," I said with a smile.

After we finished eating, he opened a bottle of Boone's Farm, then leaned his back against the tree. He wrapped an arm across my chest when I sat back against him, and he laid a kiss on me that was a little different from all those Copenhagen ones. This one tasted like strawberry wine.

"I'm still pissed about our first night together." He scoffed. "I can't *believe* I passed out on you. Fuckin' rookie move." He took another drink from the bottle, then wiped his mouth on his wrist.

I squeezed his arm as I looked out across the rolling green pastures that rested under an orange sherbet sky. "You made up for it tonight."

"I still got a little work to do, but I'm gettin' there." He put down the bottle and hugged me close to him. "That hook you set in me gets a little deeper every time I look at you, you know it?"

I laid my head on his shoulder, making myself cozy against him. "I feel the same way. This night has been perfect . . . just like every other night with you."

"You ain't seen nothin' yet."

As dusk turned to night, the first firework lit up the sky. Another one followed shortly after, then another. Every color in the color wheel painted the sky in front of us, and the stars seemed to brighten above them with every pop.

I looked up to Cass's face as the fireworks cast their glow on him, studying the few freckles sprinkled around his nose. His five o'clock shadow had gotten a little thicker since May, and his hair fell messy to one side.

Cass looked down at me, studying me in return, and I watched his eyes move from my eyes to my lips. His face was serious as he leaned in closer for a gentle kiss. Grasping the back of my neck, he pulled me in tight, then kissed me before pulling back. He moved from behind me and rested on his knees in front of me, then raised his arms and pulled off his T-shirt, the moonlight showing off his abs.

I laid down beneath him, and he clasped my hands and brought them above my head. He hovered over me, kissing from my forehead down to my neck, then ran his hands down my sides before he slipped under my shirt. I ached for him as he played with me, teasing me with every touch.

He rocked his body against mine, his hot breath lingering on my skin as he whispered, "Do you want me?"

"Yes," I answered softly.

"Do you need me?"

"Yes," I said more desperately. I arched my back and pulled him in as close as I could get him.

"Do you love me?"

I opened my eyes and stared deep into his. He'd asked me something I knew to be true for a long time but had kept to myself. I fought back the tears that came over me but failed when I saw his smile.

"Yes," I answered.

He kissed my forehead, pushing my hair away from my face. "I'm glad you do, 'cause I love you more than anything."

Passion spiraled between us. It felt like my heart was burning on the inside, hot and heavy and smoldering from the touch of his hands and the feel of his lips. A bottomless desire filled me from the inside out and I craved Cass so deep I couldn't hold back. I wanted every piece of him. Every part of him.

I'd never wanted anything more.

"I'll always love you," he said, putting his forehead to mine. "Don't forget it."

The world stood still as my innocence was swept away by a boy who'd stolen my heart. Just a couple months after meeting him, I'd fallen in love with him and knew I'd continue to fall harder with each passing moment. When he looked at me with those green eyes, touched me with his callused hands, and made me laugh harder than I thought possible, I knew I could never love another like him. Because loving him was like running through a cool June rain, like sipping on a mason jar of peach tea on a muggy summer night, like taking the first bite from a big scoop of homemade ice cream, like sitting cross-legged in a field of sunflowers under a turquoise sky. It was every good and fuzzy feeling under the sun, moon, blanket of stars, and firecracker trails. It was everything I never knew I needed.

Loving him was wild, like the wind that whipped around us as we rode his Harley into the sunset. But like the taste of his lips after a bottle of wine, it was sweet. And I'd always heard the first love was the sweetest, now I knew it to be true. Because there was no one who could ever be sweeter than James Cassedy.

Chapter 20

The Grill was a small restaurant on Main Street in Geary. Cass had mentioned it to me a few times before, saying he and his buddies spent a lot of time there. Whether after football practice, during lunch hour at school, or for an evening dinner, it was his favorite place in town.

Now I knew why.

The first thing you noticed when you walked in the little joint was the smell of greasy onion burgers. "Nothin' beats Sankey's burgers," Cass told me. "Except his chicken fry."

The pool table was surrounded by guys our age making bets, throwing down tens and twenties on the green felt like they were regular high rollers in Vegas. The east wall was lined with pinball machines and arcade games, and the Pac-Man patterns were constantly lit up by freckle-faced kids with toothless grins, wearing dirty jeans and cowboy boots.

Red Dirt Paradise

The barstools at the front of the restaurant were filled with old-timers drinking coffee, bragging about their wheat yields, and complaining about the summer heat. There was something for everyone at The Grill. I was jealous we didn't have a hole-in-the-wall hangout like this back in Houston.

Cass led us to a corner booth, where a pretty, middle-aged waitress with coal black hair and deep smile lines met us before we were even seated.

"Who's this little girl you have with you?" she asked Cass. She moved a stray hair from her eye using the eraser on her pencil, then jotted something down in her notepad.

"My girlfriend, Austin. Austin, this is Colleen."

We exchanged how-are-you's, and all the while she jotted down more secrets in her notes.

"Well," she said, "Coach Cole just came in, and he always orders the same thing. Ope, there's Doyle, let me write down his order, too." She flipped her notepad to the next page and kept writing. "I have a chicken fry with white gravy and fries for you, Cass. Same as usual. What'll you have, hun?" Her pencil stopped for the first time since she greeted us, and she gave me a no-time-to-waste look. I guess she forgot I hadn't even seen a menu.

"The same is fine," I said quickly.

She scribbled my order down with a simple nod, then jetted off to the bar, where she started filling empty coffee cups.

"Cool place, huh?" Cass said.

"It is." I scanned the walls, admiring all the old Geary alumni pictures and a painting of a bison—their school mascot.

"Wait here," he said. "I'll be right back." He slid out of the booth and walked toward the front of the bar.

I watched him as he ducked behind the counter, staying

crouched out of sight for a few seconds. He came back holding a yearbook and both of our drinks.

He laid the book in front of me and took a swig from his glass. "Vanilla RC," he said. "You'll never drink a plain RC again."

I looked at the yearbook, excited to see pictures of him and his friends, but when I read the year, it wasn't from '82 or '83. Instead, it was from 1966. And it wasn't even an annual from Geary.

"What's this?" I asked.

Cass smiled. "It's the year your mom graduated. That's her senior yearbook."

I looked down at it again and ran my hand over the dark blue, leather-like cover. I traced the gold foiled numbers, then looked back at Cass.

"You were right," he said. "You do look like her."

"How did you . . . where did you get this?"

"Sankey has all the old Greenfield and Geary yearbooks in the back. When I ate here with Larry the other day, I thought about 'em and figured you'd like seein' one with your mom in it. Searched until I found her."

A wave of tears overwhelmed me. I closed my eyes, holding them back. I'd never seen one of my mom's yearbooks before. I'd never even seen one of Steph's, come to think of it. They must have all perished in the fire, along with everything else.

I opened the front cover and saw a class picture. There were only fifteen people in her class, so it didn't take me long to find the skinny blonde seated on the front row in front of a typewriter. Her hair was shoulder-length, styled and set in the famous '60s flip. She wore a white chunky turtleneck with a checkered, knee-length skirt, and it looked like they'd snapped the picture while she was laughing.

She took my breath away she was so pretty.

"Keep turnin'," Cass said. "It gets better."

I turned to find page-length pictures of all the seniors. My mom's was the same one that was in Grandma's sewing room, only this one was much bigger and clearer. I could really see her features and how much I resembled her.

"Look, there's Tish," I said after I'd turned a few pages. Tish's dark hair was flipped just like my mom's, a little different than the bun she'd worn when we'd met. But other than the hairstyle, she looked the exact same. Her pretty face hadn't changed at all, even after seventeen years.

I wondered what my mom would've looked like had the wreck never taken her from me. Would she have looked the same, aging perfectly like Tish? Would she have lost her flip and chopped her locks, or would she have grown her hair out to look like mine? Would her smile bring me peace like it did when looking at pictures of her?

I loved everything about her yearbook and the priceless snapshots hidden like treasure on every page. Everything about her was genuine. *Beautiful.* She was active in almost everything they offered and was voted most popular *and* best smile. I didn't even know you could get more than one senior favorite. She was also the basketball homecoming queen and played the flute in band. She was absolutely full of life and had so much going for her at the time. And even though her life had been cut too short, I was thankful she'd always be remembered as that young, beautiful, and talented girl from the class of '66.

"Thank you so much," I said, closing the book. "This means so much to me. You have no idea."

He smiled, taking the yearbook after I handed it to him. "I thought it would. I know how much you miss her."

I put my arms around his neck, hugging him close. "I

wish she was here," I choked through tears. "It isn't fair." I buried my face in his neck, trying not to cause a scene, but it was hard when all I wanted to do was break down.

"I know it ain't fair." He hugged me tighter, smoothing my hair. "I wish she was here, too, darlin'. I really do."

Chapter 21

The next few weeks passed faster than I ever dreamed they could. It was approaching August too soon, and another summer would soon slip away and fade into the dreaded, lonely autumn.

The sun continued to bake the little farm town of Greenfield, making my hair lighter and arms darker. I wished I could say the same for my legs, but hidden beneath dirty jeans every day, they were as white as Lonna's Corvette.

Wheat harvest was complete, and tractors started to roll across the surrounding acres, turning the ground under and preparing for planting season in the fall. It was an easy transition from cutting wheat, as long hours and time spent in a John Deere seat were still an everyday event.

Times were busy, and the long hours Cass and I spent working ground made it difficult to spend as much time together as we preferred. When we did get to hang out, we savored the moments and used them to grow deeper in love. We told each other stories, planned for the future, and laughed more than anything—the kind of belly laughing that makes your abs sore and tears roll down your cheeks.

 He took me fishing once, which was something I hadn't done since I was a kid. We caught five catfish that Sunday, and Lonna cooked them for us the following night. Cass was impressed when I reeled in the first bluegill, and even more so that I could bait my own hook. He was blown away when I backed the trailer, with his bass buggy loaded, up to the pond. He said I was the only girl he'd ever seen do that. Grandpa taught me how to back a trailer when I was younger, and I hadn't realized it was that big of a deal. I guess to Cass, it was.

 We sat on the bank with our toes in the hot sand and a line out in the water, when I caught him staring at me. I acted as if I didn't notice, but after a few more seconds, I couldn't resist giving him a hard time.

"I could bring you a picture next time we hang out." I laughed and gave him a kiss.

"I don't want a picture. I wanna stare at the real thing forever."

"Forever? That's a long time."

"Not if I'm with you, darlin'."

"Are you gonna love me forever, James Cassedy?"

"I'm gonna love you forever, Austin Rose."

He grabbed me, and we rolled around on the bank. Before it went any further, he pulled back and stared at me, eyes solemn. He was getting pretty good at doing that.

"I mean it. I'm gonna love you forever. I need to know you'll be with me forever." He brushed the sand off my cheekbone, waiting for my response.

"I'll be with you forever," I said.

"You mean it?"

"Yes."

"No, really. You swear?"

I laughed and held his face like he always held mine. "I swear. No matter what happens, I promise we'll be together."

"I need you to straighten me out. I need you to tell me when to stop drinkin' and when to be home. I need to wake up with you every mornin' and look at you and feel what I feel right now. 'Cause I ain't ever felt like this before, and I'll never feel it with anyone else."

I saw desperation and sincerity in his eyes as sure as the sugar sand riverbanks.

"And I need you to tell me to lighten up," I said. "I need you to take me on bike rides and keep me out late and sing me to sleep. I need you to promise me every night before we go to bed that you'll always love me, no matter what happens."

"I promise I'll do that." He looked into my eyes once again, and there was nothing but honesty staring back.

A few days later, he took me on some land that Pat and Lonna owned. A canyon ran through the middle of the pasture, which we walked through, hand in hand. Trees stood tall on either side of the cleared path as if they were planted there long ago for us to enjoy. We walked miles up and down that canyon, listening to songbirds and picking blackberries from thickets.

It was the simple moments like those that really stuck with me. Those evenings and short, precious dates were the ones that made me feel the most alive. There was nowhere else on earth I'd rather be, nothing else I'd rather be doing. It was like all the problems in the world had disappeared and it was just me and Cass walking together among the wildflowers and setting summer sun.

Those moments were the best.

And then there were the times he came knocking at my bedroom window late at night. Those were my next-in-line favorite. I'd crawl through and land in his arms, and we'd take off for the wheat field. We'd stare up at the stars, talk about forever, and listen to the night for hours. Eventually, our clothes would end up in little piles beside us, and we'd spend the night rolling around in the grass or the dusty cab of a wheat truck. We even ended up on top of the barn one night, though neither of us knew how.

Toward the end of summer, I'd assured Cass many times I couldn't wait to move back and start a life with him. Each time, he argued with me and told me there were bigger things for me other than Geary, but I wouldn't let him win. I knew he wouldn't leave his hometown, Pat and Lonna, Larry, or the farm, and I wouldn't pretend like I wouldn't move back for him. I'd already considered Greenfield home more than Houston, and Geary was just a short drive away. Moving back made more sense to me, especially when I had someone I loved waiting for me.

We discussed more about our pasts, filling each other in on stories we'd never shared before. He seldom spoke of his mom, never of his dad, but brought up his Grandpa Bill quite regularly. His eyes brightened with the mention of his name. Cass spoke of how he had taught him how to fish, shoot a gun, tend to livestock, and get through life no matter what it throws at you.

"Grandpa Bill always said, 'Son, you need three things in life: The Good Book, a good woman, and a good glass of whiskey. When one ain't workin', there's bound to be hope in one of the other two.'"

Cass always laughed after quoting his grandpa, and I soon realized where he got his sense of humor. I was sad

Red Dirt Paradise

I'd never get to meet the man he spoke so highly of, but it was apparent, nonetheless, that his memory would live on through Cass.

He discussed more about a potential singing career and a future move to California. I encouraged him to pursue his music—something I knew he could easily make a living doing.

"What if we moved to California and bought some land out there?" I said. "That way, you could play your music, but we could live on a farm. You can have the best of both worlds that way."

He thought about it for a second, then shook his head. "Can't."

"Why not?" I asked. "You can make a career out of music, but you'll still be able to farm. We could live on a ranch with cattle and horses, and it'll feel like home . . . kinda."

"It ain't just the farmin'. It's leavin' Pat and Larry. I can't do that to them. I've worked for Pat my whole life, and me and Larry have everything planned out in the future. We'll start runnin' more cattle when we get outta high school, and we'll really start makin' money. We even talked about startin' a hay service, too. Swathin' and balin' for people." He tucked his hair behind his ears and put his ball cap back on. "Guitar is a hobby. Always has been, always will be. But my loyalty . . . it's with Pat."

The way he said it made me realize that was his final decision, even if his heart tugged him in a different direction.

"Maybe we'll just build a big barn one day and put a stage in it," he said. "I'll start a little band and play every weekend or somethin'. What if I did that?"

I smiled and grabbed his hand. "Well then, we better build the biggest barn around. If you're the entertainment, there'll be a full house every time."

"We'll build the biggest barn this side of western Oklahoma. I'll sit up there on an old barstool with my Gibson and a couple buddies, and we'll play Waylon and Skynyrd covers all night long. And the prettiest wife you ever saw will be sittin' front row with a smile on her face."

"And then when everyone leaves, it'll just be me and you, and you'll play me a slow Willie song, and I'll cry because it's so good."

"Then we'll go inside the house . . ." He leaned in and pinched my chin. "And we'll slip into bed . . ." He gave me the slowest, sweetest kiss under the Oklahoma stars. "And I'll love you all night long."

Chapter 22

"Well, when do you have to leave?" Billy asked as I finished greasing the plow. We'd been servicing it all afternoon as I daydreamed about Cass and his late-night visits.

"Steph is driving down here in a couple days, then we'll make the drive back."

I'd been trying to avoid the thought of having to go back to Houston. It was painful knowing I wouldn't be seeing Cass for months, and no matter how many times he said it, I knew he wouldn't be able to make a trip down to see me. That was a long drive—ride, in his case—and there was no way I could expect that to happen.

I planned to ask Steph about a fall-break trip, but deep down, I knew the chances of that happening were slim. Besides basketball starting in the fall, I'd be busy with college applications, tests, and everything in between. It would be a tough year ahead for us, but we could make it work. I had no doubts.

"I'll just be a few towns away. If you ever want to hang out, just let me know," he said, taking the grease gun from me.

I smiled and told him I'd keep that in mind, though I had no intention of giving it a second thought.

It was Saturday, and Grandma was inside preparing supper. Cass and I were going to the skating rink around eight, and I was itching to finish up work for the day. I couldn't wait to skate circles to "I Was Made for Lovin' You," hand in hand in that old gym.

"Supper's ready!" Grandma yelled from the porch, apron on and spatula in hand. "Billy, you come on in and eat, too. I made plenty."

We put away the tools for the night and headed toward the door. There were chopped brisket sandwiches and beans waiting for us on the table, so we sat down and dug into the tasty meal as if we'd been starved for days.

We were making small talk around the dinner table, talking college and crops and the lack of rain, when I heard someone pull into the driveway. It sounded like Cass's motorcycle, but I wasn't sure why he'd be here. He wasn't supposed to come for another couple hours. I looked around at everyone at the table, knowing they'd heard it, too.

"Who's that?" Grandpa asked, standing up.

"I'll go check," I said hurriedly, putting my sandwich back on my plate.

I walked to the door to see Cass parked under the willow tree. He sat on his bike, facing the house. I turned back toward my grandparents, who were looking at me curiously.

This isn't good.

"It's just my friend," I said quickly. "I'll see what he wants, and I'll be right back."

I could see Billy's questioning stare from across the room. He knew who it was, and now he knew Cass was a secret. I was already nervous for the conversation I knew would have to take place after I came back inside, and knowing Billy would be present for it made things even worse.

I left the house, hurrying down the porch. I approached Cass and immediately knew something was wrong. He looked mad—angrier than I'd ever seen him look before—and whatever it was, it had to be bad. It wasn't like him not to have a smile on his face.

"What's wrong?" I asked.

He kept his eyes straight ahead and answered with an edge in his voice I hadn't heard before. "I need to talk to you."

"Are you okay?"

"No, I ain't okay." He made his hands into fists and pounded them hard on the handlebars of his bike.

I spoke in the most soothing voice I could muster. "What happened? Tell me what's wrong."

"Jim."

"Jim? What'd he do?" I asked. "What happened?" My heart sank as I thought about his mom. Something had happened to her.

He paused, putting his head down. When he looked at me again, he seemed less mad and more hopeless. "I don't even know where to start, Austin."

I turned back toward the house, wondering how mad Grandma and Grandpa would be if I hopped on the back of his bike. What would they say if I went for a short ride? Of course they'd be furious. But they'd forgive me eventually, right?

"Uh . . . maybe we should go for a ride," I said nervously, turning and looking at the house again.

Cass shook his head. "We can't do that. I know you ain't told 'em about me, and it'll get you in trouble."

I swallowed the hard, ugly lump of guilt that had formed in my throat. "Why . . . why do you think I haven't told them about you?" I asked it cautiously while trying to come up with a good enough excuse why I hadn't.

"'Cause if you had, this summer woulda never happened."

I heard the screen door slam shut, and I turned around to see Grandpa walking hastily toward us. Cass and I were silent as he approached us, and I tried to process everything that was happening around me.

"Now listen, boy," Grandpa said with a scowl. "You get the hell outta here."

My mouth fell open as I listened to him speak to Cass like he was an escaped prisoner. In all my years, I'd never heard Grandpa sound so impolite. The sound of it broke my heart.

"You don't even know him," I said to Grandpa. "Why would you say that?"

He looked at me, then back at Cass. "I know him, all right. He's a Cassedy. Now, you get outta here, and I don't want to see you on this property or around my granddaughter ever again."

My eyes bubbled with uncontrollable tears. In that moment, I lost respect for the man who I'd respected the most.

Cass raised his eyes from the ground, where they'd been the entire time. "Yes, sir. I'm sorry I caused so much trouble. You won't have to worry about this again." Cass looked at me with so much hurt in his eyes, I couldn't stand it. "Your grandpa's right. We can't see each other anymore. It's what's best for you."

He started his motorcycle while I stood without an option. With a quick shift of his gears, he rode out of the driveway, leaving a cloud of dust behind him.

I stood there under the willow tree in complete shock, unable to grasp what just played out right in front of me. Tears ran down my cheeks as I tried to catch my breath. Grandma had come outside and was standing beside Grandpa now, with a look of horror on her face.

"What were you doing with him?" she asked.

"He's my . . . boyfriend," I choked.

Grandpa looked at the ground and shook his head, cursing under his breath.

"Austin, you can't see him anymore," Grandma said harshly.

"Why not?"

"Because you just can't."

"But . . . you—you don't even know him."

"We *do* know him."

"No, you don't know him. Not really. And you can't judge him from his past, or his family, or whatever you're judging him for." I backed away toward the truck. "Whatever you guys think you know about him, it isn't true. It's just not true, Grandma."

I couldn't stay calm. I couldn't, and I wouldn't. I shook with hurt as moisture filled Grandma's eyes.

"Honey, you don't understand," she said. "You cannot see him anymore. We won't allow it. You . . . you just don't understand."

I turned and ran to the truck. I couldn't stand to listen to her anymore. Nobody knew him like I did, and nobody was going to tell me who I could and couldn't love. After crawling in the Ford, I dropped it in gear and flew out of the driveway headed toward Geary.

Chapter 23

I remembered Cass telling me his parents lived across from the Geary elevator, so that's where I headed. My heart ached as hot tears streamed down my face. I replayed the scene under the willow tree, trying to make sense of it all. Why was Cass so upset to begin with? What *about* Jim? How did he know I hadn't told my grandparents? What did that mean? The situation was senseless. I tried my best to come up with an explanation, but each time I failed. I didn't know *what* was going on.

I neared the elevator and noticed a row of houses to the east. I spotted Cass's bike parked on one of the lawns, so I pulled around front and parked on the side of the road. The house was small, with coral-colored and hail-damaged siding. The shingles needed to be replaced, shutters were missing, and the yard needed to be mowed.

Red Dirt Paradise

I felt even worse as I gazed at it. There was no telling how much pain Cass had endured inside that house, and just thinking about it gave me chills. A darkness overcast the place, and I hated even being near it.

I sat in the truck for a few minutes, hoping he'd notice me parked outside. When nothing happened, I knew I'd have to walk to the door. I took a deep breath, hoping his father wouldn't be the one to answer, then stepped out of my truck and walked through the overgrown lawn. As I neared the door, I heard yelling coming from inside the house.

I heard Cass scream, "You shoulda stayed in prison. You ruined my life, you son of a bitch!"

A deep voice boomed back, "That girl can do a hell of a lot better than you anyway, you worthless piece of shit."

A loud crash came from behind the door. It sounded like something breaking—like glass shattering. I covered my mouth and stood frozen with fear for Cass, then waited for a few more seconds, trying to listen. When all I heard was deafening silence, my reflexes took over before I could even assess the situation. I reached for the doorknob, twisted it, and pushed the door open.

Once I stood in the doorway, my eyes darted from a frail woman standing in the corner to shards of glass scattered on the floor. A recliner was tipped over right in front of me, and bottles and cans of beer were scattered everywhere. It looked like a tornado had ripped across the room, showing no mercy to the coral-colored home.

I looked around the room and gasped when I saw the blood splattered on the floor.

My heart sank.

As I tried to take in what looked like a crime scene, Cass walked toward me from a nearby hallway. His eye was swollen nearly shut, there was a cut above his brow, and his nose dripped red. He looked scared, which was a look I wished I'd never seen on his face.

"What are you doin' here?" he asked as I tried to search for words to say.

"What the hell . . . ?" said the voice I'd just heard from behind the door. The man walked out from the same hallway as Cass, and when our eyes met for the first time, his face drained of all color. He looked like he'd just seen a ghost.

Jim looked identical to Cass, only a few more wrinkles around his eyes and the start of silver in his beard. He had a gash across his jaw and busted lip, but his battle wounds didn't compare to his son's.

The more we stared at each other, the angrier I became. I'd never been so disgusted in my life while looking at a sorry excuse for a father.

"Don't talk about him like that!" I yelled without even thinking about it. "What kind of father are you? How could you do this to him? How could you . . ." My voice was shaking so badly that I couldn't finish.

I couldn't keep it together.

Cass ran toward me, then put his arm around me and led me out of the house. He slammed the door behind him as I tried to steady my panicked breathing.

"Hey, hey. Calm down. Calm down. Breathe." He held my face, wiping my tears. "I'm okay. I know it looks bad, but I'm fine." He hugged me fiercely, and I continued to cry on his shoulder.

"I'm so sorry," I said between breaths. "We have to get out of here. You have to leave."

"No, I can't leave yet. You have to be the one to go. Please don't make this harder on me than it already is. You've gotta go home." He tried to lead me down the porch steps, but I wouldn't budge.

"I'm not going anywhere without you."

"I ain't leavin' with you, Austin."

"So, what, you just want me to leave you here with that man? Look at yourself, Cass! He's dangerous."

"It doesn't matter now. Nothin' matters."

"What's that supposed to mean?"

"It means it's over between us, so it doesn't matter anyway."

"Are you really breaking up with me? What about this summer? Did it not mean anything to you?"

"I told you things had to be over, and I meant it." Cass looked toward the door, and I had a feeling Jim was right on the other side.

"What about all those things you told me? About staying together? About forever?"

"They don't matter now."

"Why do you keep saying that?"

"What do you *want* me to say?"

"I want you to say the reason why you're acting this way!"

He shook his head. "You need to leave."

"Why are you doing this to me? To us?" I raised my voice, not caring that his parents were on the other side of the door. I didn't care if the neighbors heard me or if the whole town heard me.

Cass gritted his teeth. "I'm sorry," he said so low I could barely hear him.

I was quiet as I watched him standing in front of me. His jaw was clenched, his fists were tight, and he looked ready to fight.

"Just tell me," I said, calmer this time, because yelling was doing nothing. "Just tell me what it is. Tell me so I can fix it."

He ran his hands through his hair, grabbing fistfuls and looking ready to pull it all out. "Oh, you can't fix this."

"Well, I know I can't if I don't even know what's going on."

He shook his head and looked down at the ground. He took a second before he answered, and when he did, I knew I'd lost him. "It's over," he said. "I'm tellin' you, Austin, it has to be over."

The tears took over. They stung my eyes, blurred my vision, and ran down my cheeks. "I trusted you, Cass."

He turned around, then kicked the banister. Cursing under his breath, he paced to the other end of the porch. "You shouldn't have."

"But I did. And now you're doing this? Without even giving me a reason why? You don't think I deserve a reason?"

He leaned on the railing, looking away from me. And said nothing.

I marched over to him, getting angrier every second I didn't get an explanation. "Why." I demanded it; I didn't ask. Grabbing his arm, I turned him toward me. "Tell me why we can't be together."

Silence.

After a few more seconds of staring at him, and him doing nothing to help the situation, the screen door opened. We both turned to see Jim standing on the porch, looking our direction.

"You wanna know why?" Cass asked. He looked from Jim to me.

I didn't move.

"Why don't *you* tell her why?" he yelled to Jim.

Jim didn't speak.

"Yeah, how 'bout *you* be the one to tell her?" He shot out from my grip, bolting toward Jim.

Jim shook his head. "No." He backed away from Cass,

but Cass grabbed his collar and threw him against the outside of the house.

"Tell her why I can't be with her."

Jim grabbed at his hands and pushed Cass off him. "Don't do this to me."

"Tell her!" Cass yelled, his patience clearly gone out the window. "Tell her what you fuckin' did!"

Jim looked at me, and to my surprise, there was a sort of sadness in his green eyes. "I didn't mean to," he said. "It was an accident."

"Bullshit!" Cass shoved him, and Jim stumbled to the ground with a painful yell.

Cass went to stand above him, breathing heavy. He wiped his bloody nose and spit blood at Jim's feet.

I didn't know what to do or say, so I stood, aimlessly, staring at the man who shared such a strong resemblance to his son.

"He fucked up my life," Cass said slowly. He turned to look at me, but I couldn't take my eyes off Jim. "And he fucked up yours a long time ago."

Cass looked back at Jim, who quickly put his hands over his face.

"He was the one drivin' the car," Cass said. "He was the drunk bastard behind the wheel that night. He killed your mom."

Chapter 24

I only knew a few things about the night my mom was killed. I knew she was the passenger in a man's car. I knew the man had been drinking. I knew he'd run off the road and hit a tree. I knew she died before the ambulance arrived. I knew the man was convicted of manslaughter and sent to prison. What I didn't know was, that man was Cass's father, Jim Cassedy—the man who was shamefully lying on the porch at Cass's feet.

My knees buckled under me as realization set within me. My head spun, and my body felt heavy as the weight of a cold truth was thrown onto my shoulders. My thoughts raced from my grandparents' reaction, to Cass's behavior, to how Jim had looked at me. I couldn't see through tear-stricken eyes as I stumbled down the porch steps and across the lawn. Somehow, I managed to get the door open to the pickup.

Without another glance, I started the engine and left the man who killed my mother in my rearview mirror.

My foot was a dead weight on the gas pedal as I drove back to my grandparents' house. I couldn't recall the drive I'd just made once I arrived. When I walked through the door, Grandma and Grandpa were in the front room. They looked at me, and not a word was said. A mutual notion filled the room.

I know, and they know that I know.

I walked upstairs and lay in bed, crying tears of sadness, pain, truth, disappointment, and realization that rocked me to the core.

I'd been up for hours thinking about the previous night and still couldn't quite wrap my head around the situation. I tossed and turned, remembering the look in Cass's eyes when he'd told me. How did he find out? What did he do when I left his house? What went through his dad's head when he met my eyes? Questions I had no answers to stormed through my brain without letting up.

I rolled over in bed, letting the first rays of the morning sun warm my body. My eyes were swollen from crying, and there was a cast-iron knot in my throat I was sure was permanent. My body felt tired, but my mind was wide awake.

I kept reliving every moment, from the time Cass pulled into the driveway until I left his, until there was a light tap at my door. I dreaded talking to whoever it was. Whether it was Grandma or Grandpa, I couldn't bear the conversation that would have to take place. I lay silent, hoping the person on the other side would give up, but the knocking never ceased.

The taps got louder every time I didn't answer, until a voice that got my attention called my name.

"It's me, Austin. Can you let me in?"

I walked to the door and opened it for Steph, who swept me up in a long hug. I fought back the tears the best I could, and she smoothed my tangled hair.

She pulled away and examined my face, then wiped my cheek. "Mom filled me in. It sounds like you've had a rough time. Are you okay?"

I turned away from her, letting silence serve as her answer.

"Oh, Austin." She took a deep breath, searching my eyes. "How in this world did you end up with Jim Cassedy's son?" She sounded entirely confused, and I didn't know where to begin.

I left her arms and took a seat on the bed. She followed.

"I met him when I was hanging out with Jo." I wiped my eyes with my sleeve. "We clicked. I . . . I can't really explain it."

"You clicked? *How?*" She asked as if that notion was truly unbelievable. "Daddy said he looked just like his father—he looked like trouble. What were you thinking?"

"He's not trouble. Maybe he used to be . . . I don't know. But he's not now. There's nothing wrong with him. He's . . . he's a really good person, Steph."

"Then why did you keep him a secret? Mom said you kept telling her he was just a friend and you didn't know his last name. She thought it was no big deal and wouldn't have dreamed it was Jim's son. Why didn't you just tell them who you were seeing? Why didn't you tell *me?*"

"I don't know. I guess because I didn't know how you all would react. He isn't Billy. He doesn't *look* like a guy you'd be okay with me hanging out with." I pictured Cass riding up on his Harley sporting his Copenhagen grin, ripped jeans, and a cigarette behind his ear. No *way* Steph would've gone for that.

"Billy?" she asked. "The boy who helped you all this summer?"

"Yeah. That Billy."

"The one going to A&M to play football? And become a lawyer?"

"Yes," I murmured. Obviously Grandma had filled her in.

She shook her head, letting out a sigh. "Well, if you didn't think we all would approve of this James, then why did you still see him? Seems to me that'd be reason enough to not get involved."

I stood from the bed and walked across the room, trying not to get upset. I knew she wouldn't understand. I also knew how it sounded when it came out of my mouth, and I hated I couldn't show her how Cass really was.

"It's not like that. Cass doesn't *look* like someone you guys would like, but you don't know him. He's sweet, he's fun to be around. He might not be going to A&M on a scholarship, but he's good at other things. He's really talented and sings and plays the guitar and—and he's a hard worker, too. He's . . . he's a good person. He just . . . is."

She groaned and rubbed her head as if hearing me talk about him was a waste of her time. "Austin, this is something else." She stood abruptly and paced heavy-footed across the room and then back again. "You're seeing Jim Cassedy's son, of all people. His *son*. Did you know he was Jim's son when you started seeing him?"

"No. I didn't even know Jim's name. I just knew a drunk driver was the reason . . ." I couldn't finish the sentence. I didn't want to say it. I didn't want to believe it.

"And Jim's son didn't know it, either?"

"No. Cass found out the truth yesterday. I'm not sure how. But that's why he came over here. That's why he broke things off with me. For some reason, *he* feels guilty about it, I guess."

She took a deep breath and the corners of her mouth turned toward the hardwood floor. After a long silence between us, she cleared her throat and spoke slowly. "You know, your mother was dating Jim at the time of the wreck."

For some reason, I wasn't completely shocked. I imagined Cass's dad looking just like his son at that age. I assumed my mom fell for his good looks because I doubted his personality was any better back then than it was now.

She sat back down on the foot of the bed and patted the spot next to her. "They dated a couple months after you were born, up until the accident. Mom and Daddy didn't like him. None of us did. The night of the crash . . . he'd been drinking. Some of her friends told us she didn't want to go with him. They'd had a fight, and she didn't want to leave with him. Somehow, he forced her into it and . . ." She didn't finish. She didn't need to.

Her eyes clouded with painful memories, and I hurt with her. "I know why Mom and Daddy got so upset when they saw James in the driveway. It reminded him of your mom and Jim. You've got to understand how this looks through their eyes, Austin. This is history repeating itself. It's so hard for them to see."

I understood perfectly—to a point—and I felt guilty for lying to them about it for so long. At the same time, it didn't change how I felt about Cass.

"He goes by Cass, not James."

She sighed, tucking a strand of hair behind my ear. "Do you love him?"

I nodded.

"But you're not together anymore, right?" Her tone hinted more toward annoyance than anything.

"He ended things last night."

She let out a breath. "Listen, I know this is hard for you. I thought I was in love in high school, and it was hard for me to move on, too. But eventually, it happened, and I met Jay. Once you meet someone in the future, you'll be glad this petty little high school love never worked out."

Petty little high school love? That didn't begin to describe what I had with Cass. She had no idea.

"It's more than petty love. It's so much more than that, and I wish you could just understand it." I tilted my head to the ceiling, trying to slow the tears that fell. It didn't help much.

"Oh, now. It'll get better with time. I know how these things go." The more matter-of-fact she sounded, the less I felt like talking to her. She didn't understand how much I cared for Cass. She never would.

"I want to see him," I said. "I *have* to see him. I don't know what I'll say, and I doubt he'll know what to say, either. But I'm not okay with how we left things."

She cocked her head like she didn't understand what I meant. "Well, I planned on us leaving today. We're going on a trip."

"A trip?"

"We'll be flying somewhere tropical, and I'm not telling you where." She smiled, patting my knee. "Pack up your things, and meet me in the kitchen."

"I'm not leaving until you take me to say goodbye to him." There was a fierceness in my voice that made her eyes bulge.

"Now, Austin, I don't think that's a good idea," she said, standing from the bed.

I clenched my jaw. "I need to see him, Steph. He didn't do anything wrong, and he needs to know that."

She put her hands on her hips. "Well, I hope you aren't going to try to patch things up with him, because I'm telling you right now, you don't need to end up with a guy like him. You'll end up right here in this dead-end town, and I'll just be horrified, along with everyone else, if I'm being frank."

She tapped her foot, waiting for me to say something. When all she got from me was silence, she began again, only in a softer tone of voice. "Now, tell me I don't have anything to worry about. Tell me you're smart enough to know this relationship is not one you need to be in."

I chewed my cheek.

She tucked her chin, choosing the firm voice once again. "Austin Allison Rose, do you need me to give you *another* example as to why staying with this boy would be the worst mistake of your young life?"

I looked to the floor, choosing not to argue with her. It wasn't worth it. I'd never win.

"I just want to say goodbye to him. That's all," I said in a small voice.

Will she actually believe that?

She relaxed her arms down to her sides. "Good. I'll be waiting for you in the kitchen when you're ready." She was out the door in seconds, and I heard her greet Grandma at the end of the hallway.

I paced the floor, thinking of my next move. When nothing came to mind, I plopped back down on the bed. I was exhausted, and I wanted to see Cass, but what if I couldn't find him? And what would I say if I *did* find him?

After a few more minutes of aimless thinking, I walked over to the unsteady desk in the corner of Steph's old room.

Red Dirt Paradise

After opening the drawer, I found a notepad and pencil, then sat down and poured my heart onto a little piece of paper. That way, if I didn't get to say goodbye, at least he could read what I had left to say.

Chapter 25

I stared out the window at the blue sky and the long dirt road that unraveled in front of us. Memories of the summer blew through my mind like the wind as it blew through the wispy branches of the willows mangled in the fencerows. I leaned my head back against the headrest and closed my eyes, holding the letter next to my heart.

I imagined Cass's smile and the way his nose crinkled when he winked at me. I pictured him clapping his hands together like he always did when I made him laugh. His eyes, his cockiness, his drawl. His uncanny ability to keep a smile on my face. I tried to remember every little thing about him that made me fall in love with him, from the way he held my face when he kissed me to the promises he'd made me. All the times we'd walked barefoot along the riverbank, chased each other through Grandpa's pastures by the silvery light of the moon, and the night we drove Lonna's Corvette way too fast singing along to Springsteen.

Why did it all seem like it was just a dream?

After Steph slowed the truck to a stop, I got out and walked the few steps to the front porch and lightly knocked on the door. A small calico kitten shot out from under an old, wooden rocking chair and ran in the direction of Cass's bike, which was parked on the front lawn.

High heels clicked noisily as someone made their way to answer the door, and I took a deep breath in hopes to relax.

Lonna answered dressed in her Sunday-morning best, Bible in hand and a soft smile like she'd been expecting me. "Hi there, Austin." She looked around before speaking low. "Come on in."

I stepped inside, and she closed the door behind me.

"Sorry to bother you all this morning," I said. "Is Cass here?"

"Oh, you are no bother, honey. We were just on our way out to church. Yes, he's here." She bit her lip and looked around nervously. "He's in the spare bedroom, last I knew. I think something happened between him and his parents. He came in late last night, and Larry told me he didn't want to be bothered. Do you know what happened?"

I shook my head. "I'm not sure what happened."

She pursed her lips, skimming my face. I took a nervous swallow.

"I think . . . I might know what happened," she said quietly. "And I think you might know, too."

I looked at the floor, then hugged my arms to my stomach. "Yeah . . . I know what happened."

She smiled sympathetically and squeezed my shoulder with a gentle hand. "Come on in here. We'll have a little talk."

I followed her to the kitchen, where she pulled out a

chair for me at the small wooden table. She leaned against the counter opposite me and took a deep breath. "I'm trying to put together the pieces without actually talking to James, but I'm thinking maybe you two found out about Sandy and Jim?"

I nodded and looked to the floor.

"I thought so. Who found out first, and how?"

"Cass found out. I think from Jim, or maybe his mom." That part of the story was still unclear to me, and I wondered how the event had unfolded. Did he mention my name in passing and Jim heard it? Did his mom question him on who he'd been seeing and then slip the truth? Did his mom even know I existed?

"I'm not sure exactly how," I said, "but when he did find out, he came over to my grandparents' to talk to me. My grandpa came outside and kinda blew up, so Cass left. Then my grandma came out, and she wasn't happy, either. They didn't even know I'd been seeing Cass. It was a shock to them. And knowing it was Jim who killed my mom . . . that was a shock to *me*."

Lonna shook her head. "Whew. This is heavy for you kids." She took a seat in the chair next to mine. "I'm so sorry you have to go through this. It's bad enough what happened to your mother, but to know James's father played a part in it?" She leaned an elbow on the table and brought a hand over her mouth. "I should've said something. I thought long and hard about it when James told me he was seeing you, but I just couldn't do it. It didn't feel like my place. I was just at a loss for words every time I thought about saying something. And then when I saw you guys together . . ." She shook her head. "It felt almost a sin for me to interfere."

I bit my cheek, wondering how the summer would have

Red Dirt Paradise

gone if the secret had slipped sooner. *Would we still be where we are now?*

"It's okay," I said. "I should've said something to my grandparents about him in the first place. I've spent all summer wanting to. I just had this gut feeling I should keep him away from them."

"Well, don't you feel too guilty about that. James is a little ornery, and truth be told, he doesn't exactly have the appeal that most grandparents like to see. Regardless of who his father is." She smiled and squeezed my knee. "But we both know the kind of heart that boy has on the inside, don't we?"

The sincerity in her voice made a knot find its way to the back of my throat.

"You ready, Lonna?" Pat stepped into the kitchen, buttoning the sleeve of his striped western shirt, but Lonna quickly shooed him from the room.

"I'll meet you in the car," she said.

He nodded, then gave me a smile.

Larry snuck out from the opposite end of the hallway, tucking his white T-shirt into clean jeans, and met Pat at the door. He looked my direction, offered a small wave, then followed his dad out the door in silence.

Lonna looked back at me and placed her hand on my knee. "I know it's hard when the world is against you, whether that be history or distance or grandparents." She smiled and gave me a soft pat. "But honey, sometimes you shouldn't care what the world thinks. You have to do what *you* want to do, no matter the circumstance." She stood from the table and pointed toward the hallway. "It's the last door on the right. Go talk to him."

I stood, and she pulled me in for a hug the second I did.

"I'll see you next time you visit," she whispered, giving me one last squeeze. Lonna grabbed her Bible from the counter on her way out of the kitchen, and before I knew it, I was alone in the house with Cass.

I swallowed my nerves and walked toward the hallway, not having a clue what I would say on the other side of his door. I hesitated before knocking, trying to think of the right things I *could* say to him. I tapped the wood a couple times and knew I had to think fast, because like Lonna said, I shouldn't care what the world thought. Even if my grandparents were against us because of history, and Steph was against us because of who he was, and we lived in different states, none of that mattered.

Because he was what I wanted.

And I didn't want to lose him.

"What is it?" Cass asked in a voice so low it didn't even sound like him.

"It's . . . it's me."

After a long moment of ringing silence, I heard the bedsprings squeak and footsteps walk toward the door. I braced myself before he opened it.

"Come in," he said, cracking the door.

I followed him in, closing it behind me. He sat on the edge of his bed, staring at the ground. I could see his split lip and black eye, though it was obvious he was trying to hide it from me. He had his right hand wrapped, and there was a cut on his shoulder that needed a bandage and maybe some stitches.

I put my hand over my mouth, trying to keep my tears at bay. Neither one of us knew what to say or do, so the room was silent. After a long moment, I walked over to the bed and sat next to him.

"I'm sorry about everything," I said slowly, fighting to keep a steady voice. "Jim, my grandparents . . . last night. I hope you're okay."

"You shouldn't be the one apologizing," he muttered.

Cass stood and walked to the corner of the room. He faced the wall and looked at the floor. I slipped the letter under his pillow so he wouldn't notice it until later.

"You know it's over," he said, his voice tight. "Why did you come here?"

My heart crumbled.

"You don't have to end things because of him, Cass. None of that stuff is your fault. And—"

"It's over." His words were cold and emotionless, as if he'd been drained of all feelings for me. He felt distant. It was like someone had replaced the guy I'd fallen in love with, with someone I didn't know at all.

"I don't wanna end it like this," I said.

"We ain't gotta choice." He looked at the ceiling, still keeping his distance from me. "After everything Jim's put you and your family through, it ain't gonna work."

"That doesn't have anything to do with you."

"I'm his son," he said firmly.

"That doesn't matter," I said, matching his tone.

He scoffed. "It matters."

"You aren't anything like your dad."

"Yeah, well, I ain't the fuckin' boy next door, either." He rubbed his forehead, then continued in a quieter voice, though it was through tight lips. "There was a reason you didn't tell 'em about me." He turned his head in my direction but kept his eyes on the ground. "And that probably had somethin' to do with it."

I was silent. Guilt dug its claws into my gut so hard I winced at the pain. "I'm sorry," I choked.

"It's better for both of us if we just act like this summer never happened."

The phrase came too easily for him. He might as well

have stuck a knife in my chest and twisted it mercilessly. It would've felt just the same.

"I'm tellin' you, it's over. And there ain't nothin' you can say."

And that's when it hit me. I lost it.

I lost it because I'd lost him, and there was nothing I could do about it. I lost it because of the tenseness between us, the sound of his voice, and the fact he hadn't looked at me since I entered the room. It left me no choice but to believe I couldn't talk him out of whatever conclusion he'd come to.

It was over.

The tears came fast and hard. I let everything out I'd been trying to hold in since morning, shaking from the sadness that filled my soul. When he lifted me up and hugged me hard against him, I cried even harder.

I cried for him. I cried for the future I would have without him and the memories we wouldn't get to make together. I cried for my mom. I cried for the years I'd had to live without her, and I cried for the guilt I knew Cass felt because of it.

"I don't wanna lose you," I heaved, hugging his neck as tight as I could, hoping it would help to remind him how much I needed him—how much he needed me.

When I finally calmed down enough to catch my breath, he pulled away from me. Holding my face in his hands just like he always did, he stared at me with watery eyes and a broken spirit as visible as his swollen lip. He wiped the tears from my cheeks, then dropped his hands and grabbed a T-shirt that was on the bed. Without another word, he left me standing alone in the bedroom.

I wanted to follow him. I wanted to scream at him and tell him not to leave me. I wanted to shake him by the shoulders

Red Dirt Paradise

and make him see things from my perspective. I wanted to do all those things, but I didn't do any of them. I couldn't bring myself to move. Instead, I slowly slumped to the edge of the bed and listened to him start his bike. The sound of the engine shook the walls of my heart, and I jumped to my feet, rushing out the door in a last-minute attempt to catch him, but it was no use. He was already pulling onto the blacktop and jumping gears without a look back in my direction.

    I watched him until he disappeared, then stared ahead at an empty road, with questions left unanswered and a heavy heart left in pieces.

Dear Cass,

If you're reading this letter, it's because I couldn't find you or I couldn't change your mind. Either way, I hate how things ended between us. I hate that they ended at all. I know you had your reasons and I'll try to accept the fact that it's over, but know I don't want to. I wish things were different.

I want you to know I'm so thankful for the time we spent together. Memories were made that I'll treasure forever. You brought out another side of me I had no idea existed, and I'm a better person because of you. I'll never regret or forget this summer, and I'll always miss those conversations we had under the stars and the way I felt wrapped in your arms.

Maybe if I wish hard enough, our paths will cross again in the future. But if that never happens, I hope I left a good enough impression on you so you may remember the good times we had. You're a truly wonderful person, James Cassedy. Don't let anyone tell you any different. All I ask is you stay true to the man I fell in love with.

Austin

P.S. There won't be a day when an Aerosmith song comes on that I don't remember you singing it to me.

 ## Chapter 26

"Oh, look at this one!" Steph said, pointing to a picture of a dreamy summer Hawaiian sunset. I'd taken the photo the first night we'd arrived, and I'd forgotten how beautiful that evening really was.

"This one is good, too," I said, pointing to one she'd taken of a lone sea turtle who'd found his way onto the beach one evening.

"It's nice, I guess, but I think it's safe to say you won this competition."

Anytime Steph and I took a vacation somewhere, we had a competition of who could take the better pictures. At the end of our trip, we'd get them developed at a Fotomat and compare them on our plane ride home.

"I don't know," I said. "I think you won this one."

"No way, honey. You're the clear winner. That sunset proves it."

"You're just being nice."

"Oh, I am not," she insisted. She took the pictures I was holding and grouped them with hers, then put them back in their envelopes and slid them in the front pocket of her carry-on bag.

"What are those?" she asked, pointing to a separate envelope underneath the seat in front of me.

"Just some pictures from this summer," I answered.

"Well, come on. Let's see them." She reached for the envelope, but I snatched it before she could touch them.

"I don't want to look at these right now," I said.

Usually, she would've argued with me, but this time she didn't. Instead, she gave a simple nod and reached inside her purse.

"Well, I'm tired anyway," she said. "I think I'll get some sleep before we land." She yawned, leaning her seat back what little she could, and covered her eyes with a black satin sleep mask.

I reached for my Judy Blume novel and began reading where I'd left off, but my eyes kept drifting to the envelope nestled beside me. I'd promised myself I wouldn't look at them. I even made sure at the Fotomat that they separated those pictures from the Hawaiian pictures so I wouldn't accidentally see them. But now, knowing they were right beside me, the thought of what was inside sparked my curiosity. What did Cass look like on his bike that day on Pat and Lonna's land? What about those pictures we'd snapped at the concert? The pictures I took of him one night while we were on the riverbank?

The envelope wouldn't leave me alone. It poked my side, beckoning me to move it. Grab it. Open it. Dump its

Red Dirt Paradise

contents out all over my lap and rifle through them like they were newfound buried treasure.

"Damn it, Karl!" a man yelled from across the aisle.

I looked over, and the boy, whose name I now knew to be Karl, held the headphones away from his ears. "Can't I just listen to my Walkman in peace?" he yelled back in a surfer-boy accent ridiculously close to Jeff Spicoli's from *Fast Times at Ridgemont High*.

Karl was my age, maybe a little younger, and looked like he could've been Cass's brother. He wore ripped jeans, a Marlboro shirt, and a ratted bandana around his head, with dirty high tops on his feet. His sandy-blond mullet grazed his shoulders, and there was a single dimple on his left cheek. I'd noticed it when he boarded the plane behind us.

"I've been talking to you for a minute now," said the man, "and you can't listen to a thing I say because of that damn Walkman!"

Karl dropped his headphones around his neck. "I told you we can talk after I finish this new Van Halen tape!" He pushed the stop button on his Walkman. "You're killin' my groove, old man!"

The man, who I assumed was his dad, laughed. "You kids and your godawful music. You wouldn't know good music if it bit you on the ass."

Karl threw his head against the headrest and rolled his eyes. "If you don't think Van Halen is good music, you're really off your rocker this time."

"Hell, the music we had when I went to high school blows Van Halen out of the water. Zeppelin. Sabbath. There'll never be better music than what those guys played."

"Pops, you gotta stop livin' in the past. Keep up with the times, man. It's all about Van Halen now. Diamond Dave and Eddie—"

"Ha!" his dad cut in. "You wanna talk frontmen? Let's talk Robert Plant. You wanna talk guitarists? Let's talk Jimmy Page."

"Diamond Dave is a legend."

"Diamond Dave is a phony."

Karl shook his head, ignoring him. "Man, whenever we get home, I can't *wait* to blow out the speakers in my Firebird to 'Panama.' Burn some rubber on those S-curves west of town singin' 'Drop Dead Legs.'" He laughed maniacally. "Oh, *hell* yeah."

"You listen here . . . I paid for those speakers, and if you're gonna blow them out, it better be to 'War Pigs.'"

"Black Sabbath isn't even together anymore. And don't tell me it's the same with Dio. Original lineup, or it doesn't count."

"Ozzy will be back."

"Are you kidding? Ozzy is doin' his own thing now. *He's* keeping up with the times. You should follow his lead."

His dad scoffed. "After Ozzy's done parading around, he'll get back with Sabbath."

"He got fired. It's not like he just quit. They'll never get back together."

"They'll get back together."

"How do you know?"

"Because, son. They always get back together. These bands are good together, make great music together, then something happens and they break up. Then they go off and piddle, and once they realize they were better together, they reunite. Happens in every aspect of life."

I glanced at the envelope. It was stabbing into my hip, demanding my attention. I couldn't look away from it.

"No matter the problems they had that broke them up,

they work them out. May take some years, but they'll find their way back together."

I couldn't stop myself.

I grabbed the envelope, flipped the top, and pulled out the pictures I had forbidden myself to look at. The first one I saw was from the concert. It was taken before we went into the venue, by an older woman I'd caught walking past us in the parking lot. Cass had his arm around my shoulders, looking down at me while I smiled at the camera. The way he was looking at me—the love that filled his eyes and showed in his Copenhagen grin—made tears cloud my vision and rush down my cheeks.

"Mark my words, son. They'll get back together. Give it a little time. That's all they need."

May the nostalgia of days gone by light the fire in your tired eyes, flourish your aching heart with little pockets of vintage sunshine, and spark your memory one Springsteen song at a time.

ACKNOWLEDGMENTS

Special thanks to my dad. Thank you for allowing me to see the '80s through your eyes. Stories from your childhood and teenage years truly give me life. I could sit starry-eyed and listen to them until you run out of things to say. Thankfully, that's yet to happen. Love you, Dad.

Thank you to all my beta readers and editors. You all have made this book into what it is. I have both laughed and cried while reading your feedback, and every bit of it has helped me grow as a writer. Thank you for going on this journey with me.

Thanks, Morgan, for selling me that little Suzuki. You're the reason I'm familiar with the special kind of peace that comes from being behind the handlebars. You rock.

Thank you, Aunt Lori, for introducing me to rock n' roll. Growing up, you made sure I had the coolest Walkmans and iPods, and the hair metal playlists you made me were always out of this world. The influence that had on me kind of speaks for itself in this book. Thanks for being my hero.

ABOUT THE AUTHOR

Brooke Cowan is the author of the Red Dirt Series. She, her husband, and their son live on a farm just a wheat field away from where she was raised.

If she's not working on the farm, she enjoys watching Roseanne reruns, chatting with her dad about the good ol' days, working in her flowerbeds, or listening to decades-old music. She can often be found with a cup of sweet tea in her hand and her head in the clouds plotting her next storyline. Her love for rural Oklahoma is wholeheartedly woven into her stories, through which she loves celebrating small-town living and invoking the nostalgia of teenage love.

Made in the USA
Columbia, SC
02 October 2022